Undercurrents

A Cape Breton Anthology of Speculative Fiction

Edited by:

Sherry D. Ramsey | Julie A. Serroul | Nancy S.M. Waldman

Third Person Press
Cape Breton, Nova Scotia
Canada

Third Person Press
Email: thirdpersonpress@gmail.com
Web: www.thirdpersonpress.com
Cape Breton, Nova Scotia, Canada

Undercurrents: A Cape Breton Anthology of Speculative Fiction
ISBN: 978-0-9811025-0-4

Acknowledgements

We would like to thank our families for their continuing support through all phases of this project, all those who submitted stories, and our contributors, who worked so diligently and willingly with us to bring the stories to their full potential.

~ *The Editors*

Contents

Introduction

The Idea

As speculative writers, we are keenly aware that our stories are "out there," and that "out there" is where we have to send them. Our markets are predominantly in the United States, with occasional opportunities in the larger cities of Canada. But closer to home, one is left with the impression that the East Coast is bereft of either speculative fiction writers, or more importantly, speculative fiction readers.

We, the editors of Third Person Press, suspected that this was not the case. It was our belief that fiction about coal mining, the fisheries and the very real, poignant tales of surviving in economically depressed areas overshadowed the other fiction—perhaps in the same way that the Celtic music phenomenon has overshadowed the rest of the burgeoning East Coast music scene. There has been a movement to bring these other music genres into the spotlight that has inspired us. In one of our first meetings the concept and the title "Undercurrents" were born.

The rest of the world seems to be awakening to the vast possibilities of speculative fiction. Television shows about supernatural abilities, ghost mediums, unusual phenomenon and space travel are experiencing otherworldly success. Movies are following suit and the entire industry groans under the weight of speculative fiction tales. It seemed "illogical," as a certain pointy-eared alien would say, that the imaginations of people here in our part of the world would be any less entranced by the growing genre.

We found it just as unlikely that all local writers were ensconced in reality-based fiction and content to sail in charted waters. We decided to act on our intuition that more lurked beneath the surface. And so, we plumbed the depths for the powerful speculative fiction stories we knew swirled in the undercurrents. We were not disappointed. We hope you will feast upon our bountiful catch. Enjoy.

~ J.S., October 2008

The Process

The stories in *Undercurrents* are written by authors who have a connection with Cape Breton. Some are life-long residents. Others were born or lived here earlier in their lives, but do not currently reside on the island. Some have adopted the island as their own. All have some attachment to Cape Breton.

It is our pleasure to note that the authors represent a wide range of age and experience. *Undercurrents* includes contributions from previously-published authors, brand new talent, and much in-between. The publishing history of the writers was not a consideration in our deliberations. Instead, we looked for compelling, complete narratives with well-drawn characters and solid plots. As well, one or more speculative genres had to be in evidence for a story to be accepted.

The number and quality of submissions was impressive. We had many difficult decisions to make and were not able to accept every well-written story. Our focus was to balance *Undercurrents* stories as to length, subject matter and, most importantly, genres. Often, the primary reason behind a dreaded rejection letter was that need to balance and diversify the overall collection.

We wish to thank everyone who submitted stories. We salute both your writing and your willingness to put your creative endeavours out there. Our hope is that each of you has been encouraged by this process and that you continue to write.

Undercurrents represents a collection of great stories, but also a collaboration. From beginning-to-end, reading, evaluating, editing and polishing so many wonderful stories was a delightful learning experience for us, the editors of Third Person Press. We arc gratified to present proof of what we knew from the outset: Cape Breton breeds not only strong writers, but also strong speculative fiction writers.

~ N.W., October 2008

The Stories

Since my colleagues have dealt with the "why" and the "how" of this book, it falls to me to address the "what." If you are not familiar with the term "speculative fiction" you might be thinking, "isn't all fiction speculative?" And in one sense, you would be correct.

Speculative fiction as a literary descriptor, however, and as we've chosen to use it, encompasses a variety of fiction genres, all of which share perhaps only one common feature—they speculate about worlds, characters, times and places that are unlike what we fondly call the "real world" in some important regard. By stepping outside these boundaries, speculative fiction allows the writer to answer that vital question of fiction—"what if?"—from an infinitely expanded range of possibilities. In fact, it changes even the parameters of the question itself. No wonder speculative fiction is sometimes called the "literature of the imagination."

Still unsure what you might find in the following pages? When we wrote our submission guidelines, we tried to put a very fine point on it: we asked for stories from any of the speculative sub-genres: science fiction, fantasy, horror, magic realism, the paranormal, or combinations thereof. The writers who responded took our request to heart and showered us with a wealth of stories from all corners of the speculative realm.

So in *Undercurrents* you'll find, we hope, stories that will resonate with or possibly awaken your "sense of wonder." Stories that will open your eyes to new possibilities, that will spark your imagination, that will encourage you to see the world through a different lens, even if only for a short time. Stories that will take you to places beyond the "real world"—places that did not, do not, or cannot exist. Or perhaps they have, or do, or will, and we simply don't know about them. Yet.

~ S. R., October 2008

Magic Show

"Coming out then, Rob?"

Rob looked up from his desk. Anthony from Receiving stood in the entrance to his cubicle, looking at him expectantly.

"Oh. Sorry, Anthony, I can't tonight," Rob said, closing down his workstation.

"Oh, come on. It's trivia night at the pub. We can watch the drunk college students try to remember when Kurt Cobain committed suicide."

"I really can't."

"Oh?" Anthony raised his eyebrows. "Got a date?"

Rob hesitated only a second before taking the easy way out. "Yes," he lied, feeling his heart speed up a little. "I want time to get home and change before I meet her."

"No worries. Good luck, Rob."

Rob continued to power down his computer, but his ears strained to hear Anthony finally leave, whistling tunelessly to himself. It was only when the door had clicked shut behind his co-worker that Rob started to relax again.

Quickly, he shuffled into his coat and pulled on his gloves. He looked at his father's watch. If he wanted to get there before everything started, he'd have to hurry.

It was a blustery night, the kind where darkness seems to fall early and all at once, like it was waiting around the corner for the day to drop its guard before leaping out and beating it into submission. Rob's grandmother had called these 'border nights.' She'd never said what she meant by that, but Rob could hazard a guess. You only had to look at the way people hurried home more quickly than usual, away from the thick, heavy darkness and the tugging wind, to know that there was something passing close tonight, something strange and not quite human.

Not that Rob really thought about that kind of thing anymore.

As he scurried through the streets with the same startled rodent run everyone else seemed to have on these nights, he listened to Robert. Robert was the name that Rob had given to his inner voice of logic. Robert didn't have any truck with nonsense about border nights or strangeness or anything that didn't have some immediate explanation. He calmly explained to Rob that it was just another early spring evening, when the weather was unpredictable and odd because of changing wind patterns. There was nothing strange about the night. There was nothing hiding in the shadows. Robert could be very comforting.

Occasionally, Rob thought that Robert was an annoying old windbag who was just fooling himself with platitudes and false hopes. But not very often. Most of the time, like tonight, he was glad to listen.

The fitful breeze shivered around him, tugging at his coat like a child trying to get his attention. He ignored it, and kept walking.

Finally, he reached the small, dingy club that was his destination for the evening. He wasn't there for a date. He wasn't sure why he had lied to Anthony, except maybe that he didn't want to become known in the office as the kind of guy who went to these shows. He'd never dealt very well with ridicule, and if anyone found out about his secret passion, he'd have to give it up.

He looked around nervously, just to make sure, but the only people outside this little dive were the local drunks and junkies who were too messed-up to bother getting inside against the eerie night. They paid him absolutely no attention, although it should be said that most people paid Rob absolutely no attention. It wasn't that there was anything wrong with him. He was perfectly normal. That, in fact, might have been part of the problem. He was so normal that he became almost invisible, an unremarkable tree in an average forest.

Still, he looked around, mostly to assure Robert that there was no one there who knew him. Robert wasn't crazy about Rob coming to such places to begin with, and if there were the slightest chance of being seen by someone who mattered, then he'd force Rob to walk away. Rob turned up the collar of his jacket and went into the theatre.

The poster on the door said, in the bright and slightly desperate lettering of such posters:

MAGIC SHOW!!!

Rob didn't relax until he was seated at a small table by himself with a beer before him. A careful scan of the crowd revealed no one he knew, although there were a few other regulars there, people that he'd seen at other shows in the city over the years. They carefully avoided each other's gazes.

Rob reflected on this as he sipped his beer. It was as if they all had a little Robert inside them somewhere, telling them that this was wrong and stupid and immature, and that they should go before anyone important saw them. He wondered if everyone had that little voice that told you what you should be doing. He hoped not.

Robert was that nagging feeling of insecurity that made you show the world an acceptable face. It was a survival voice, a voice that told you to go with the herd and not to stand out, because standing out makes you vulnerable. It was the voice of safety and security. Rob listened to it a great deal now.

When he was younger, he hadn't listened so much to the voice. Instead, he had listened to another, rather more attractive voice, although voice wasn't the right word. It was more like a feeling, an intuition. His grandmother had called that one the Dark, because it came out of the darkness at the back of the brain, the parts that had been shut away by civilization and Robert, and because it was attracted to the hidden things of the world. Things no one remembered or wanted, or at least that no one admitted to remembering or wanting. Rob called his voice Bobby, the same name his grandmother had called him until he was seven and she died and everything changed.

His grandmother loved magic shows. Rob had many memories of being taken, over his father's objections, to see jolly men in bad suits performing their wonderful tricks. He'd enjoyed seeing the cards fly and the rabbits appear. But he had been more interested in the assistants, those skinny girls in sparkly tights who could be cut in half and put back together, who could float over the stage, who could vanish without a trace. That, the young Rob had known, was the real magic. Not the conjurer and all his words, but the women who were the focus of it all.

Back then, Bobby had been the voice he listened to, with all his excitement about the danger of hidden things. And he had known, with all the surety of a seven-year-old, that the border nights brought something with them. Once or twice, when he was about on those nights, he would have sworn that he had caught *something*, a glitter where there was nothing to shine, or a scent where there was nothing to make it, wild roses and pine, wet fur and sweat.

But growing up is hard to do, and the rest of the world had quickly moved to shake him out of that habit of listening to Bobby and his grandmother. Rob's father disapproved of the things his mother was teaching his son, although as Rob remembered it, his father disapproved of almost everything. *Be logical*, he said. *Be productive. Do well in school. Be normal.*

But Rob had persevered, and Bobby had lived until his grandmother died. Then there was no one to take him to the magic shows or to remember the Dark. The other kids, having outgrown their own Bobbies by now, started to make fun of him for believing in the strange and unseen. And the voice of Robert, who sounded strangely like his father, had grown stronger.

And so, through a combination of ridicule and social stigma, Rob had stopped listening to Bobby and had started listening to Robert more and more. He did well in school. He got a good job. He worked hard at it, and was plodding up the ladder of promotion. He was a good and productive member of society, and he never worried about things he couldn't see. His father had given him his good watch when he had gotten his job, a congratulations for doing so well. Rob wore it every day.

But sometimes the pressure of it got to be too much, and then he had to go to the shows. He couldn't stop. He told himself that these were different, that they were harmless entertainment, that everything was done with tricks and angles and mirrors and wires. That he did it to remember his grandmother. That there was no *magic* in it. But, just occasionally, when there was a very well done trick, he'd feel the stirring of something deep inside himself, and remember the feral smells of roses and pine and sweat.

~ Undercurrents ~

Not that there was much hope for tonight, he thought as he looked at the stage with the practiced eye of a man who had seen eight magic shows already this year. It was barely even a stage. Only a small raised platform, the type usually used for bad live music and comedians who fail to elicit a single laugh. A ragged piece of fabric, possibly an old bed sheet, hung from a wooden pole to serve as a curtain. In front of this, on a wooden easel, someone had optimistically placed a sign. A scattering of glittery stars clung to it, shedding their glitter every time the door opened and a breeze blew in. They flared briefly in the light from the candles on every table and the neon beer signs around the club, and then died as they tumbled to the floor. The sign read: "The Amazing Santiago, with Special Assistant Gloriana!! You WILL Be Amazed!!!"

Probably not, Rob thought, finishing the lukewarm beer. But it was better than a night at the pub with Anthony and his friends, whose conversation inevitably turned towards sports or television. Most of the time he could deal with it, even welcomed it, because it was normal. But sometimes he was afraid that he would smash a glass over someone's head for being so relentlessly boring, and those were the nights he went to the magic shows.

The club was only about half-full, but the barman went up in front of the stage and announced that the show would start in five minutes, so they should order their drinks now. Rob snagged a second beer and settled down in his seat with a bowl of peanuts.

There was a click and the hiss of tape before a tinny fanfare played. A female voice from behind the curtain said, "Ladies and gentlemen and children of all ages, we welcome you to the show. You will see things to amaze you, things to astound you, and maybe even things that will make you question what you know about the universe! Including...the Amazing...Santiago!"

On the last word, the curtain was pulled aside by a hand, revealing a small, pudgy man in a shabby tuxedo and a slightly crushed top hat. His face was almost covered by a large, bristly mustache. The addition of a red velvet cape did nothing to make him look more amazing.

There was some half-hearted applause from the audience, but the Amazing Santiago bowed and waved as if it was an emperor's welcome. He blew kisses to a middle-aged woman near the stage and waved graciously as the last few handclaps died.

"Thank you! Thank you!" At least he had a good voice for the job. It was rich and round and carrying, the voice of a god passing commandments to a cowering prophet. "Thank you for that wonderful welcome! I am, as you have guessed, the Amazing Santiago! I have studied magic for many years. I have travelled far, perfecting my art and learning ancient secrets of magic from the hidden masters of the craft. I have performed for the kings and queens of the earth! And now I perform for you!" He waggled a finger. "But not alone. I bring with me the jewel of the world, the most talented and magical woman alive, the beautiful and mystical Gloriana!"

Rob paused with his beer halfway to his mouth as the woman stepped from behind the curtain. She was beautiful and delicate and sharp, like a sword blown from glass. She stepped gracefully onto the stage as if it were the ballroom of a palace instead of a beer-soaked piece of splintery wood. The sequins of her costume made the air around her sparkle, a cold clear glitter like frost in the moonlight.

The applause for Gloriana was, due to the predominantly male audience, more enthusiastic than that for Santiago. There were wolf whistles and cat-calls, noises men make when they feel the beast in them stir. But Rob just stared. Not that he'd never looked at a pretty girl before, but he'd never been so fixated, so hypnotized by only a presence.

He continued to be transfixed as the act started. Santiago wasn't bad; he knew all the classic tricks, plus a few of the more obscure ones, and did them all competently. There was no fumbling of coins, no tell-tale shine of fishing line holding up his floating rings, no waterfall of cards slipping out of his sleeve. He was good.

But Robert had eyes for no one and nothing but Gloriana. He watched as she assisted Santiago with each trick, sometimes holding his hat so that things could appear from it, sometimes waiting unafraid for a sword to fall, sometimes doing nothing more than standing and smiling. Rob sat mesmerized by her, until he was almost blind from the sparkle of her sequins. Her eyes flashed green and gold in the dim light, like a hunting cat.

When the vanishing cabinet came out and a volunteer from

the audience went in, Rob held his breath. For a few wild moments, he had believed that the man, Philip—who told them all he was a delivery man and had come to the show with his lovely wife Enid—was gone forever, never to reappear. Packages would go undelivered. Enid would wander home alone and confused. And Philip would have simply...vanished.

But then Santiago bellowed a few words and waved his hands and Gloriana threw open the door to reveal Philip, alive and well inside the cabinet. He looked bemused, and he stumbled when he left the stage, but he had returned.

Before Rob realized it, the show was over. Santiago was bowing to the sound of applause that was more enthusiastic than it had been at the show's opening. Gloriana smiled and glittered next to him.

Rob looked at his watch and realized that the show had been going for hours. It was past eleven. *You should be getting home,* the voice of Robert said. *You need to sleep before work tomorrow.*

But again tonight, Rob ignored Robert, and stayed in his seat. He was waiting for something, although if pressed he couldn't have said what. The other patrons of the club left, talking amongst themselves about the surprising quality of the show. Rob ignored them, and waited.

The club was empty by the time it happened. Gloriana slipped through the door leading to the storage room that had functioned as her dressing room. She no longer wore the sequined costume, but there was a hint of sparkle around her even in street clothes. She smiled when she saw Rob and walked over.

"Did you enjoy the show?" she asked in a low, musical voice.

"Yes," Rob replied, his voice cracking like a thirteen-year-old's. Embarrassed, he cleared his throat. "Yes. I did. You were very good."

She made a dismissive little noise. "Parlour tricks. Basic stuff for the masses." She looked at him with those feline eyes. "But you...you seem like the type that might appreciate something different."

"Different?" He felt Robert stir again. "It's not dangerous, is it?"

She laughed softly. "No, no. Just different. I'm doing another show tonight at a different club. Would you like to see it?"

Robert chimed in with a vehement *no*, saying that he needed to get home, he had to pack his lunch and go to sleep, he had work tomorrow with coffee and spreadsheets and Anthony telling him about the girls at the pub. Normal things. But Rob, after a moment's hesitation, said, "I'd love to."

Gloriana smiled. "Good. Then let's go."

She led him out of the club, winking at the bartender as she passed, and out into the night. It was as strange as it had been before, a true border night. The junkies and drunks in the street turned as one to watch Gloriana pass.

They whirled through the darkened streets, she leading him by a hand. Rob passed places he saw every day, and saw how different they were at night. Things loomed more, shadows deepened, and everything looked subtly wilder, as if a jungle had become concrete and hid unnatural, more dangerous beasts.

All the while, Robert kept up a steady stream of nagging, telling him how stupid it was to be out on the streets this late when the dangerous people were around, how silly he was being over a girl he had just met, how ridiculous he was going to feel in the morning when she was gone—

But Rob barely heard the voice. He followed in a daze, enveloped by the strangeness of a city he thought he knew, feeling the dark undercurrent of the border night pulsing through everything. Without warning, Gloriana pulled him into a darkened doorway and kissed him, crushing her body against his. Her heat seared through his coat as he tasted the ripe-berry sweetness of her mouth. The sparkles shimmered in the air. He reached up to hold her, but she slipped away and pulled him onwards again, and he followed the sound of her laughter in the dark.

Finally she stopped next to a door in a small back alley. Rob paused to catch his breath and looked around. "Where are we?"

"At the club." She pointed at the unmarked door.

"There's a club here? Are you sure?"

"Very. Not many people know about it." And she opened the door and led him inside.

The new club was dark and smoke-filled, an oddity since the city had passed stricter smoking laws. Coils of it hung in the air, clouding Rob's vision. Blindly, he followed the pull of Gloriana's hand to a small table near the stage.

~ Undercurrents ~

"Sit here," she said, pushing him down into the chair. "I'll go get ready for the show." She kissed him again, quick as a cat, and was gone.

From outside, this place had looked like a small room, the kind of dive bar that fills back alleys in every corner of the world. Inside, it was the size of a theatre, filled with gilded tables and huge, comfortable chairs. Many of the tables were occupied. Rob found it hard to make out details through the dimness and the smoke, but some of the occupants were far too large to be human. Others were too thin, too fat, too...odd. A waitress brought a tray of drinks to one table, and he could have sworn that a paw reached out to grab a glass.

Inside, Robert was gibbering in terror, but Bobby had woken up and was watching the scene with wide eyes. Rob felt the stirring of those same feelings of fear and wonder that he had felt all those years ago, when his grandmother had told him about the darkness.

The waitress came over to his table. Dimly, Rob noticed that she was covered in fine, downy fur. She placed a glass in front of him, filled with some golden liquid. "For you," she said. "From Glory." And she was gone into the smoke, a tawny tail flicking behind her.

Rob lifted the glass and drank. The thought that there might be something wrong with it never crossed his mind. It tasted like winter, a clear blue sky on a cold day, when the air takes your breath away and every surface shines with frost. He gasped, feeling the delightful shiver of it spread through him.

A spotlight speared down into the dim smoke, illuminating the stage. This was a much better one than the sad affair at the previous club. Red velvet with gilded trim hung from every corner, and candles flared to life on the stage. Music came from nowhere, not the tinny, tape-hiss-marred music of before, but real music, a triumphant fanfare.

Gloriana stepped out onto the stage and the theatre erupted with applause. She was naked, and Rob saw now that he had been wrong to think that the sparkle of before had come from anything so crude as sequins, shiny bits of plastic. She needed no help to shine. The air around her shimmered and coruscated, the northern lights brought to earth.

She smiled and waved, acknowledging their adoration. She

looked directly at Rob and winked one green-gold eye. And then the show began.

This was no trickery with wire and mirrors, trap doors and secret switches. Gloriana made fire leap around the stage, danced with it as it coiled itself around her like a python. Dragons roared from the shadows, dragging their shining scales over the stage and crushing a small table to splinters. A rain of golden coins fell from her hands, tumbling over the edge of the stage. Flowers burst into bloom before fading and withering before their eyes, only to bloom again.

The audience roared and applauded, hooted and howled and screamed in voices that were never human. Rob gaped.

Finally, Gloriana held up her hands for quiet. "And now," she said into the silence that followed, "it's time for my favorite trick: the vanishing cabinet!"

The audience applauded again as a battered wooden cabinet appeared on the stage, materializing into sight. Aside from its entrance, it looked normal. A few painted stars adorned the sides, but it was still just an upright wooden box with a door.

Gloriana turned, her skin glittering like frost. "And now, I shall need a volunteer." She smiled at Rob.

Applause and cheers greeted him as he stood from his seat, rising so quickly that the chair fell over. He walked to the stage and climbed the stairs, the spotlight following him the whole way. Robert shrieked for him to stop. Bobby cheered him on.

He reached her and stood before her, unsure of what to do now, but confident that she would tell him. Gloriana looked at him, mischief in her eyes. "Well, Rob, are you ready?"

"Yes," he said, drowning out Robert's voice. "I am."

"A round of applause for my brave volunteer!" She smiled and took his hand as the audience roared its approval. Her other hand opened the door of the vanishing cabinet. "All you have to do is step inside, Rob."

"That's all?"

"That's all." She smiled at him again, and he saw that feral sharpness return.

Rob turned toward the cabinet. The inside had been lined with spangled velvet, and the stars shone in the stage lights. It was only a few steps away.

Stop it! Screamed Robert. *Think about what you're doing! You don't know what will happen in there! You have a life, a real life, and you're going to throw it away for a trick! She could be anyone, could be anything! You don't know what you're doing! This is insane! What about your life?*

Rob paused. Even with all the enchantments around him, it was a moment of perfect clarity. He looked back on his life thus far. A clean, empty apartment. A boring social life. A job with no purpose. He could see forward, too, all the way to his clean and empty middle-age and sterile retirement, ending in a cold, clinical death surrounded by beeping machines that had never believed in magic at all. The way his father had died.

He smiled. And stepped into the cabinet.

Gloriana closed the door behind him with a click that echoed loudly in the sudden silence from the audience. She stepped back and waved her hands, shining and beautiful as a star in the winter sky. She called out magic words in her musical, powerful voice. And, when all was still again, she opened the door to the cabinet.

Inside, it was empty. A wristwatch lay on the floor. The velvet and stars hung in place.

And drifting out, faint and unnoticed by the cheering audience, the delicate smells of wild roses and pine, wet fur and sweat.

⁂

Stephanie Short escaped from academia in 2006, waving diplomas and cackling madly. Now she writes full time and cackles hardly at all. She was last seen living in Sydney, Nova Scotia, with her fiancé/partner in crime, John, and three enormous cats. Trained in fantasy writing, three combat sports, and knitting, she should be considered dangerous. Approach with caution.

Improbable Mission Force

Lt. Daniel "Sapper" Westphal slouched in his flight harness and fiddled with the range selector for his onboard radar. *Max. Min. Max. Min.* Nothing, nothing, nothing. He and his eleven squadmates had been floating near a dim little star at the intersection of nothing and nowhere for over four hours, and hadn't seen so much as a stray wisp of free-floating hydrogen, much less a Former warship.

As far as Sapper was concerned, this wasn't what fighter pilots were for. Their skills could be put to better use strafing transports and dogfighting with the enemy. Leave the early detection to a beacon or something.

Sure, they didn't know much about the Formers. They could be aliens, robots, even some sort of human separatist movement. In fact, the name "Former" had come from the one thing they did know for sure. After the first encounter, Earth's president asked his Secretary of Defense "Do these things mean us harm, or is there potential for cooperation here?" The Secretary's response was: "the former." But all that was no excuse to waste perfectly good combat pilots on pansy info-gathering missions.

Max. Min. Max. Min. Electronics were pretty small these days. Couldn't they have fit some sort of video game player into the cockpit? *Max. Min. Max.*

Ping.

Resolving into view on the other side of the star were three small Former fighters. The Formers had two models of fighters. The heavily-armed, wedge-shaped manned ones, and unmanned drones that looked like lawn darts and handled like rocks. These were the drones—no living pilot, short-range fuel capacity, basic weapons. Sapper grinned wolfishly. His *Accipiter* would make mincemeat out of them.

"Contact noted. Do not engage," came the voice of Lieutenant Commander Jody "Buster" Kyte, his squadron commander.

What? Three fat, helpless little drones against twelve top-of-the-line starfighters and they were passing it up? *Accipiters* might still look like old-school atmospheric fighters, but they had more firepower than the average cruiser. Sapper whacked the side of his flight helmet to make sure his headset was working. Surely he couldn't have heard right.

Jody, floating on his left, glared angrily at him through two layers of Lexan canopy. "I know you heard me, Westphal. Do not engage. That's an order."

Sapper should have obeyed. After all, Jody had earned her callsign from busting other pilots' asses. Instead, he looked past her to the three escaping Former drones, and without a second thought, reached down into the footwell and tripped the circuit breaker for the comms.

Putting on a confused look, Sapper tapped his helmet again to indicate he couldn't hear her. Purple-faced, she was probably yelling loud enough to rupture the eardrums of the other pilots. He shoved the throttles forward, thumbing the weapons selector.

A well-placed missile and a brief burst from the cannons later, the three dart ships were reduced to a cloud of debris. Sapper headed back to the formation, only to discover that it had left. No big surprise there. Jody liked to get in first so she could be waiting angrily for him on the flight deck.

Sapper goosed the throttles and rounded the star, rocketing out toward the edge of the system and the waiting bulk of the Oberon, his home carrier. Over fourteen kilometers long, it was nothing more than a speck in the empty blackness until Sapper was practically on top of it.

He cycled through massive primary airlock, his single fighter dwarfed by the space designed to process entire squadrons of much larger spacecraft, and emerged into the flight deck, which was swarming with pilots and technicians.

As he guided his fighter to its berth, Sapper looked around for waves and thumbs-ups from the other pilots. Usually they celebrated when one of their own made a kill, but despite the number of enemy fighters he'd downed, he was an exception to the rule. His squadmates, as usual, were avoiding his gaze, using both hands to cradle their aching ears. Well, at least the hearing damage was Jody's fault.

Ah. Speaking of which, Jody was waiting for him near his berth. She couldn't have been much older than Sapper's twenty-three but she somehow managed to project an aura of strict, middle-aged momness. Her long brown hair was perfectly tied back, regulation style, and her flight suit was wrinkle-free. How she managed that after six hours in a fighter cockpit was beyond Sapper. As usual, she was the living embodiment of the Officer's Drill and Deportment manual and she was pissed.

Petty Officer Tunny, the deckhand who looked after Sapper's fighter, unrolled the refueling hose. He was twenty years older and fifty pounds heavier than the diminutive squadron commander, but Tunny took one look at Jody's face and backed off to a safe distance to wait until the inevitable blowout was over.

"The Commander wants to see you in her office," Jody said as soon as the canopy was open enough for Sapper to hear.

Sapper put on a confused face as he stripped off his gloves and helmet. "Why? I mean, I was having comm trouble, then as soon as I noticed everyone had left—"

"Save it," Jody interrupted. "I know you heard me."

Sapper dropped the confused act. "All right, yeah, I heard you. But you know that order was crap. I did what I had to do. We're in the war to win, not to watch."

Jody regarded him very seriously. "Everyone thinks they're Aaron Roth these days, Sapper. But there's nothing noble in disobeying orders."

The story of Aaron Roth was very hush-hush because it had taken place during a classified op. So of course, everyone in the fleet had found out about it from their mechanic's sister's brother-in-law's nephew who claimed to have been working in the mess hall of Roth's carrier.

The story went that a month back, Roth's squadron was cut off from their carrier, facing scores of Former fighters. Roth's commander, in his panic, ordered everyone not to engage. He wanted them to group together in a stationary huddle where they'd be sitting ducks for the approaching fighters. Aaron Roth disobeyed the order and fought a path through the mob. Because of it, he was the only one who survived. Scuttlebutt had it that he'd blamed the Fleet for the others' deaths and resigned.

~ Undercurrents ~

So, if there were one person in the entire Fleet who didn't think Roth was a hero, it would be Jody "follow-my-every-stupid-order" Kyte.

Sapper opened his mouth to argue with her, but Jody was already walking away, without yelling, browbeating or threats. She didn't even seem angry. Just...exhausted.

Surprised, Sapper called after her. "Wait! Where are you going?"

"Just go see the Commander, Sapper. You're not my problem anymore," Jody said without turning around. She passed through the main hatch and was gone.

"That was weird. Did she take an anger management course or something?" Sapper asked Tunny as he unstrapped himself from the cockpit.

Tunny dragged over the refueling hose. "She got sacked, actually, is what I hear. Something about failing to keep control of her pilots."

Sapper vaulted down onto the deck. "I suppose you're going to tell me that's my fault."

"Doesn't matter what I think, sir. I just look after the equipment. But the Commander will probably see it that way," Tunny replied.

Sapper helped Tunny hook up the hose. "Come on! She pansied out. They can't blame me for that."

Tunny watched the numbers on the refueling gauge tick by. "We talking about the same Jody Kyte here? 'Cause the one I know has a citation for bravery under fire. You ever think maybe she was working a plan out there?"

Since the short answer was "no" and the long answer would make him more than fashionably late for his dressing down, Sapper just shrugged.

But Tunny persisted. "Well, what did she say in the briefing?"

"Dunno. I didn't go."

Tunny crossed his arms. That meant he was about to go into lecture mode, so it was time for Sapper to bug out. "Love to stay and chat, old buddy, but I gotta go get yelled at," Sapper said as he scooped up his gear and headed for the lift.

"You know," Tunny ventured, "you might try listening to people before they start yelling."

Sapper waved dismissively over his shoulder. "You forget I

don't listen to them even when they do yell."

"And that's why your only friend is a forty-five-year-old aircraft mechanic," Tunny retorted as the lift doors closed behind Sapper.

Sapper stuck a hand between the doors and pushed them open again. "I heard that! It's not my fault they're jealous I can outfly them. Which reminds me: add another three to the scorecard."

Tunny frowned at the fuselage of Sapper's fighter, already crowded with hash marks denoting kills. "I guess there's room on the forward landing strut."

§

Sapper got off the lift on twelve and approached Commander Valence's office. He spotted a head and ducked in for a second to look in the mirror. He ruffled his hair. It was sweaty and about two inches longer than regulation, so it flopped into his face. Bedhead: check. He unzipped his flight suit a little at the top and shook his pant legs out of his boots. Rumpled flight suit: check. He practiced a smarmy grin, making sure his brown eyes projected just the right blend of sheepishness and self-confidence. Perfect. He was far too adorable to be demoted. He left the head and turned up the corridor, barging into the office marked "Commander, Air Group."

"You wanted to see me, ma'am?" Sapper asked in a bored tone, head lolled back as if to say this meeting was a big waste of his time.

"Yes, Lieutenant. Please have a seat."

The voice and the words threw Sapper. What was this "please" nonsense? Usually his little talks with the CAG started with "Goddammit, Westphal," and ended with "if you ever do that again I'll make sure the next time you see space it'll be without a pressure suit."

He took his eyes off the ceiling and looked at the Commander —or rather, at the chair behind the desk where the Commander should have been. Instead, a stuffy-looking little man sat straightening a stack of paper. He was balding and looked like he would've been more at home in a cheap suit than a Commander's uniform. Maybe the Fleet was getting desperate enough to recruit from the ranks of insurance salesmen.

"Who the hell are you? Where's Commander Valance?" Sapper blurted.

"I am the Commander you've been summoned to see," the man replied brusquely. "Now have a seat so we may begin."

Sapper was thrown for a loop. He couldn't think of anything smart-assed to say. So he sat.

"Excellent," the little man said, putting on a pair of bifocals and taking up the first sheet in the stack. "Now then, how often, on average, would you say you find it necessary to disobey orders? A: always, B: often, C: sometimes, D: rarely or E: never?"

§

Tunny was still cataloguing the dings Sapper's *Accipiter* had acquired flying through the debris field when Sapper wandered back down to the flight deck in a daze. Tunny turned at the sound of Sapper's footsteps and asked, "Well? Am I gonna have to learn to tolerate a new upstart pilot or what?"

Sapper sank down onto the deck and leaned up against the front landing skid. "Looks like."

"Yeesh," replied Tunny, putting away the clipboard and turning his attention on his friend. "They finally fired you?"

"Not exactly," Sapper hedged, hiding a grin.

Tunny's eyes narrowed. "If you weren't getting reamed out, where have you been for the past three hours?"

"Filling out evaluations on Jody and the Commander."

Tunny's eyes widened and Sapper couldn't hold it in any longer. He started laughing. "They're sending me...to an elite squadron!" Sapper managed to choke out.

"I'll be damned," said Tunny.

§

Sapper hauled his issue duffel out from where it was jammed behind the ejection seat of his fighter and slung it over his shoulder. He hopped to the deck and looked around. This new carrier's flight deck wasn't like any he'd ever seen before. Everything on the *Asgard* was clean—the deck, the bulkheads, the fighters—even the deckhands seemed to be free of their usual sheen of engine grease. Absent too was the harried atmosphere, with people running back and forth shouting orders at one another. The personnel here were cool, collected, and for the most part—absent. Apart from a few technicians, the only people there were other arriving pilots.

"Tally ho!" a British-accented voice shouted from above him. Sapper jumped back just before a duffel thumped to the floor at his feet. He looked up to see a scrawny blonde woman standing in the cockpit of an *Accipiter*. She waved.

"Sorry about that."

"Uh, no problem." Sapper regarded her as she followed her bag—which no doubt weighed more than she did—to the floor.

"Jamie Markham. Callsign Firecracker. What do they call you?" she said, sticking her hand out.

Sapper shook it. "My parents call me Daniel, the Fleet calls me Lt. Westphal, and everyone else calls me Sapper."

Jamie laughed as she picked up her bag. "Sapper? How'd you end up with that one?"

"Things keep blowing up in my face."

"Me, I go off without thinking sometimes, see? Like, one time my instructors sent me to—"

"Crackers! Wait up!" shouted another voice from the other end of the hangar.

Jamie turned. "Wally! How goes it?"

Sapper looked back. A cheerful-looking redheaded man was heading for them. "Wally what? What's his callsign?"

"Wally is his callsign. On account of talking to him is like talking to a wall. If you're his superior officer, that is. His real name is Tobias something-or-other. He was in my squadron for about a fortnight a few months ago. My CAG moved him along 'cause he couldn't stand him, same as everywhere else. Fourteen squadrons in two years is what I heard."

Tobias caught up as they reached the main hatch and were stopped by a young gray-uniformed ensign with a clipboard. "Sign in, please."

"Chill out, mate. We can do it after lunch," Jamie replied as she tried to edge around him.

But the ensign sidestepped to block her way. "Sorry, all pilots are to sign in, drop off their gear, and proceed to the briefing room on six."

~ Undercurrents ~

"Oh, shove off," Jamie said as she pushed her way past. "Last to the mess buys!"

The ensign extended the clipboard toward Tobias. "Please, I'll get put on report if I don't get—"

"Whatev," Tobias replied, ducking under the clipboard and following Jamie.

The ensign turned to Sapper with pleading eyes. Sapper was about give the guy the slip, but he hesitated. No doubt Tunny would get on his case if he didn't cut this guy a break. So Sapper grabbed the clipboard. "What do I have to do?"

"Thank you, sir. Next of kin goes here. Then personal history, flight history, and medical records. Sign here, here, and here for the confidentiality agreement, and list all personal items in the space below. Then..." the ensign added two more sets of forms. "One for each of your friends."

Sapper sighed and started writing.

§

Two hours later, Sapper dropped into a seat in the back of the briefing theater. It was designed to hold at least a hundred, but there were currently only eleven other people present. Jamie and Tobias were a few rows in front of him. Sapper opened his mouth to tell them off for ditching him with the indoc papers but before he could say anything a tall black man in Captain's bars stepped up to the dais at the front and called for their attention.

"Welcome to the Improbable Mission Force. All of you have been specially selected for your skill, your ability to assess situations, and your self-reliance. We've brought you together here because we need you to take on missions of vital importance. Missions too difficult or dangerous to entrust to a regular squadron." He stopped to let that sink in, gravely eying the smattering of assembled pilots.

Sapper rolled his eyes. Was everyone here this melodramatic? If that Captain up there expected anyone to be impressed, he'd obviously forgotten who he was talking to.

A hand went up. It was Jamie Markham. "'Improbable Mission Force' sounds frightfully bureaucratic," she quipped. "How about Impossible Mission Force?"

Laughter flowed through the group.

~ Undercurrents ~

"There was already an Impossible Mission Force," the Captain replied matter-of-factly.

"Was? What happened to it?" asked Tobias.

"CBS canned it in 1973," Jamie replied, just as the Captain said, "The pilots were all killed attempting an impossible mission."

Silence in the room.

Then the Captain smiled. "That was a joke."

Everyone laughed again.

Sapper forced a smile, but something was nagging at him. He didn't know whether it was the senior officer with a sense of humor (which until now Sapper had thought to be impossible) or the fact that he just wasn't used to having his talents acknowledged, but something felt wrong. Damned if he knew what it was.

"In all seriousness," the Captain continued, "the name Impossible Mission Force would have been inappropriate. We would never risk our best pilots if we didn't think the mission could succeed. I believe in this program. I've been pushing the brass for it for a long time. It's only the recent...circumstances that have forced them to reconsider their view of more skilled and independent-minded pilots. So let's show them what we can do."

Heads bobbed in agreement throughout the room. Sapper knew what they were all thinking—Aaron Roth. What happened to him had forced the brass to give them a chance.

"Leadership in this squadron will be chosen on a rotational basis," the Captain continued. "The commander for the first mission will be Lieutenant Westphal. If there are no further questions, please proceed to the flight deck. Skids up in fifteen."

§

"Remember," the Captain's voice crackled over Sapper's headset, "we'll be monitoring the situation closely. If at any time we judge the risk to be too great, we'll issue the order to break off."

Sapper hardly paid attention to the announcement as his fighter shot out of the airlock into the blackness of space. He flipped over and followed the carrier's hull until he met up with his squadmates near the stern. His was the last fighter to arrive,

~ Undercurrents ~

so they formed up in a loose wedge and set off for the belt.

As Sapper throttled back to cruising speed, he regarded his new squadron. Their formation was manoeuvreing like a single entity. It was gorgeous to look at. Every pilot exuded talent through their pores—which was why it seemed weird that their supposedly big important mission was to retrieve a damaged probe from the asteroid belt.

Maybe the Captain was trying to ease them into it or something. Maybe. More likely their talents were going to waste again. No doubt the Captain was really no different from the brass at all, and this whole IMF thing would turn out to be just another example of command incompetence.

Soon, though, there was no room in Sapper's brain for pondering. They entered the asteroid belt and he had to turn his thoughts toward not getting pulverized. The formation broke up, each pilot finding his or her own route through the asteroids on the same general heading. Sapper grinned as he darted through the rapidly closing opening between two humongous rocks. Now this was more like it. Not every half-trained freight hauler could fly like this.

He looked to starboard and saw Jamie and her wingmate, Tobias, playing chicken with an asteroid the size of Puerto Rico. It looked like it was going to be Rock: 1, Pilots: 0 but Tobias rolled out an instant before impact. Jamie followed a fraction of a second later, shaving it close enough to shear off the landing struts if they'd been out.

"Loser!"

"Yeah? Well, watch me invert through that canyon!"

Sapper closed in, intending to join the fun. Then his screens beeped at him, reminding him that he was carrying the enhanced electronics package. He brought up the info on the contact. It was the probe.

"I've got it. Three o'clock. Near the northern pole of that potato-shaped one," he reported to the squadron. "Cracker, time to fire up that arm."

Jamie, who was flying a specially-equipped fighter with a magnetic grapple arm mounted behind the cockpit, immediately became the center of the formation as the others regrouped around her.

They swooped in as one on the target while Sapper hung

back to keep scanning. The ten other fighters spread out to cover Jamie as she manoeuvred close enough for the grapple arm to reach the probe.

"Two minutes," Jamie reported, setting her *Accipiter* down next to an object that resembled a giant crushed soda can. "Then we'll see who can tag the most asteroids, Wally."

"Hah. Might as well hand over your money right now. I'm 98 over 100 on accuracy."

As Jamie hurried through the checklist to switch her flight controls over to the grapple arm controls, Sapper watched his screens—to scan for trouble, of course, but also to mentally catalogue which rocks looked like the best targets for the shooting contest. Suddenly there was a blip. Yellow. Unidentified. He sent the Identification Friend/Foe signal and waited for it to be returned. The IFF pinged back and the blip changed colour to red.

"IMF 1 to *Asgard*," Sapper announced. "I'm reading one enemy drone on an intercept course."

"*Asgard* to IMF 1, we copy. Be advised that the early warning buoys on the far side of the belt read three squadrons entering the area, approximately forty fighters. Chances of mission success are now less than 6%. The Captain is issuing a recall. Repeat: all fighters are ordered to return to the ship."

Sapper checked his screens. He was still only reading the one dart ship.

"IMF 1 to *Asgard*. I think we have time to—"

A chorus of "you're damn right" and "let's get that mofo" interrupted his suggestion. Immediately the ten-fighter cordon of protection around Jamie broke up and headed off willy-nilly toward the dart ship.

"Hey, cheaters!" Sapper shouted, "Wait for me and Cracker to —" but he was cut off by the *Asgard* controller.

"*Asgard* to all fighters! Destroy the probe and return immediately! Do you copy?"

But nobody was listening. Somebody (Tobias?) hissed into his radio, faking static, and transmitted a few words to the effect of "no we don't copy." Sapper rolled his eyes. Did he honestly think anyone would fall for that?

He switched over to squadron frequency (as the *Asgard* controller was no doubt also doing) and listened to them arguing over who'd get to make the kill.

"Fifty says I get it in one shot."

"Yeah? Well I got a hundred here that says I get there first."
They'd turned it into a competition—one they were cutting him
out of! "Goddamn cheating sons of—" Sapper muttered, shoving
the throttles forward and moving in to help Jamie ditch the
probe.

"No, Sapper, it's okay," Jamie protested. "Gimmie a sec to
shut down this arm and we can join the fight."

But Sapper barely heard her. As he slipped into a lower orbit,
he had a different angle on the asteroid field. A biggish rock that
had blocked part of his scans was no longer in the way. His
screens blossomed red. Ten, fifteen, twenty-five, at thirty he lost
count. They just wouldn't stay still long enough. And they were
right in position to jump his squadmates from behind.

"Guys!" Sapper shouted into the comm. "Get out of there! I'm
reading—"

But Tobias stepped on his transmission. "*Kssssshhhh* not
reading you *kssssshhh*," he lied.

"Goddammit, Wally, listen to me! There are forty fighters—not
the stupid dart things, but real fighters, about to fly up your
tailpipe!"

No reply. "Tobias!"

Still no reply. The green blips on his screen continued to plow
toward the lone red blip, the red swarm close on their tails.

"Forget the probe, we're out of here," Sapper snapped at
Jamie. Then, swearing, he started flipping through the comm
frequencies, looking for the one his squadmates had switched to.

The rearmost green blip winked out as the swarm caught up.

Sapper flipped faster. Static, static, static. Two more blips
winked out. *Come on come on, where were they?* Static, weird
pulses. *Wonder what that was, no time, keep going.* Static,
static...

"—got my port thruster, I can't—"

A green blip winked out.

"—somebody get this bastard off my—"

Another blip gone.

"This is Sapper!" he shouted, "Head for that big round one!
Use its gravity to slingshot out of there!"

Amazingly, they complied. The remaining five blips made for

the radar shadow on his screen that marked the asteroid. The red swarm followed.

While he waited for them to reappear on the other side, he switched back to Jamie's frequency.

"Firecracker, switch up to channel 9."

She joined him on the new frequency a moment later. "Sapper! What the hell is going on?"

He ignored the question. "You ready to go?"

"Yeah, I got the probe and everything—"

"Good," Sapper replied. "Turn around. Throttles to the wall on my mark."

They turned their backs on the fight. On Sapper's screens, green blips appeared from the edge of the shadow. There were only three.

"Now!" he shouted. He and Jamie firewalled their throttles. A few seconds later the three sling-shotted green blips caught up to them. The five ships closed formation and rocketed toward the edge of the belt.

On his port side, Tobias's fighter was so close Sapper could see into his canopy. Tobias was dead white and sweating. He caught Sapper's gaze and swallowed. "Thanks, man."

§

As Sapper maneuvered his *Accipiter* into its berth, he noticed an officer waiting for him. He sighed. Some things never changed. But one thing had—he didn't seem to care as much anymore. Maybe it was all the empty spaces on the flight deck. He popped the canopy and tossed the officer his helmet before the man could open his mouth.

"Yeah, yeah. The Captain wants to see me," Sapper said as he trudged out of the landing bay, leaving behind a very confused-looking deck officer.

He stepped into the lift and pushed the button for the command deck, his mind not on the motion but on the seven dead pilots. He agonized over whether he could have done more to save them, while simultaneously fuming that they hadn't listened to him. The result was an aching confusion. It was a new feeling. As his feet mechanically carried him off the lift and down the corridor, he wondered if this was how Aaron Roth had felt.

~ Undercurrents ~

He didn't bother to stop in the head and check himself out in the mirror. Over half of his squadmates were dead. Who cared if he looked presentable or not? Who cared if he got fired or not? He found he was actually sort of hoping for it. He entered the Captain's office without knocking and sat down.

"You wanted to see me, sir?" he asked listlessly.

"Yes, Lieutenant. Good work today."

Sapper blinked at him, waiting the requisite few seconds for the Captain to say that he was kidding, that he was just having some fun at Sapper's expense before busting his ass back to ensign for failing to keep his pilots alive. But the Captain's face stayed straight.

"To be honest, once I saw how many Former ships responded, I didn't expect any of you would survive," the Captain continued. "Commander Valence thought there was a fifty-fifty chance that you yourself would pull through. But the fact that you not only managed to escape but to save nearly half your squadron and the probe...well, frankly, that's amazing."

Sapper's thoughts whirled around like particles in a synchrotron. Didn't expect them to survive? He thought about his squadmates—all troublemakers. The mission they were sent on—how it seemed so easy. The fact that they were sent on a mission at all when none of them could work as a team. Then he remembered the weird pulses he'd found flipping through the frequencies and anger seared through the confusion.

"You set us up, you son of a bitch!" he shouted at the Captain, leaping out of the chair. "You put one of their distress beacons on that probe to call the Formers down on us!"

"Yes," the Captain agreed. "I set you up. I set up a group of loose cannons who were constantly endangering their home squadrons with their reckless disregard for orders. I sent them out on a mission in which they would have to obey an order on blind faith or they would be in serious danger. I taught the survivors a lesson the hard way, since all of the easier ways had failed."

Sapper collapsed back into the chair, stunned. A lesson? Seven people died to teach him a lesson? He stared at the Captain, brimming over with mixture of hatred and self-loathing.

The Captain's cold gaze met Sapper's. "Listen to me, son. More fighters than we expected responded to the call. But those

~ Undercurrents ~

seven people, they have no one to blame but themselves. We tried to save them. You tried to save them. But they wouldn't listen."

Sapper stared in horror at the Captain. "This is why the brass kept turning you down. You're playing with pilot's lives. But why? Why did they say yes?"

"I was telling the truth back there," the Captain replied. "It was because of Aaron Roth. The story is wrong—Roth didn't live because he disobeyed an order, his squadmates died because he didn't obey one. If he'd stayed in that huddle, the carrier's long-range cannons could have taken out enough of the swarm for them all to escape. But Roth wandered into the gunner's firing solution, and she wouldn't take the shot. The rumour mill took the story and distorted it, making Roth into some sort of hero. The number of pilots who wanted to believe Roth had known better than his superiors was alarming. So the brass let me have my program to identify and re-educate reckless pilots. It's simple math—potentially lose one pilot from a squadron during the program, or leave them in place and run the risk of having them wipe out their whole unit."

Sapper felt drained. He didn't know what to think anymore. The only thing he knew for sure was that he couldn't listen to any more of this. He got up to leave.

"Sit down," the Captain said. "You have not been dismissed."

Sapper didn't sit, but he didn't leave either.

"Tomorrow you will take your remaining pilots and return to the Oberon, where you will take command of your old squadron and complete the mission formerly assigned to Lieutenant Commander Kyte."

Sapper knew it would cost him, but he had to ask. "What mission?"

"As you would have been aware, had you attended the briefing or bothered to keep your comms open, her mission was to find and tag a group of Former warships, track them back to their base, and destroy it."

Sapper swallowed. So Tunny had been right.

"The random skirmishes you're so fond of are an unacceptable waste of your talents. Now that you've learned you can do better, I expect you to continue to do so."

The Captain placed a set of Lieutenant Commander's épaulettes on his desk, halfway between himself and Sapper.

~ Undercurrents ~

"You have a choice. Either take these and go find out where the bastards are coming from, or hand me your wings. Do we understand each other?"

Sapper looked at the épaulettes, weighing his response. He wanted to tell the Captain where he could shove his promotion. The bastard had set them up and killed seven people. But no matter how many times he told himself that, he couldn't make himself believe it. Those pilots had been following his lead. Their deaths were his responsibility.

He could still say no. But suddenly saying no for the sake of saying no didn't seem like fun anymore. He removed his Lieutenant's bars and placed them on the desk. Then he picked up the Lieutenant Commander's bars and slid them on. Along with the bars, the weight of the lives he'd just lost, as well as the ones he would now be responsible for, settled permanently on his shoulders.

With a smart salute, he replied, "Yes sir."

Katrina Nicholson's first published work was a ten-line story about a butterfly named "Batrina." (She was eight). She spent the next dozen or so years avoiding becoming a writer for fear of ending up living in a cardboard box. But after six years in Air Cadets, two pilot's licenses, a stint as a lifeguard, a season as assistant director of a summer camp, and four years of history at Dal, she finally gave in. Since then she has earned a Writing for Film and Television diploma from the Vancouver Film School, won a writing contest for the film *Serenity*, and been published in *Carousel* magazine. As far as living in a box goes: so far, so good.

The Reality of Dreams

Ernie kept his eyes shut and didn't move. Cupboard doors slammed and dishes crashed but he kept quiet and still. If he stayed motionless, Karen would think he was still sleeping. That was the best he could hope for in the morning. Because if she thought he was awake, she would call him names and make fun of his thick glasses and receding hairline. The house shook as the front door slammed. Ernie opened his eyes and relaxed by listening to the quiet after the storm.

As usual, Karen had left a trail of destruction through the house. Dishes lay strewn here and there in the living room. Part of the Cape Breton Post was on the floor, part on the couch, and still more was stuffed into the easy chair. Ernie started to pick up the mess when he saw the hint of orange and white peeking out from the hall closet.

He put down the paper and pushed Karen's things aside to see it more clearly. He heard the crowd chanting his name as he traced the letters on the back of the jacket the Capers had given him for leading them to victory. He carefully took it out of the closet and slipped it on. The memories went silent. It didn't fit anymore. He was too fat.

He threw it into the closet and shut the door. How could his life have ended up like this? He had been popular and good looking in high school and university. He had even dated Julie Simmons and been the envy of everyone on campus. And now? Now he pretended to be asleep so he didn't have to speak to his wife. Now he was going to spend the day answering phones at a seed catalogue for minimum wage.

Ernie piled the dishes in the sink and poured himself the dregs left in the coffeepot. He sat down at the computer to see what sort of spam filled his inbox this morning. He had forty-two new messages. Most were promising him improved vigour in bed, something he really didn't care to think about. Others promised him financial windfalls. As if.

Are you happy? the last message in his inbox asked. It had no return address, no date or time that it was sent, just the question in the subject line.

"No, I am not happy," he said as he deleted the message.

Would you like to be happy? a new message asked, again with no return address, date or time. Ernie sighed. Must be the build-up to some sort of sales pitch.

"Sure, who wouldn't," he said as he clicked away that message as well.

What would you pay to have life the way you want it? Another new message asked. He deleted it.

Well, what would you pay to have life the way you want it? A fresh message asked.

"Pretty much anything," Ernie said as he skipped to the next message.

Really? Flashed in his mailbox.

Ernie paused. This was a great marketing gimmick. They had anticipated his answers and he had to admit he was curious.

"Yes," he typed in reply.

What would you want? Asked a new message the instant his was sent.

"I want to be married to Julie, my university girlfriend, have a full head of hair, perfect vision, and a better job," he answered. That will teach those spammers. There was no way any herbal supplement could do all of that.

And what would you be willing to pay for all of that? the reply inquired.

"If you can do that you can have anything you want." Fat chance of that happening. He clicked send and waited to see what product was being advertised.

You wake up in the morning married to Julie Simmons, have a full head of hair, 20-20 vision, and work as a call supervisor at August Seed Company. Everything else stays the same. All it will cost you is your soul. Is it a deal?

Ernie shook his head. This was someone's idea of a sick joke.

~ Undercurrents ~

A prank. He deleted the message. He looked up at the clock and realized he needed to get ready for work.

As he got into the shower he started to wonder. What if it could be true? Julie really had been hot with long legs and a great body. It would be a pleasure to wake up next to her each day, and with a full head of hair and a better job, life would be perfect. He would be happy again.

When he dried himself off he wished he hadn't deleted the message. He'd like to respond to it. This could be someone else's way to laugh at him, but who cared? Everyone did anyway. Not that what he wanted would ever happen, but who knows? He went back to the computer.

Ernie, do we have a deal? a fresh message asked.

"You have a deal." Pain stabbed through his index finger and a tiny smear of blood stained the mouse buttons. Ernie waited with his sore finger in his mouth for new messages but none came.

The day progressed as every other day progressed for Ernie Johnson. Customers called to complain and order seeds. He ate his lunch in the break room by himself. He went home to find new dishes scattered around the house. He watched reruns on television until ten and then slipped into bed. He heard Karen come in but pretended to be asleep.

The next morning, the first thing he noticed was that he could see the clock clearly without his glasses. His hand went up and he felt a thick full head of hair. He sat up quickly and looked over. Lying next to him was Julie Simmons. She was a bit older than he remembered but was still blonde and shapely. Damn, he was living the good life.

Ernie dashed off to the bathroom. He was as handsome as he remembered. Life was now better than he ever dreamt it could be. Julie was still sleeping when he finished getting ready for work but that was okay, he could enjoy her later. He kissed her cheek and headed off to spend the day as a supervisor instead of as a drone. Ernie was living his dream.

§

Julie waited until she heard the door slam before she opened her eyes and got out of bed. She had almost ruined it by flinching when he kissed her. Pretending to be asleep was easier than listening to him prattle on about his great hair and important job. Why did she ever marry a superficial shell like Ernie Johnson? Sometimes she thought she could see a glimmer of something else in him but then he would go on and on about his lush hair and his perfect vision.

She trudged out to the kitchen and poured herself the dregs of coffee. With nothing else to do, she sat down at the computer to sort though the morning spam. The last message was strange. It had no date, time, or return address.

Are you happy? it asked.

She typed her reply without any hesitation.

Peter Andrew Smith makes his home in Antigonish, Nova Scotia with his wife Meredith and their two dogs, Willie and Barkley. Peter is a member of SF Canada as well as the Nova Scotia and New Brunswick Writer's Federations. His diverse fiction and non-fiction publications can be found listed at www.peterandrewsmith.ca.

For the record, Peter is happy with his life and has never been tempted to reply to spam, even on the day he won the UK Internet lottery three separate times.

Emoters

Stephanie flipped colourful cards one by one and studied the face of the woman sitting across from her.

They sat on either side of a tiny table swathed in a white linen cloth. Draped in elegant folds, the material pooled on the floor at their feet.

Stephanie's cubicle walls formed a close square around them. On the floor a CD player emitted soft nature sounds, masking the distant mall noise of bustling weekend shoppers.

The client was forty-ish, tall and thin, her close-cropped hair feathered with grey. A cool assessing stare was the sole expression on her face.

Great. A skeptic. Why'd they bother...

The card she'd just flipped elicited the faintest scent. Her nostrils flared and she breathed in deeply. Gone. The scent had been as soft as the brush of a butterfly's wing. A laughing couple graced the card.

"Are you married?"

"Yes." The woman's face remained an unreadable mask.

Stephanie would get no help there. Her partner, Carly, read the clients by facial expression, body language and tone. That wouldn't work with this one. Her own special talents might yield better results.

Rifling through the packet of cards, Stephanie thought of the talented artist who'd created them for her. His dark eyes, long curly hair, and those hands...she thrust the memories away.

She found the card she wanted and flipped it over. The card of the Entwined Lovers, their limbs tangled in ardent lovemaking. Stephanie closed her eyes to focus.

An acrid, earthy scent assaulted her. Anger. It splashed into

Stephanie's nasal passages like acid and she gasped.

Her client, still expressionless, raised an eyebrow.

Stephanie flipped another card, a bride and groom laughing under a shower of confetti.

A complex array of scents hit Stephanie. The sweet, nutmeggy scent she associated with sadness meshed with loss, laced with wisps of the acrid scent of lingering anger.

Stephanie scooped up the cards, reorganizing them into their places in her plastic container.

She glanced up at the woman's confused face. "You still love him." She reached over to touch the woman's hand. "Are you sure he's done this?"

Her client's mouth twisted into a sharp denial, but then her face crumpled and she gave a single, abrupt nod.

She needed to talk then, and Stephanie let her. Let her release her flood of pain, anger, fear, sadness and humiliation. Wave after wave of powerful scents. Stephanie struggled mentally under their weight.

Afterward, the client encompassed Stephanie's hand in both of her own. "Just saying it. Just saying the words. I feel...lighter. Thank you."

Her powerful emotions suffused the booth.

Then the scents disappeared. Stifled. Muffled. Gone.

A bad head cold could cause it, blinding Stephanie to her pheromonal sensing. But she didn't have a cold, so it must be... Evan.

Her client waited expectantly, but Stephanie had no idea what she'd just asked her. She closed her eyes. *Back off, Evan, please. God, I wish I was telepathic instead of what I am.*

Carly poked her head inside Stephanie's cubicle. She took one look at Stephanie's face and then came right in, steering the client out and chatting.

Stephanie, on tiptoes, scanned the milling crowds for Evan's head. And then the blackout lifted. Faint emotional odors lingered in the cubicle, and, if she strained, Stephanie could pick up the emotions of the closest passers-by. She slumped back down in her chair, waiting with trepidation to see if Evan would appear.

It wasn't him she didn't want to face, it was their shared past. A history that bound together eighteen "special" children kidnapped from their families and kept, under guard, at the compound. "Patients" to the scientists and military officials, the kids called themselves "inmates."

Carly strode back in, whispering, "Are you okay?"

Stephanie smiled slightly as she took in the spectacle of the "Amazing Carlita Capone".

Carly's tiny face seemed too minute to bear the towering mass of unruly curls in a most unnatural shade of burgundy. A vivid orange silk scarf contained most of it and was meant to complement her wispy, flowing orange and purple dress. Sparkly gold sandals matched the golden array of bangles, chains and hoop earrings. A thick application of makeup made Carly appear ten years Stephanie's senior. They were the same age.

"You look terrible," Carly said. The sharp, peppery scent of her concern wafted over Stephanie.

Evan must have left the vicinity, but he was close. He'd be back, and he never brought good news. Stephanie took a deep breath to push down the curdles of fear and panic in her belly and attempted a relaxed smile.

"I'm fine. Headache." She massaged her temples and forehead. It wasn't a lie.

"Sorry. That client was a tough nut. I used every ounce of my skills on her and came up dry, so I thought I'd send her to the real deal. It must have worked, she looked content."

Stephanie moved her massage to her face. "I told you I'm no psychic, Carly. I just have a way of reading people, and sometimes I throw in a little of what you taught me." Stephanie shook her head. "I keep waiting for one of them to blow up at me for not being able to tell them their future, only verify what their own instincts are telling them about the present."

"But that's really what most of them want. Just guidance."

Stephanie laughed. "So they come to the two most messed-up chicks in the world and pay us for advice. Beautiful."

"Hey," Carly said, chin jutting out with fake indignation. "I'm great at other people's lives. Just not my own!"

They packed up their cubicles, leaving the mall by a back service entrance. For Stephanie it avoided the barrage of emotionally-charged scents of a public place. For Carly it avoided any potential run-ins with her violent ex-husband, Albert, or one of his private detectives.

Carly's on-the-run lifestyle suited Stephanie's. It made Carly the perfect business partner and the only true, long-term friend she'd had in her adult life.

The two women hovered in the shadows cast by the mall until satisfied that nobody seemed interested in their camper parked in the far corner.

"Looks good," Carly muttered.

As they climbed inside their aging fifth wheel, Stephanie felt a familiar flush of guilt at her friend's practiced subterfuge. Carly remained in grave danger, but it was because of Stephanie, not her bully of an ex.

Stephanie adjusted the blinds from closed to half-shuttered and peered outside. She bit her lip. She knew she should stop being so selfish and tell Carly the truth, but she was terrified of going it alone again. Carly seemed happy with their life together.

Justifying never worked. Guilt chewed her insides.

Carly emerged from the tiny bathroom, her face pink and gleaming without its garish makeup. She sighed. "I'm me again."

Unless you watched "Carlita" enter the bathroom and "Carly" come out, you'd never recognize them as the same woman. Carly's cap of dark, pixie-cut hair, mascara-only makeup, jeans and tee-shirt look was natural and youthful.

The two woman shared a light lunch and pored over mail-order catalogues. Stephanie sat content, steeped in the light, perfumey scent of their happy companionship.

Then it was gone. Like a switch had been thrown.

Trying to seem casual, Stephanie parted the blinds.

A figure stood against the building, face shrouded in shadow. Evan. She knew his posture even without the effect of his talent pressing upon her. With a twist of his head he lifted it and the pheromonal scents returned. That was his signal.

Stephanie released the blinds and winced, waiting. It didn't take long.

"Let's go for a drive," Carly blurted. "I feel the need for speed and ocean breezes. Let's unhitch the truck and go for a spin along the shoreline..."

Stephanie let Carly babble and her own thoughts drift, the scene playing out as it must. Just like the last time—nearly two years ago now—that Evan had come. When she was forced to leave Jessie. The artist she'd been living with and just started to trust, maybe love. Oh God, not again. Poor Ev, he was just the messenger. She fought to keep her eyes from filling. The air was thick with the pheromones Evan was pumping into her friend to give her this restless excitement. Guilt nudged her in the ribs again.

Stephanie helped Carly disconnect the truck, then begged off, pleading her headache. Carly set off alone.

Evan slipped into the trailer moments after the truck roared away, ducking to get his long, lanky frame through the door.

He looked the same. A few grey hairs at the temple, but otherwise the same quiet, brooding expression.

"They found me again?" she asked, throat tight.

"No." He inspected her head to toe as if looking for imperfections.

She waited and fought off an irrational urge to scream at him to spill it. No point trying to read his scent for clues. His ability to block and smother pheromones was unmatched by any of them. They could all do it a bit, but Evan was the master.

"Then why are you here? They can track us more easily when we're together." Stephanie glanced out the window, chewing on a thumbnail.

"They didn't. And they won't again."

"What did you do?" A flicker of fear rose, but Evan stepped closer and smothered it.

"Don't do that," she snapped.

"Sorry."

"So...answer me. What did you do?"

He scratched his unshaven face uneasily. For a millisecond his blanket thinned and she caught a cocktail of conflicting emotions. Frustration, fear, pain, affection. Only one person could do that to him.

"Donnie?"

Evan nodded. "Can we sit down? Carly should be good for about an hour."

Stephanie sighed. "I hate it when you mess with her." She waved off his defensive comments. "I know, I know, we need to talk."

He looked hopefully at the leftover sandwiches and cookies, and she said, "Help yourself, I'll make tea."

She put the kettle on while he munched, a calm settling over her. Evan made her feel safe. He'd always had that effect on her, on all of them. Even before they understood why. Familiar memories thrust into her mind and for the first time in a long time, she let them come.

"It's okay. Take my hand."

Stephanie was hunched on a soft patch of fake grass, her bony knees pulled up, and her forehead pressed into them. She knew it was the boy with the soft, brown eyes and nice voice again, but she didn't look at him. She wanted to pretend the grass was real. She knew it wasn't because it had no smell. Nothing in this room had a smell, except the other kids in it. Some smelled afraid, others angry. This boy smelled nice, but when she looked at him she couldn't pretend that she was in her backyard and that the familiar smells of home, Mom and Dad surrounded her, snug and safe.

"She's just being a baby. Ignore her, she'll get over it. We all did." The second voice belonged to a boy she didn't like very much. Or at least, most times she didn't. Sometimes she liked him a lot. Like at the cafeteria last night. She'd suddenly liked him so much she'd given him her chocolate fudge sundae. Which was weird, because she'd really wanted it. She hadn't felt like crying again until the boy with the long, curly hair wiped his mouth and walked away with a smirk. Then she'd felt worse than ever.

"Come on, give me your hand, please."

She lifted her head to look at the nice boy reaching down to her.

When she didn't take his hand, he flopped down beside her. "Forget Donnie. He can be a real jerk."

"Yeah."

"My name is Evan."

She remembered now. He'd told her before, but there were quite a few kids here. "Why can't I go home?"

"Try not to think about it."

"Why?" She felt the lump in her chest swelling painfully.

"It makes it worse."

They sat on the fake grass and looked at the fake pond with the real fish in it.

"I like the fish," she whispered.

"Me too."

They watched the orange, red and yellow shapes darting

under the dark, rippling water.

"Is your scar sore?" Evan asked.

She realized she'd been fingering the bare patch of skin on her scalp. Sliding her fingers to the raised ridge in the center, she gave it a gentle probe. "Only if I touch it."

He turned so she could see the side of his head. The area around his scar had a nice thick stubble.

"Your hair's growing back!" she said.

"Yours will, too."

They smiled at each other and Evan took her hand in his. The lump in her chest dissolved and the tightness in her body melted.

She sighed. "I can't smell anyone anymore."

"Or how they're feeling."

She drew her eyebrows together and looked at him, surprised.

"It's what you're good at. Donnie and I have been snooping. But you'll be a lot better at it now that your surgery is over."

"Are you good at something?"

"Yeah. I'm doing it. If I let go, the smells will come back and you'll feel stuff again."

He started to loosen his grip but she clutched his hand. "No, don't." She leaned her head against his shoulder and they watched the fish in silence.

Stephanie was so absorbed by the memory she didn't remember bringing Evan his cup of tea. She put it down and touched his hand, letting his emotional blanket envelop her. When he raised his eyebrows at her, she just smiled and withdrew her hand, sliding into the seat opposite him.

Between bites and sips of tea, Evan explained. "I became aware of someone trying to locate me...my usual ways."

She knew what he meant. He had a dozen false addresses and aliases. If someone nosed around one he'd go to ground again, ditching his current alias.

"So I checked with my sources to see what the old gang was up to now, and they told me there'd been an industrial accident at the compound."

Stephanie's eyes widened. "How bad?"

"Looks like a bomb site."

Gone. The place she'd spent so long running away from no

~ Undercurrents ~

longer existed. The intensity of Evan's stare burned away her relief. "What? Was someone hurt?"

"Well, officially, it was just a storage facility, and the accident has been blamed on an error by the workers. They're admitting to six government employee deaths, but you and I know there were a lot of untraceable people there. The numbers must be a lot higher."

"But our program was shut down. There weren't any inmates there anyway, just scientists analyzing our data, right?"

Evan looked at the ceiling. "After we escaped, three kids died over the years on assignments. The other thirteen were allowed out into society, but were monitored. After a couple of incidents, they decided to re-institutionalize them, but only grabbed a few and the rest took off, including Wayne. When the program was officially shut down, the nine kids returned to the facility 'volunteered' to have their implants removed and be monitored for life. Seven of the nine survived the surgery. And you know about Nell and Tony."

"They shouldn't have stayed together," Stephanie muttered.

"Yeah, well, love—who can explain it? So, that just leaves you, me, Donnie and Wayne with implants."

"That's everyone?"

"Well, I went to see Gina and she said that should account for everyone up to when she left two years ago. She was one of the lucky 'volunteers' who survived the surgery."

Evan gave her a strange look. "By the way, they removed her vomeronasal organ too."

Stephanie shivered. The organ, commonly associated with dogs, was once part of human anatomy as well. Back when humans depended on pheromones for survival. It died off as one of many unnecessary attributes over the centuries. However, the kids "selected" for the program all had the genetic throw-back organ, along with unusual sensory abilities. Ordinary humans could detect the subtleties of thousands of different scents, but those with the vomeronasal organ, or VNO, were vastly superior. The implant—an advanced microchip inserted in the sensory center of the subject's brain—aided in the detection and translation of scent, pheromonal and hormonal emissions from animals. Although her enhanced sensory ability had greatly complicated her life, the thought of it being surgically removed made her feel ill.

"If Gina's being monitored, it was risky to go see her."

Evan leaned forward. "Well, Gina doesn't think she's being monitored anymore. Her 'social worker' hasn't kept his appointment, the number he gave her to call is disconnected, and the web-log for her daily diary entries has been dropped from its server."

"Weird."

"This is weirder. I went to see Wayne." Wayne kept in touch with both Evan and Donnie. Stephanie worried about that all the time.

"Yeah."

"He's dead."

"What!"

"I have a key to his place. In case I needed to crash...because his place was so secure from the compound."

Wayne worked for the mafia in New York. Dangerous, he admitted, but he was safe from whoever the Company sent hunting him. He was confident in his abilities to control the gangsters around him. They didn't understand what he could do, just that he had a good "feel" for what people were thinking.

"The mafia killed him?"

Evan gave her a hard look. "Not unless they can kill someone by making them bleed out of their nose and ears."

Stephanie's heart thudded. Only a pheromonal battle between Emoters could do that. That was their name for themselves—"Emoters." The effort to manipulate each others' emotions, suppressing and emoting back and forth, could cause pain and nosebleeds. If prolonged, the nosebleed became a gusher, your ears started to bleed, you'd have convulsions and, if unchecked, you could die. It was played out like a game of Mercy, with the stronger Emoter backing off at will. That was how Nell and Tony had died, hunted down by the Company's best, Donnie —the turncoat. Donnie had offered himself as a hunter rather than have his chip removed. Whether he'd have come after her and Evan at some point was speculation.

Wayne had told them, "No way man; Donnie's playing them. He'd never give up us three. And Tony and Nell should'a given up, not fought back. The Company had them pinned down. Donnie had no choice."

~ Undercurrents ~

Wayne. So street-smart, but so stupid when it came to Donnie. Just like all of them, including Stephanie. But not Evan. He'd stopped falling for Donnie's act years ago.

Evan stood up and put his dishes in the sink. "When I got home, the alias I'd given to Wayne alone had been contacted. And obviously it wasn't him. From the smell, he'd been dead a few days."

"Donnie killed Wayne and then tried to contact you."

"Yeah, and considering what he'd done to Wayne, whom he actually liked, I really didn't feel like catching up on old times. Especially since it was likely about finding you."

A cold finger of fear traced her spine. "Do you think the Company made it look like the compound was destroyed so that we'd get complacent and they could send Donnie in?"

"Maybe." He crossed his arms across his chest. "Whatever's going on, I wasn't going to hang around until I was forced to run again." His eyes surveyed the trailer. "I don't have your great setup, but I'm comfortable."

"I'd hardly call this four-star."

"You're not alone."

Stephanie's eyes filled. "I'm sorry. You're right, I'm lucky to have Carly. I wish you could stay with us, Ev, but you know—"

"I know." He gave her a grim smile. "Anyway, I decided to find Donnie and see what the hell he's up to."

"And?"

He pulled out a piece of paper with three cities written on it. "And he's moving around a lot."

"My God, that's our last three stops!"

"Yeah, he's closing in on you. But I'm going to close in on him first. I know where he's going to be at three o'clock today."

One hour away. "Are you going to confront him?"

"No, not yet. I'm going to do some recon. See if I can't figure out his game."

"So, where is he?"

She listened while Evan described a park on the opposite side of the city. The flyers were posted everywhere. Donnie was passing himself off as some sort of Rock-n-Roll Preacher. Only he wasn't promoting Christianity, but something called Clarity.

"His followers are growing with each whistle-stop, like a cult. And here's an interesting tidbit—his stop in upstate New York coincided with the destruction of the Project facility."

Thoughts churned through Stephanie and she looked up to see Evan watching her.

"It's up to you," he said.

"What?"

"I know you're deciding whether to come with me, and it's up to you. You're giving off that scent you always do whenever you're faced with running into Donnie. I'm not going to lie, I'm hoping you'll come with me. If things go south, I could use backup."

She looked into the eyes of that little boy so long ago by the fish pond. "Let's go."

They were pulling away in a cab when Carly returned.

Carly's shocked expression filled the driver's side window of the truck, her eyes flicking from Stephanie's face to Evan's.

"Shit." Realizing her face showed dismay, Stephanie flashed Carly what she hoped was a reassuring smile.

Stephanie glared at Evan. "She's back early. You're losing your touch."

He shrugged. "She must be very strong-willed."

To survive what she did, she'd have to be. Stephanie sighed. "Yeah, she is—very. Oh well, I'll come up with a cover story."

He smirked. "About me? Cool, can I help?" His shield thinned enough that Stephanie picked up a faint trace of the sweet, fruity smell of his playfulness, and a hint of...musk. That was a surprise.

She chuckled, but flushed and looked away. Evan firmed up his barrier.

In the awkward silence, to her annoyance, she thought of Donnie. Sex with him had been amazing. Even better than with Jessie, who'd had an artist's sensitivity and intuition. Donnie had driven her insane with desire. One time, afterward, saturated in sweat, they'd argued.

"I don't know if it's really me...if I'm truly feeling these things, or if you're influencing me with your talent. I know it's at least partly your talent, I can sense when you're using it," Stephanie said.

Donnie laughed, tossing back his long hair. "Who cares? You enjoyed yourself, so why complain?"

Stephanie watched him as he lay there. After sex was the only time she could be sure he wasn't using his talent.

~ Undercurrents ~

"Don't you ever feel guilty about manipulating people's emotions?" She swallowed. "Because I do."

He rolled his eyes. "I told you to stop spending time with that whiner, Evan."

"He's part of our team."

"Yeah, well, aside from training, I mean."

"So you don't."

"Don't what?" He sat up and started getting dressed.

"Feel guilty?"

He didn't answer. Zipping his jeans, he gave her a slow smile. Then sighed. His brain chemicals weren't recovered enough to use his talent on her. "No, okay. Satisfied? Not a bit. We were born with active VNOs. Like animals. Sniffing out danger, sexual partners, prey, allies. Then these scientists take us from freaks to super-humans and all we have to do is work for them? Big deal."

He'd be back on his game soon. Evan had taught her to temporarily block him, but she couldn't sustain it. She got up and pulled on her clothes. Sex was all she could ever expect from Donnie. In her clear-minded moments she understood that. Still, her eyes filled as she escaped from the room, hurrying before he either saw or sensed her despair.

Down the hall, she gave in to her tears. He was right about one thing. Her real life was stolen from her and she was stuck here, so she might as well perform. They were by far the top team. She was the best at reading people, Donnie at manipulating them and Evan at smothering emotions. She wasn't proud of all of their work, like when they'd affected big business and influenced politics. But they'd defused dangerous criminal situations and resolved three kidnappings with only one death. A kidnapper had blown his own brains out. Donnie pheromonally "persuaded" him it was the right thing to do. He'd then convinced their handlers that the man had been about to shoot the victim, the ten year old son of a prominent CEO.

Stephanie hadn't sensed any sign of aggression or hopelessness from the kidnapper. Even more telling had been her sense of Donnie's frustrated boredom with the long resolution process. But Stephanie and Evan didn't dispute the story. In the past they'd come to regret challenging Donnie. It did serve to sicken them enough that they found the courage to follow a dangerous plan and escape the compound less than two weeks later. They knew Donnie would never forgive them for leaving him behind. They hid as much from him as from the organization.

After a couple of close calls they'd split up.

"I'll find you," Evan had promised her. And he always had. She knew he followed her and covered her tracks. She remained terrified, however, that one day it would be Donnie, not Evan, standing in front of her trailer.

Stephanie sucked in her breath and met Evan's eyes. "I don't know if I can face him."

He covered her hand and her panic evaporated. "Today's recon only, okay?"

"Okay." But getting close to Donnie carried inherent risks. Although manipulation was his strong suit, he'd always been sensitive to Stephanie's scent. And one inkling of a pheromonal blackout and he'd start looking for Evan.

The cab pulled into a large, sprawling park. This corner was partitioned off with high portable fencing, like a circus used when it came to town. Campers, port-a-potties and a huge tent sat inside.

Stephanie shook her head at Donnie's three-ring circus. They walked toward the tent. Stephanie hesitated when she saw the large man outside collecting tickets.

"Don't worry," Evan slid two tickets back and forth between his fingers. "I've got you covered, fortune-teller."

She grimaced at him playfully as he handed them to the man. Her face went blank, however, as the flaps were opened. She and Evan staggered back at the onslaught of pheromones flooding their senses.

Evan closed his eyes, pinching the bridge of his nose. "God, this is killing me, and I'm not nearly as sensitive as you. Are you going to be okay?"

She slid trembling fingers into his and nodded. "I am now. We have to find out what's going on."

A second man joined the ticket-taker outside the tent and they whispered, looking Stephanie and Evan over.

Even without her ability Stephanie could have sensed the aggression and animosity behind their cold, assessing stares. They stepped inside.

Excitement and anticipation thrummed through milling people. The majority of the crowd were in their twenties or thirties.

The buzz of voices in the darkened tent hushed as a beam of light illuminated the small stage, throwing into silhouette a single figure carrying a guitar. Sitting on a wooden stool, he began to play and hum. The lights did not illuminate his face until he began to add words to the tune.

Donnie's voice was powerful and lilting with a gentle tone.

The crowd sang along with enthusiasm, seemingly knowing every word.

"He's good," said Evan.

Stephanie nodded. *I wonder if he's manipulating hormones in the first couple of rows?* And then the wave of pheromones lapped over them. Evan and Stephanie glanced at each other wide-eyed.

"No way he can reach way back here!" Evan shook his head in disbelief.

It was impossible. None of them had that kind of power.

The mood of the crowd began to shift into one of the most basic of human emotions. Sexual desire crackled like static. Bodies began to rub together much more than accidentally and lusty looks were exchanged. Stephanie resisted the flickers in her own belly and noticed that Evan's palm within her hand had become sweaty. "How's he doing this?" she asked. Evan shrugged.

They peered through the semi-darkness to where Donnie sat, playing the same few bars over and over as he concentrated on the crowd. The pheromones pulsed from him. It was his signature. Sexual manipulation had always been Donnie's favorite game.

Stephanie squinted. There was other movement on the stage. Five large men emerged, their faces seemingly devoid of features. Donnie conversed with them briefly, pointing into the crowd with one hand covering the microphone.

The men, all wearing some type of breathing apparatus, climbed down from the stage. Unaffected by the pheromones sluicing around them, they moved through the crowd, separating entwined people and bringing some of them to the stage. This took considerable force because those selected seemed most affected by the pheromones, making love with abandon.

Stephanie turned to see if Evan saw what was happening. He was looking behind them, eyebrows knotted with concern. "Uh,

Steph..."

She craned her neck to see a familiar brunette, pressed up against a man, kissing him.

"Carly!" Stephanie gasped.

Carly raked her fingers through the man's hair and pulled him closer.

"Oh God, she must have followed us!" Stephanie shoved her way through the bodies, Evan close behind.

As she neared Carly, the pungent, musky odour of the couple's desire swirled around Stephanie. Glancing back, she cursed as she saw Evan hopelessly ensnared in a cluster of people, fighting to extricate himself. The young man slid his hand under Carly's shirt. *I can't wait for Evan's shield.* Barrelling through the last few people, Stephanie grabbed Carly's arm and yanked. "Carly!"

"Steph?" Carly turned swollen lips and glazed eyes toward her.

"Come on, Carly, snap out of it."

Carly returned to the kisses of the enamored man.

Yanking Carly's arm again, Stephanie slapped her, hard.

Gasping, Carly held her cheek. Confusion flooded her face as she regarded the man who held her. He moved to kiss her again, but Carly struggled to pull away.

"Let go of her!" snapped Stephanie.

The women's struggles seemed to inflame him even more and he engulfed Stephanie with his arms as well.

"Enough, friend," said Evan. The man's grasp slackened and the two women pulled away.

It was the young man's turn to look confused and ashamed.

Dashing away from his sputtered apology, they made for the exit.

Stephanie glanced back at the stage. Donnie spoke to the men leading away five audience members. Then he approached a screened-off area of the stage that Stephanie had not noticed. A young girl in a long, flowing dress emerged and took his hand.

Stiffening, Donnie pivoted and faced Stephanie, who was silhouetted by the light spilling in from the open tent flap. She slipped out.

Evan and Carly were just outside. "What were you looking at?" Evan asked as he rubbed a hand down Carly's arm, calming her.

Stephanie crooked one finger and they all went to the edge of the tent. Peeking around, they saw Donnie, the child and nine men walk away from the back of the tent. They entered a small trailer nearby marked "Security".

"Who's the kid?" asked Evan.

"I don't know, but I bet that belongs to the star of the show." She pointed at a huge motor home parked against the fence.

Trying to look casual, they walked toward it.

Stephanie grabbed Carly by the hand. "Listen, go home, okay? I'll explain all of this to you later, I swear."

Carly's mouth tightened. "I'm not going anywhere without you."

"You really should." Stephanie took a deep breath and began to focus on her friend.

Evan smothered her efforts. "You don't want to do that. For three reasons."

Stephanie gave him an annoyed look.

"First, you hate using manipulation on a friend. Second, as soon as she steps away from the park she's going to snap out of it, fast, because she's strong-willed, and third..." he nodded toward the back of Donnie's trailer. "She's the only one who can fit through there."

A minuscule window had been left open, the curtain fluttering in the breeze.

They slunk closer.

Stephanie eyed the opening. "I doubt even Carly can fit through that."

"I will, if you tell me what that singer did to me, and how you snapped me out of it."

"It's a long story. Look, Donnie controls how people are feeling through hormones...it's a special talent. And I, well, I slapped you because it was the quickest way to end it. Pain neutralizes some of the effect."

Carly was eyeing them strangely. "And why didn't it affect you two?"

Evan was shoving the screen out of the window. After a moment of effort, it clattered to the floor inside. They all held their breath. There was no reaction from inside.

Carly raised her eyebrows pointedly at Stephanie.

"We have talents too. Evan can block Donnie as well as mute someone's feelings."

"And you?" Carly said it like she already knew.

"Let's just say that even if we'd never met, you hadn't spoken...even with my eyes closed, I'd know you were annoyed, angry, and," Stephanie's eyes filled, "afraid of me."

Carly took a deep breath, held it and then let it out. She walked over to the window by Evan. "Give me a boost."

Evan looked to Stephanie first. She nodded.

After a struggle, Carly wriggled inside.

Evan and Stephanie went around to the door and waited, scanning the security trailer for signs of movement.

Several people staggered out of the big tent, disheveled and dazed.

"Come in," muttered Carly as she opened the door, "quick." Carly's tee-shirt was torn and her stomach scraped.

They scrambled inside, re-locked the door and looked around. The camper was luxurious and elegant with an abundance of oak, leather and brass.

"Yeah," said Carly in response to Stephanie's open-mouthed stare. "A hell of a lot nicer than our little tin can. Now tell me what you guys are looking for, because you're obviously not waiting around for a chat with him."

Evan was already rummaging through drawers.

Stephanie joined him. "We're trying to figure out what he's up to, just dig and if you find anything interesting or unusual let us know."

Stephanie didn't meet Carly's penetrating glare. The scent from her friend was chiefly disappointment, and she just couldn't deal with it right now.

The table held remnants of lunch and a sketch pad with a childish but excellent rendering of a horse and rider, galloping. A pillow, blanket, sheets and a teddy lay folded on a seat.

"Where'd he pick up the kid?" Stephanie pondered aloud.

Carly was flattening out a map of North America which was highlighted and marked. "Any chance she's his?"

"Maybe. But he's careful about that."

"That sounds like personal experience. And there's no such thing as 'careful enough' when it comes to making babies. Unless he's celibate."

~ Undercurrents ~

"No way that much has changed."

Carly gave her a look of frustration. "You *are* going to tell me everything soon, right?"

"Yeah, sorry."

"Oh my God!" said Evan from the back room.

The girls joined him in what was the master bedroom. One end held a desk and filing cabinet that Evan had eviscerated. Papers lay scattered over the floor and bed.

Kicking papers out of the way, the girls moved to examine several photos Evan fanned out.

Stephanie peered at one of a man in a business suit. He looked familiar. "Who is that?"

Evan's barrier was down and Stephanie could pick up on not only his alarm, but also his excitement and fear.

"Well, of these five men in the photos, three of them have something in common. They're dead. One was a CEO from Ottawa and two were gang affiliates from Toronto." He pointed at the others. "This guy I don't know, but this last guy, the one you asked about, he's the mayor of this city. Not dead, though. Don't you guys watch the news or read papers?"

"Not much," said Stephanie.

"You know," said Carly. "Toronto and New York were our last two stops, and that's what I was going to show Stephanie when you called out. Come here."

They followed her back out to the map she had spread out.

Carly traced her finger along a trail of yellow highlighter. "Yeah, see Steph, this is almost exactly our route. That can't be a coincidence, can it?"

"So what, he's following us *and* murdering people along the way?" Stephanie asked Evan incredulously.

"These are high profile individuals or mob targets."

"So Donnie's become a hit-man?"

Evan shook his head. "I don't know. These men were either shot or stabbed. Donnie doesn't need to get his hands dirty like that to kill someone."

"So what's the rock singer/puppet master shtick about—" Stephanie broke off and inhaled sharply. She shoved Carly toward the bathroom door. "Get out, Carly! They're coming. Evan and I will hold them off."

Carly dashed toward the bathroom and Stephanie slid the

folding divider door closed. Evan moved toward the front.

"Evan, buddy. Always a surprise to see you, you sly dog with the sneaky barrier. And my sweet Stephie," Donnie inhaled as though smelling a bouquet of flowers. "You, baby, I could sniff out of a crowd of a thousand. And I did, by the way," His eyes met hers and he gave her a slow, sensual wink. "I knew you were out there and I was so hoping you were coming to see me." He grimaced at Evan. "Minus one tight-ass."

Stephanie could still faintly smell Carly, no doubt fighting to get back out the tiny window. Donnie had never had her skill in sensing, but he seemed so powerful now she needed to distract him.

She filled her mind with sensual images from her last night with Jessie to elicit the right flare of pheromones.

Evan shot her a look of shock.

Donnie's nostrils flared. "Mmm, happy to see you too, baby," he whispered.

The door opened and a man stood there with the little girl. "I brought her, sir."

"Perfect. Stand outside, and if anyone other than me comes out, shoot first."

"Yes sir. Uh, do you want me to call the police?"

Donnie gave him a withering glare. "Just send someone *with* a brain back to check that our new recruits are properly armed and memorizing the photo. Nicky and I'll be over for their last motivational speech shortly."

The willowy little girl in the flowing dress entered. She had long, dark hair and looked to be around eleven. She clutched Donnie's hand, keeping her eyes cast down. She only looked up at Donnie's face.

Donnie smirked at Evan and Stephanie's obvious interest in the girl. "This is my niece, Nicky. Or, at least, that's what we're telling people." He crouched and touched Nicky's face. "Blood relation or not, it doesn't matter. We're family because of what we can do, right, Nick?"

The girl gave a slow, tentative smile, still refusing to look at the other two adults.

"This is Evan and Stephanie, Nicky, and they were once part of my family too, but they left us." Donnie stood and met Stephanie's eyes. "Maybe they're sorry and they want to come

~ Undercurrents ~

home, or," he shifted his gaze to Evan, "maybe they're here to hurt us and we'll have to deal with that."

For the first time Nicky's eyes shot toward Stephanie's face. "Uncle Donnie, let's just make them promise to leave and never come back. If they come back, we'll know they're bad and we'll..." she pointed to the security trailer. "We'll make a soldier who can stop them. But only if they come back—"

Donnie was shushing her, but her voice rose with fear and anxiety. It was a sour tang in Stephanie's nose.

As the child began again, Donnie barked, "Enough!"

Stephanie sensed the smack of intense fear he shot into the child, stilling her into pale acquiescence.

Evan spoke, "My God, Donnie. You're brainwashing people to murder for you?"

Donnie's smiled at Evan with evil promise. "Evan, you have always been a thorn to me. I wanted it to be different, I really did. Your ability, mine, Steph's, we could have done anything."

Evan stared at the ceiling, apparently deep in thought. "How's it even possible? No matter how hard you dose someone, the pheromonal influence would never last long enough for them to pull off these types of murders. You'd have to follow them around reinforcing it. It would be easier to do it yourself. But then, where's your alibi? I guess you're long out of town by the time it happens."

"You never give me enough credit, Evan. I found the perfect way to start building my dreams with my music and then I catch wind of renewed research at the compound. A second phase of kids whose vomeronasal organs were manipulated genetically to be even more powerful than ours. Well, I couldn't let that happen."

Evan and Stephanie looked at each other in horror. There'd been children in the compound when it was destroyed.

"When I found out about Nicky," he put his hands on the girl's shoulders, "and that she could make my suggestions louder, stronger and longer-lasting, well, the opportunities it presented were irresistible. My dreams grow every day."

"Yes, well, using people always was your true talent," said Evan.

While the men argued, Stephanie tried to catch Nicky's eyes. She never held her gaze for more than a second. Whispers of emotions flitted between them each time.

Donnie must have picked up on it, because he shot Stephanie a look and squeezed Nicky's hand. "No, Nick, we'll make friends with Steph later." He leveled a look at Stephanie. "*If she stays out of this. Evan's become a problem. Help me.*" The last two words were not a request.

The child riveted her attention on Donnie.

Evan stiffened.

The pulse of pure emotions that shot from Donnie was so powerful, the outer edge of it lanced into Stephanie and she gasped.

Evan seemed to be in agony, his mouth open in a soundless scream. He gripped the table, writhing.

"Donnie, stop it!" yelled Stephanie. How could little Nicky be responsible for Donnie's incredible jump in ability? The child trembled with effort as she sent her enhancing ability to Donnie.

"Steph?" came a tiny whisper behind her. It was Carly. She was still here. She had edged the folding door open a crack and was staring at Evan in alarm.

"Go!" Stephanie mouthed at her, glancing at Donnie. He seemed too engrossed in torturing Evan to notice.

But Nicky had, her gaze flicking toward the rear of the trailer. As she did, Donnie seemed to falter and Evan drew in a shuddering breath.

Carly and Stephanie's eyes met. The girl was the key.

Carly pulled deeper into the shadows and Stephanie reached out to Evan, sending him soothing, calming emotions.

"Stay out of this, Stephanie," warned Donnie.

"You're hurting him, Donnie, please let him go." As she spoke, Stephanie looked into Nicky's eyes, not Donnie's.

"I'll let him go. Right after I make him hemorrhage." He shrugged. "I'll try not to kill him, baby, for you, but there's no guarantee." He shot a look of impatience at Nicky. "What's the holdup? Is something wrong?"

Nicky glanced at the folding door. "Um, no."

There was a crash from deep inside the trailer, followed by the tinkling sound of falling glass.

Oh God, Carly hurt herself trying to get out.

"What the hell was that?" asked Donnie.

He moved toward the back, but Evan stretched out his hand

and attacked Donnie with a barrage of emotions.

Donnie froze and shot a stream back, gesturing at Nicky to help out.

The little girl leveled her stare at Donnie.

Evan groaned.

"Nicky, please stop," Stephanie knelt by the child and took her hand.

The folding door opened and Carly walked out, disheveled and pale.

Donnie looked shocked for a moment, but then focused his glare on Carly.

For a second she faltered, and then continued toward Stephanie and Nicky. Teeth gritted, she fell to her knees in front of the child.

"I understand," she said, panting, "I do, honey. Better than anyone. He's your family—all you have. You feel like he'll only love you back if you do what he wants? But if he loved you, he wouldn't make you do things you didn't want to do."

Donnie, enraged his attack on Carly was having little effect, kicked her in the ribs.

Carly saw it coming and threw herself backwards to absorb some of the impact, grabbing Donnie's leg as she fell.

He landed hard and twisted, struggling to get back on his feet.

Evan leaped on him, joining the tussle on the floor.

Nicky was crying. Stephanie took the girl's face in her hands.

"We have to stop him, Nicky."

Nicky widened her eyes. "I hate it when he makes me hurt people, or makes them do stuff they don't want to do...but I won't hurt him. I can't."

"Okay, but you don't have to help him."

Nicky lowered her face to her knees and sobbed.

Stephanie told her, "Close your eyes and cover your ears. I promise we'll only do enough to stop him."

I hope. Standing, she faced the scrabbling forms. Carly was curled under the table, cradling her ribs. Donnie sat on Evan and seemed to be getting the upper hand.

Stephanie concentrated on Donnie, thrusting a stab of fear at him.

His face contorted. "Stephanie!"

Evan shoved him away and struggled to stand.

"Nicky!" yelled Donnie.

The child sobbed louder and began to hum, plugging her ears and keeping her eyes shut.

Evan shielded Stephanie and she slammed Donnie. He squirmed on the floor, calling to Nicky, unable to retaliate through the barrier.

Stephanie knew the one emotion that would end it. The one that Donnie's brain seemed unable to conceive on its own. Remorse. She flooded him with it, tapping easily into her own.

He struggled and thrashed. Blood dripped from his nose. Evan laid his hand on Donnie's head and Donnie went suddenly still. Evan had done this before, smothering a target's consciousness, but it took everything he had. Evan slumped into the seat at the table, lowering his face into his arms. "He was weakened enough for me to put him under," he said in a muffled voice.

Stephanie laid one hand on his shoulder. He rubbed his face across her knuckles.

"Can you keep him under?"

He lifted his head. "Maybe. I'll need a minute."

Stephanie crouched by Carly. "Are you okay?"

Carly still cradled her ribs. "They're not broken. I remember what that feels like."

Stephanie laughed. "You *are* the amazing Carlita Capone. The one person in this room without heightened abilities stood up to Donnie first. How?"

Carly grinned weakly. "Remember what you said earlier? About pain keeping you immune?" Carly dropped an object that hit the floor with a tinkling sound. A bloodied, jagged piece of glass. Her palm was deeply lacerated. "It does help."

Stephanie grabbed a linen napkin from the kitchen counter and bound Carly's hand, whispering, "You are the toughest chick I know."

Carly's grin spread.

Stephanie crawled over to Nicky and pulled the still-crying child into her arms.

"It's over, sweetie."

The security guard began pounding on the door. "Donnie, sir? Is everything all right in there?"

~ Undercurrents ~

Reaching up, Stephanie slid the lock into place.

After a moment of silence, the guard ran off.

"Evan, we're going to have company," Stephanie said.

He rummaged in Donnie's pockets and pulled out a set of keys, shaking them in victory. He tossed them to Stephanie. "You drive; I'll baby-sit."

She climbed into the driver's seat and was just shifting into drive when the security guards came pelting outside.

"Hang on." She narrowly missed the lead man who was pawing at his shoulder holster for a gun.

"Too late, big boy." Gravel sprayed as she peeled away.

After a moment, Nicky and Carly curled up together in the passenger seat.

"What's going to happen to Donnie?" asked Nicky.

"We're taking him to a hospital where we'll 'persuade' a surgeon that a mysterious growth in his sinus cavities has to come out immediately. We'll 'persuade' them to destroy the organ. And we're leaving Donnie in their capable hands after 'suggesting' a psych evaluation."

"What about me?" Nicky whispered.

Stephanie raised her eyebrows. "What? What about you? You're family." She met Evan's smiling eyes in the rearview mirror. "We're all family."

Carly wrapped her uninjured hand around Nicky's two. "Damn right."

Although it was likely that Donnie's goons had come somewhat to their senses without the constant influence of Donnie and Nicky, Stephanie drove two towns over before slowing down.

She sensed Evan giving Donnie another dose and began to worry that Evan would injure himself. She bit her lip as she saw him dab at blood that dripped from his nose.

A kilometer later she passed a sign for a hospital and released her tension.

Stephanie looked over at Carly, deep in conversation with Nicky. At the hospital she'd tell her friend the truth. Stephanie had 'influenced' her monster ex into a very long prison term. Carly was free to stay or go, although she'd be a welcome addition to their little troupe. There were so many things they could do together, not the least of which would be finding their families.

~ Undercurrents ~

Stephanie filtered through all the emotional currents lapping through the camper. She latched onto one she was delighted to realize was resonating in her own chest. An emotion she'd felt only vicariously for so long. Hope.

❦

Julie A. Serroul lives with her husband and two children in a log house overlooking Bras d'Or Lake. She routinely turns her back on mundane reality to delve into the fascinating realms of speculative fiction. Julie writes short stories that must be beaten, threatened and coerced down from obnoxiously long-winded novellas. Giving in to her wordy muse, she is currently finishing a dark fantasy novel started during National Novel Writing Month.

Under duress, she is accepting applications for a four-legged friend of the canine variety to join her clan. Must be willing to sweep up own hair, have impeccable hygiene, an aversion to jumping onto furniture, and excellent bladder control.

~ Undercurrents ~

My Grandmother's Hologram

"Luna!" My grandmother barks at me. It is just her way. "Don't fiddle with that, child."

I am no longer a child but I resort to childish ways, toying with the remote, randomly altering her reality out of nervousness. Gran is squatting on her rocklike hassock in an absurd little corner of our habitat, gazing across an ocean that exists only in her memory. A sailboat vanishes on the western horizon, reappears in the east in the same interval as the passing clouds. Waves lick rhythmically at her feet. With just the right combination of settings I can make them rise and thunder onto the beach in a churning foam but they disappear before they can recede. There are no tides. My father, who was only fourteen when he designed the hologram for her, has never seen the ocean and did not consider this. It is an oversight for which she still reprimands him when she is in one of her moods, or he is in one of his.

The weak morning light filters through the adjacent solarium and at this early hour appears to dance and sparkle upon the water. She says it is a sickly light, without warmth, nothing like the vibrant, blazing sun of her childhood. Still, it is her favourite time of day, when the illusion seems most real.

A dozen times this past year, with my commencement looming, Gran and I have spoken privately of my going off-world; I am hoping my news will not disappoint her. This is why I delay telling her until my father arrives. For once the certainty of his response is a steadying influence instead of a weight on my heart.

I settle the screaming seagulls to a gentle long-interval swoop and turn away from the hologram to the alcove window. I scan the forest floor far below, hoping to please Gran with the sighting of some rare species, but the only evidence of the existence of any animal is the subtle meandering trail among the wild grasses and bracken. High above, a sky dome caps the entire sector. It reminds me of the bell jar in our science lab in grade school with its scientific proportion of flora and fauna, a self-supporting environment. Karlof says the state has no interest in conservation, that the wildlife here is in service to the human population much like the canaries in the coal mines of history, measuring with their lives the qualities of our filtered air and artificial sun. It is one more argument for the breakfast table. Gran would have them all released. My father echoes the propaganda that they would be worse off in the wilderness where airborne toxins, polluted water and the lethal rays of the once-healing sun are culling them to extinction. To me, it is obvious that the same thing is happening within the enclave. No young are born here. The adults do not mate. New additions appear full-grown, lively and curious, until they too lapse into the stress-patterns of long-term captivity. But where do they come from, if not the outside?

My father's creative genius in the field of holography has earned us this lofty penthouse habitat. Like the animals, I have grown to adulthood encased in this elaborate cocoon—not wholly of my father's design, but of men like him, men who reward their own by removing us beyond the fringes, sealing us off from the filth and violence and disease we are told infest the city. On one side a windowless facade keeps us blind to the smog-encrusted cityscape, on the other we enjoy a panoramic view of one of the most exceptional wilderness fantasies in the suburbs, more of his work. The illusion of distant fields and mountains merges so smoothly with the narrow band of wooded parkland no one but the keepers could ever find their way to the feeding cages.

When I was very young my Gran and I conceived an elaborate plan of escape. We would live where we could run beside the ocean, the real ocean, under the free and open sky, wading knee-deep in the cold strait waters where she lived as a girl. "An old woman's foolishness," my father said, "feeding the fanciful dreams of a child." Lately I look at her and I see myself sixty years on, and I wonder: is this my future? Basking in a re-engineered past so that I might forget for a time that we are living in a bell jar?

~ Undercurrents ~

These days Gran says she is content, that she has lost her desire for adventure. But I see how her eyes light up when Karlof arrives with tales of the streets and the people he meets there. He brings her word from the underground as if she is a trusted member of the conspiracy, keeps her updated on men and women whose aliases are legendary. For these are the ones who are surviving—who have survived for years—in the uncontrolled environment, who slip in and out of the city at weak points in the sentinel and breathe words of encouragement into the ears of those who would listen and believe, as Karlof and I do. And he listens with the same rapt attention as she maps her memory of the natural forest beyond the city walls, of pristine rivers and lakes she remembers like yesterday, of water that does not taste of purification and air that is cleaner than the sealed oxygen-infused atmospheres of living complexes such as ours. Of the sun's healing rays—not diverted by vast energy recovery domes to be sold back to us reconstituted—but full spectrum light, greening the earth at no cost to anyone.

My father shakes his head and repeats the stock lines of officialdom, reminders of failed attempts at escape, the trials that followed and the harsh sentences imposed by proxy on entire families—all of it carefully scripted in order to counter the romantic illusion that a better world, a better life might exist beyond the world we know. Occasionally there are news clips of bodies sighted by patrolling drones. Bodies, we are told, that are not recovered because of the danger of exposure to the rescue crews. Exposure to what, they do not say.

Karlof and I have a plan, a single vision we have arrived at by vastly different paths. I have woven a dream of my future like a tapestry here on the beach with Gran, threading together the history and story books and memories she has shared from a time long past. He comes to it from an attitude of rebellion. For just beneath his refined manners lies a defiance of the social order that punished his entire family for his father's crime.

Five years ago, when my above-average results on the mandatory board exams delivered me all but physically into the hands of residential school masters for a course of advanced study, both Gran and my father cautioned me. It was time to come down out of the stars, find a practical application for my imagination. But my school experience did not bring me down to earth. Rather, it gave me wings.

For that is where I met Karlof, this older boy, a dropout from an inferior school who had taken a job at our library so that he might have access to historic texts normally reserved for those who could afford tuition. In the lounge he drew us into conversation and filled our heads with ideas that conflicted with what we were being taught, showed us their sources in books our grandfathers might have studied and explained the history of erasure, the concept of revisionism. Soon I was a class of one, exploring with Karlof a curriculum that was not part of the calendar: the art of reading between the lines, the religion of soul-searching, the science of deception, the wisdom of questioning authority.

§

Last night I sat next to Karlof in a tiny bar on the fringes of Sector Bravo, acting casual, avoiding the subject that was uppermost in my mind.

"When I was a little girl," I said, "my mother told me I would leave the Earth and never come back."

I don't remember much about her, but I remember that. Gran says it didn't mean anything, that she said it only because she met my father too young and married too soon. She didn't want the same for me. But I continued to give it the power of prediction, accepting that I would enlist for a tour of duty off-world.

I toyed with the fringe of my scarf. "You must know, it's not where my heart is."

I should not have been disappointed by his silence. We have never declared our feelings. He has been at different times a best friend, a companion, a brother. And yes, we have crossed a line that brothers and sisters should never cross. In the quiet moments of many dawns we have discussed my career options and planned out a utopian future. His incomplete education qualifies him for no more than basic wages but three years of my off-world credits would set us up nicely, enabling us to spread our purchases of survival gear and provisions over time so that it might seem to be for adventure vacations and leisure pursuits. That is where many others have gone wrong, acting too quickly,

~ Undercurrents ~

drawing undue attention by making too large an outlay on suspicious goods.

In the sharing of dreams there have been no promises made. But I have hoped. More than hoped.

I forced a brave smile. "It's only three years. And by the time my tour of duty is up you will have everything in place."

He shook his head slowly. "I don't think that's going to happen."

"But you will wait, won't you? You won't go without me."

"At the end of three years," he said, "you will be trained in weapons and self-defence. But—"

"But what?"

"You're so—"

"What? Young? Is that it?"

"Idealistic," he said, ignoring my outburst. "It's a noble trait. But you lose yourself in it. Like tonight. How many patrons have come in while we've been talking? How many have left? Who is sitting behind us? No, don't look. Where are you now, Luna? You are not here in this bar, alert to what is happening around you. You are in your own head, making pretty plans. But would you sense the animal stalking you? Could you kill it, eat its meat when there is nothing else? Could you draw your weapon on a man, knowing you stand between him and the first food he has seen in days? Or because you are female and he is in need? Or would you hesitate, even in that moment, to rationalize the value of human life?"

This is how it is with him. He inflames me to anger, and in the same breath silences me with the truth. I envy him his freedom—not just the freedom of experience, breaking rules and traversing the extremes of society from the elite to the subhuman, but the freedom that comes from within, that allows him to assimilate into any milieu without ever losing himself. At the same time I resent how he flaunts his lower class experiences as something more enviable than my privilege. How can he compare his vague feeling of entrapment within the broader bounds of society to the confined existence I have led, when he wanders the city at will? Or reproach me as if I have chosen to be born into this class? Anyone can see my life has been far more repressive than his.

There was no point in lashing out. Since we entered the bar

~ Undercurrents ~

the Karlof I knew had been regressing into the tough persona he dons with a seasoned actor's aplomb, a fad among a certain university crowd. None of them are friends of mine. Individually, on campus, they are much like him, intelligent, curious and law-abiding. After curfew they come together like a swaggering band of thugs, challenging the law for sport, not quite criminal but pushing boundaries, secure in their group mentality. To them it is a game. Whether they graduate or not, their success is already mapped out for them or will be bought by their fathers. To Karlof it is a key that opens doors that would otherwise be shut in his face. Doors that will eventually lead us to the outside. This sport, he says, this ability to develop a whole new personality and wear it like a mask, may one day make the difference between life and death. For both of us.

I worry that this act of his—of theirs—is changing him, making him into something he is not.

"You follow their lead," I once accused him, "because you don't want anyone to see who you really are."

"And who am I?" He waited, maddeningly amused.

"Nothing like them."

"Uneducated, you mean? One of the lowly masses having to work for a living?"

"Be serious. You know it's nothing like that. They are brats—crass and unfeeling. And they take pleasure in it. That's the worst of it."

"While I, on the other hand, am what? One of those 'sensitive loving men' from your Gran's collection of romance novels?"

I blushed. What would he say if he knew the hours I have spent playing and replaying those discs?

"If I did think that," I said, "it would be a compliment."

"Is it? And what chance does a man like that have in a world like this?"

At the time I supposed he spoke of himself. But I have come to believe it was his father he meant. Karlof has never mentioned him, except to say he died in prison. I am left to assume it was a crime against the state. It is a punishable offense to speak in defence of one convicted of such a crime. This would explain not only Karlof's reticence, but why his family was stripped of privilege and relocated to a welfare compound. It was in that environment that Karlof grew to adulthood, his hard strength

~ Undercurrents ~

drawn from one world, his refinement and intellect a remnant salvaged from the other.

What little I know of Karlof's past I learned not from him but from a concise report on my father's flash drive. Through the social protocol of investigation I have been welcomed as extended family into many homes. But I worried that Karlof would not consider such a request the compliment it is meant to be, that prior approval and Safe status would be not merely meaningless to him but repugnant. But he signed the waiver allowing access to all of the documented details of his life. When the report came he confirmed its contents without apology, made no excuses for his undesirable connections and activities. His honesty seemed to please my father. Their conversation drifted to politics and I entertained myself by watching the memory screen on the desk. It was on a short loop through my father's military service, a professional compilation of action shots and stills. A group of troopers moved about, getting into line, draping their arms fraternally over each other's shoulders. The lens zoomed in on my father and the man to his left, captured them in a smiling, programmed pause before fading to the next sequence. The man might be Karlof in a few years.

Karlof signalled the barman to refresh our drinks.

"I don't understand," I said. "What about our plans? In three years when my tour of duty is up am I just supposed to go back to my father's world, to the hologram he has built around me? No. I can't. If I am going to break free, it has to be now, when I go off-world."

"Free," Karlof said. "You give the word more power than it deserves. There are limits no matter which path you take. Yes, I edge into dark circles, but cautiously. I have my own criteria of Safe people and Safe places. I make acquaintances here, not friendships. I ask questions, I answer none. I keep my eyes lowered and my ears cocked."

But you make your own rules! I wanted to cry out. Didn't he see the difference?

"You forget," he went on, "even your Safe friends were once strangers to you, to your family. We were strangers too until our families arranged—"

Only in retrospect would I see this was no slip of the tongue.

"But they didn't," I said. "We met at Althea's—"

~ Undercurrents ~

"Think about it," he said. "A Safe event. The room secured, the guests registered, the activities monitored. What did you think? That I crashed the party? Outwitted an entire security detail assigned to protect a Senator's only daughter?" His eyes held mine. "I have been designated Safe since I was sixteen. Do you really think we would have met otherwise?" He leaned closer. "You saw the image screen that night in your father's office. Do you think he paused it on some random frame? Our fathers were friends once. But protocol must be followed. He had to treat me like a stranger so that questions would not be asked. Look at me, Luna. I shouldn't have told you. Promise me. You'll never mention this to anyone."

I nodded, unable to speak. This changed everything. The giggling, heart-pounding escapes from the dorm that my friends and I plotted so carefully, the nights of partying in the plaza after curfew, racing under the Parkway lights, dancing in clubs with fake IDs, then creeping back across campus in the tipsy dawn. Were they Safe experiences after all? He was right. We might have been able to outsmart the residence dons, but never the security details of our high-profile friends like Althea. We had sometimes joked about scholarship students from the lower classes of society, speculated on which of them might be financing their tuition by monitoring, even manipulating, Althea's social life to ensure a rounded, fun-filled education that was as close to normal as possible, while keeping her—and us, her friends—abnormally, impossibly safe. I had no need of private security but my father, with his connections—of course he would have made sure he was advised of my every move. I pictured his computer directory, a folder with my name on it, an array of hidden files and images I would one day download to a memory screen and share with my grandchildren as fond reminiscences.

Karlof spoke, bringing me back to the present. "This doesn't mean you shouldn't go off-world at the end of term. It will be good for you. And maybe it is for the best." He smirked, "Maybe you were only attracted to me because of my disreputable character, my unsavoury connections." He thought a minute and added, "And I to you, because of your status."

I studied the stained rings on the table surface. At times I see him so clearly, and other times, like now, I cannot read him at all. "You don't mean that," I said.

~ Undercurrents ~

Karlof lifted my face. I waited for the kiss but the barman shouted, rushing around the counter, twisting a towel in both hands.

"Hey, you! You don' start nuttin' in here. Dis ain' one a dem places. You wan' dat, you go somewheres else."

Karlof stood to face him, clenching his fist, ready to fight if it came to that.

"I don' wan' no trubble. No trubble, pleez. Jus' go." The barman mopped his bar rag across the band of sweat forming on his bald head and, shrinking visibly, waved toward the door.

I laid my hand lightly on Karlof's. He pulled away to feel inside his jacket where he wore a civilian-issue Taser. But it was a wallet he withdrew. He parted a flap to reveal a compartment and thumbed through a thickness of bills. I tried not to stare. Though legal tender, they are rarely seen in my world. They are the currency of the streets, of criminals and anyone who does not want his activities traced.

"I don't want trouble either," he said to the man. He laid a generous denomination on the table. His eyes, looking down into mine, mirrored regret. "It was nothing. Just a kiss goodbye."

On the street I tugged at his sleeve. "What was that about?"

"House rules. No skin-to-skin contact."

Rules. Even here on the fringes.

It was late. But instead of heading back to our cruiser we were moving deeper into forbidden territory. My heart quickened. This was where the underground met, where shady commerce was conducted between suppliers with the highest of ideals—or none at all—and those who escaped to the outside.

I raised my hood and pressed my shoulder into the crowd. The night thickened around me like syrup. Real darkness, a darkness such as I had never experienced, hung above us just out of reach of the constant electric twilight. It gathered on the horizon of long cross-streets, poured out of deep alleys. I peered down each one, wondering which of them might conceal the gateway to freedom.

Karlof steered me onto a pedestrian concourse where lights recessed into building facades created a brighter but still eerie semblance of daylight. Impersonal elbows and shoulders nudged me aside. Hands groped at me. Voices whispered lewd invitations and sexual threats. I swung around, ready to accuse, but the

~ Undercurrents ~

faces were uniform, blank. I stopped suddenly, put two fingers tip to tip with my thumb, and drew a slow deep breath as my Gran had taught me, a fragment of a meditation ritual she practices. Breathe, relax. On the exhalation its calming effect swept over me and the foul utterances melted away, tickling my ears like raindrops, and were absorbed into the night.

Karlof pointed upward. Far above the streetlights the air shimmered like diamond dust on black velvet with a mist that never fell. I gasped, stunned by the alien beauty, alien to me, witnessed before now only through the remote perspective of another's lens.

A cylinder of glaring light blinded me. I tilted my head to the source, shielding my eyes with my hand. The hoverpatrol singled us out. A mechanical voice inquired, "Do you require assistance?" And then concluded, "Move along," before I could have answered.

Karlof gripped my arm more tightly and manoeuvred me among the street-walkers who bent their heads from this beacon, a glare stronger than the brightest natural daylight they would ever know. We 'moved along' obediently. The spotlight followed our progress for some ten or fifteen metres. The faces we passed did not acknowledge the light or the persons within its circle, only shuffled on obediently, heads bowed. Respectfully, one might think, were it not for the darting eyes narrowed into devious slits, missing nothing, and lips barely moving but hissing forbidden words. They 'moved along' nonetheless.

Literary texts of the previous century had predicted this future veiled in the pretext of fiction. I wondered now at the bleak picture so uniformly portrayed by their many authors. Had they drawn a brighter map of the future, would it now be so? With this thought we were plunged into shocking darkness. The hover-patrol whirred into the distance.

As my eyes readjusted to the twilight state I wrapped my cloak closer around me, thinking of Gran and the night she gave it to me. Surely she knew of my explorations far afield from my home territory with my new friends from school. As my father said, it was a frivolous gift for one who need never feel the chill of external air. And when I bent to thank her she pulled me close and whispered that if I was going to hedge propriety I might just as well go warmly. I never conceded to her, or even to myself until now, that our expeditions were well within the restrictions of our level of society, travelling from roofport to roofport in our father's cruisers, testing boundaries that were no doubt preprogrammed into their Global Positioning Systems.

I had heard of these street-walkers, the homeless masses who seemed neither to eat nor sleep, who walked on and on along the maze of intersecting malls and sidewalks without purpose or direction. But before tonight Karlof would never take me into the underworld. Now as I walked among them, seeing them at close range, I was, for the first time in my life, acutely embarrassed by the opulence I took for granted. I prayed to my Gran's God that they might be as ignorant of my life as I was of theirs.

"Don't stare."

With that warning Karlof steered me into a narrow arched alleyway. We were inside now, in a concourse similar to the shopping malls I was accustomed to, except for the hordes of aimless people and the accompanying stench of filthy humanity: tobacco smoke—long-since banned—stale sweat and urine and...I swallowed hard, buried my nose in the luxurious softness of my hood and tried not to think what else. I saw an Exit sign and bolted through the door, only to find myself in a narrower and only slightly airier service passage, gasping, still tasting humanity with every breath.

"Why would you bring me here? It's horrid!"

"You wanted to see the city before you went. The streets."

"But not here! Not this!"

"Then what?"

"You said, before we escaped—"

"Ssh!" Karlof moved in protectively. "Don't use that word. Not even here."

The only witnesses were service staff at the far end of the corridor who were making a racket, tilting large metal garbage bins to the lips of underground chutes and tossing them aside with a clanging echo.

"You said," I repeated, softly, "we would have to lose ourselves in the city for a time before...going out. Three years is a long time. I just wanted..."

How could I admit it to him now? It was an image of him I wanted. Karlof going about the business of planning our escape, so that when he sent grinning, arm's-length clips of himself I could say, "Yes, he took me to that street. I remember that café."

~ Undercurrents ~

I drew in air that was rank with other people's lives and half-lives. Deaths too, I thought, horrified.

He sighed. I read it as exasperation. "How can you consider going off-world when you can't bear it here for five minutes? Out there, you'll find it as barren as your world is contrived and as corrupt as this one is foul. Maybe," he said, "you are not so different from your father after all, or the men like him who conceived your perfect world."

His voice was a strand of gossamer floating in the smoky air. "Your grandmother's hologram. It does not exist. And I think that is what you really want."

I tapped my foot impatiently. "Take me home," I choked.

§

Last night I did not sleep. Hour by hour my decision was made and unmade as question mounted on question and revelation bore revelation. The one who has been my trusted guide has led me to this crossroads unprepared. To blame him would be perverse. I have been a willing captive of Karlof's vision of the future. Willing to suspend reality—that is how I see it now. For the freedom I sought does not exist. Except inside of him. In this moment I know nothing so clearly as that I want it to exist inside of me too. There is only one way I know this can happen.

My father steps through the doorway. I tell them what they have been waiting to hear.

"I am not enlisting. I am taking the contract at the Central Office."

Gran cannot resist a twitch of her mouth, the beginning of a self-satisfied smile. Why did I think she would be disappointed?

My father releases me from his congratulatory hug to grip Karlof's shoulder in a rare display of affection. "And you, lad? You have news as well?"

"I've been awarded a scholarship," says Karlof, telling my father what, clearly, he already knows.

"From an anonymous donor," he adds. For my benefit, it seems.

So this is the reason for his change of heart. But why could he not tell me himself? I am happy for him. I flash him a smile, a private message of understanding. Our plans are not to be

~ Undercurrents ~

discarded, only delayed. But he cannot meet my eye. He is serious, subdued, looking at Gran. I sense in him a movement like a phantom of my peripheral vision, a nod, a facial tic, a shift in posture. I'm not sure what. I might ignore it except, as I turn to her there it is again, another encrypted signal.

Two gestures, a mutual acknowledgement which I witness and comprehend. Objection rises to my lips, but in that moment he slips his hand into mine.

D.C. Troicuk grew up in Glace Bay, NS. She lived 'away' for 20 years, experiencing six of Canada's provinces before succumbing once more to the lure of Cape Breton. Her work has appeared in *Canadian Living*, *The Antigonish Review*, *Pottersfield Portfolio*, *Gaspereaux Review*, *The Nashwaak Review* and in the anthology *The Day The Men Went To Town* (Breton Books).

Water

The creature was of the water, liquid in human form. On land now, its phosphorescent-blue scales lay taut over its unhealthily slim frame and continued to flow like the element from which they came. With a heavy grace it glided up from the harbour, through the brackish waters where the river widened. The air was weighted with salt, and cold as November.

The creature moved over the rugged landscape between the erratics, ancient reminders of the devastating glaciers. The stones looked like they had fallen from the sky; they waited in the fields, lakes and rivers. Pain sparkled in the creature's liquid grey eyes: its blood coursed with poison. Its heart beat twice, skipped a beat, and then beat again. With anguish it moved steadily, straight and determined.

§

This was not how Jeffrey had pictured spending his twentieth birthday. It was ridiculous to be jealous of his parents' new (not yet born, actually) child. But then, he wasn't jealous. There was just something about it that was unsettling. Of course there were all of the obvious problems like the child's health, his mother's health, and the whole economic situation, but this wasn't what was troubling Jeffrey. His parents were too old to be having a new child, and thinking of his parents as aging made him feel older than he expected to be. And this too was ridiculous, and not exactly it.

A weight seemed to have descended on him, like a fog that rolls in from the river at night, or hangs low to the ground over a swamp and dampens all sound into silence.

~ Undercurrents ~

And so, on this, his birthday, he was at the river just fifteen minutes from his home, waiting for his forty-one year old mother to go into labour. He sat on a stone and stared at the shimmering water. Everyone used to swim in it, but no one dared now. It depressed him to think his father's mill was the reason for this—for the poisoning of a whole ecosystem. Picking out a ripple he tried to follow it, got lost in its course, and only recovered long enough to get lost in another. There was a dark sleepiness in the flooded river at this time of year, between the rain and the snow, between the highlands and the ocean.

Jeffrey knew the river was a metaphor for just about everything. Right now it flowed over its muddy bed, touching the mud but separate from it, like his mind flowing over what was really burning at him. But even knowing this he couldn't find it. There was the scare with Angela last month: she'd missed a period and had begun to panic. It was nothing. It was nothing when they learned it was nothing, but before that it was something.

Maybe, he thought, this existential crisis or whatever it was just happened to people around his age, people who don't know where they're going in life. It probably happens again at fifty or sixty when you wonder where your life has gone. If that was true, he preferred this crisis.

He wasn't sure how long he'd been at the river, but he'd been expecting the call for a while now. Time was a funny thing. For a while it had been lost completely in the river's current, but now that his butt ached from the hard stone, time was back. He looked down at his cell phone and saw that the battery was dead. *Idiot!* Jumping to his feet he felt the rocks skitter out from under him, and for just a moment, between heartbeats and the sinking feeling of gravity, he realized how ridiculous his falling into the river would be.

Then he hit the water. It was like being pummelled from all sides at the same time; as if he had entered a new and completely hostile world, a new planet, a new universe. There was a moment of hesitation before all of his nerves screamed "cold." Jeffrey kicked and beat at the water as he was pulled further into the river. He pushed his head through the surface, spit out the foul stuff and gulped some air. At this instant he was colder, heavier, and more panicked than he'd ever been before.

~ Undercurrents ~

The river may have seemed sleepy, but it was awake now. The current moved with a sort of patient power that looked calm from the riverbank but was terrifying when you were immersed in it. Jeffery wished he were naked. The freezing silver water pushed him downstream and the weight of his clothes forced him to struggle for breath. His arms and legs grew heavier and he railed at himself. He knew this was not a particularly fast or large river —there were no rapids, and it wasn't even particularly deep most of the time; he could not—or at least should not—drown here.

Taking a deep breath, Jeffrey let himself be pulled under again, and struggled to unzip his jacket. The wet material stuck to his arms and all his movements were slowed, but he finally managed to pull it off, and rise to the surface for air. His arms wouldn't move the way he wanted them to, and his legs felt like miniature anchors holding him back as he tried to swim to the riverbank. He felt as if his body were filling with a kind of poison, something that was drowning him inside, clogging his arteries and muscles and keeping his body from listening to his desperate commands. With disbelief, Jeffrey found that he couldn't get out of the current, that he could move his limbs less and less.

As he started to sink beneath the dark-silver surface of water, holding a few seconds worth of oxygen in his lungs, he was thinking of Angela. Thinking that he couldn't have lived with himself or her if...but his thoughts stopped when he hit a rock, his numb leg erupting to life with pain.

Jeffrey bounced from rock to rock but soon felt his feet start to drag on the bottom. He stood up. Here where the river widened out, the water was only up to his waist. Shivering, he picked his way across the river to the shore. It was a painfully slow process in his waterlogged and freezing state.

From the shore he tried to figure out where he was. The whole world seemed lifeless. The sky was the solid grey of the river and the trees all around him were straight and bare. A few bushes held onto some red berries that had refused to fall. Beneath his blue lips and chattering teeth, Jeffrey felt the strange hollow feeling and weakness that comes with the dissipation of adrenalin. Clutching his arms in front of him, and not thinking very clearly, he walked into the woods, hoping he'd find a trail. He regretted giving up his jacket to the river.

After five minutes of thinking he'd freeze to death lost in the

~ Undercurrents ~

woods, he found a cabin. Fortunately it was fishing season and someone was there. As he collapsed on the couch, he made sure to tell the fishermen that he wanted to be taken to the Dunvegan hospital, where his mother was giving birth.

§

A mile away, the creature moved steadily inland. With strides fluid and faltering it crossed the alien landscape. Beneath its phosphorescent skin, its blood coursed and ached, as its heart struggled to pump that which was foreign. But it continued with inscrutable purpose, toward the hospital.

§

Jeffrey's father, Harold, looked like he'd been loading two by fours all day alongside the slingers at one of the mills he owned. His pale skin bagged beneath his eyes. A nagging cough seemed to start below his lungs and rattle up. His wife, Anne's, troubled delivery of Sarah, and the news that his son had nearly drowned showed themselves in his dark-circled eyes and lined face. But he wasn't too tired to order a maintenance worker out of his way as he pushed Jeffrey, wheelchair-bound, to see his new sister.

They rounded the corner of the maternity ward, just in time to see something that stopped them dead: a creature, blue and wet and smelling of salt, stepping into the room, two guards trying to stop it. Harold let go of the wheelchair and rushed into the room. Jeffrey stood up and followed, feeling every step in his bruised knee and aching frame.

§

Inside the room, Jeffrey watched in horror as the creature, smooth-scaled and luminous, eased the newborn Sarah from his mother's terrified grip. The nurse, his father, and the two security guards were all moving toward it. But as they closed in on this creature, in which—despite everything—Jeffrey saw a strange beauty, they seemed to slow down. As if the closer they got to it, the denser the air became, so that they could not quite reach it. The creature, cradling Sarah tenderly to its chest, moved lithely around their absurdly slowed hands. Only Harold, whose eyes and face burned with rage, managed to touch the creature. It glared at him with a kind of revulsion that seemed personal. Harold's fingertips slid off its arm.

Jeffrey moved to block the door as the creature came toward him. Its eyes were black now, its scales dark grey beneath its phosphorescence. Jeffrey realized it was ill. Lifting its sleek head from the baby, still pink and unbelievably tiny, it looked at Jeffrey.

For a moment Jeffrey felt as if he were still drowning...or had drowned, and his oxygen-deprived brain was hallucinating the entire thing. When the creature reached him and Jeffrey reached out to stop it, he saw and felt an unimaginable pain. The creature's eyes swam and sparked in its head. Jeffrey felt the air thicken around his hand, like the densest of liquids, as he reached out.

He knew that he could touch the creature, that he could grab its arm, but his hand stopped short. The pain was a wall he could not cross. The creature ducked under his arm and was behind him, moving down the hall before Jeffrey could change his mind. He collapsed on the floor; his mind aching as if a bright light burned behind his eyes.

§

It walked back along the river to the sea carrying the baby in its arms. The infant's pink skin and dark hair contrasted with the smooth blue-grey chest she was cradled against. The crowd of people all straining after it had no effect. Its heart beat twice— *thump-thump*—and then missed another beat before thudding again.

At the ocean now, past the erratics, the creature descended over the wet stones. It picked up speed while the crowd behind it, held back by an invisible density, slowed. The creature stumbled once, marring its beautiful gait, before reaching the water. The baby did not cry.

The liquid creature was waist-deep in the water when it paused for a moment, as if even its home had turned against it. It looked over its shoulder at the people who had not yet reached the beach, and then slipped beneath the surface. The pink and the grey disappeared beneath the water. What one heart lost, the other gained.

                              🙟🙝

Bruce Miller grew up in rural Cape Breton, migrated to some nearby cities, and then returned. While away he won some prizes in a few poetry contests and spent one entire night writing a play, and another entire night reading *Ulysses*. Currently he is teaching, working in the garden, and making tzatziki. The rest of the time he spends time in his rather ancient house with his beautiful wife, reading, pondering world problems, and composing songs he cannot sing. Also, he is envious of his wife's built-in grammar machine.

A Cat Named Wellington

I had never seen the widow Dunsmire so alight as she was on the day she paid a visit with her new kitten. I sat in my study in the early eve as per usual, a single candle burning as the last dim light of day slipped out of the sky, when I perceived a rapping at the door. Startled, I advanced the front door with caution; I lived in the wood far from town and few souls ventured that way.

As I approached the door, I kept my cane tight-fisted in my hand, ready to defend in case the visitor was of an ill manner and desired to rob or abuse me in any fashion. The door, cracked slightly, revealed the small white face of the widow Dunsmire, wrinkled with a smile.

"Mr. Cobbit," she said, "I apologize for disturbing you but I have something I greatly wish you to see."

"Mrs. Dunsmire" said I, relieved at the sight of her, "Please come in."

I opened the door to its extent and found that the old woman held something small in her arms. It was a kitten. She had wrapped it in a blanket and held it like a baby.

"How delightful!" I said, and let the lady in.

I poured tea for us both and we took a seat in the front room. The widow gingerly stroked the kitten as we talked of the recent industrial boom on our beloved, isolated Island. The widow had gone to town that afternoon, and found the people all a-bustle with talk of coming prosperity. The widow and I shared the same mother country, but we rarely spoke nostalgically of it.

The kitten remained content in the widow Dunsmire's arms, silent and obedient as any well taught student. It seemed almost to be listening to our conversation, and appeared to have a look of agreement upon its face. I requested her to let the thing down so that it may inspect the room, and I in turn inspect it. She unfurled it gently from the blanket and it stepped lightly onto the wood floor. A handsome grey tabby it was, no bigger than my fist. The little thing circled round a bit and contented itself to curl up by the fire as I talked with its adopter.

I inquired how the lady had come into possession of the little thing. It had been scratching at her door but an hour ago. The widow Dunsmire had been frightened, anticipating it was a rabid raccoon or some other undesirable creature that would cause her harm or disrupt her garden or home. The scratching persisted and finally the old woman gained the courage to examine the noise. The widow Dunsmire spoke with such vigor that it pleased me to see her so happy. Nettled with arthritis, she seldom held a smile as movement was painful, and it manifested in the daily conducting of her person. Normally, she was old and frail as withered rope, but on this day she looked ten years younger, and one would never think she'd experienced a flicker of pain in her life.

Over three cups of tea, we talked of trivial things, and of her dead husband for whom she mourned more and more since the war had taken him so many years ago. She felt that the kitten was a gift from the late Lieutenant Dunsmire, an act of kindness to give her pleasure in her last years before she could reunite with him in God's welcoming Heaven. Having no children and being the last of her kin, the widow Dunsmire was utterly alone in the world.

As we conversed, the little cat sat humbly by the fire, not sleeping, but pondering it seemed. It did not exact the mischievous behavior of most kittens, which I thought strange. The thing seemed to me a very refined creature. I suspected it might be sick and dying because of its calmness, but was relieved of my worries as its body and countenance suggested otherwise.

"Have you chosen a name for it yet?" I inquired of her.

"Wellington," she said firmly, giving no explanation or reason.

I nodded my approval but was inwardly appalled. *Wellington,* I thought, what a name for a cat.

The widow Dunsmire desired to use my facility, and in her absence I inspected her little pet. I crouched beside it and lifted its chin in order to inspect its face more thoroughly. It obliged me and did not rebel, but the moment its eyes struck mine, it seemed to scowl. I smiled for a moment, amused with its attitude, but soon became bothered. The expression its face held was undeniably spiteful and annoyed, and eerily intelligent. The animal did not respond to my intimidating stare, which I thought strange. It held my gaze with no sign of surrender.

What happened next I must relate carefully, for no words, no matter how meticulously chosen, can adequately express the bizarre horror. The cat narrowed its eyes, opened its little lips, and mouthed the words *"Go to hell, you stupid man."* I must beg pardon for using such a vulgar phrase, but I am only relating the scene in honesty. I am not accustomed to such language, which made the general impact of the experience all the more sickening. I swear to my God and on my dead mother's grave, the kitten wished me harm.

I jumped back, gripped with shock. I was so jarred by the experience that upon the widow Dunsmire's return I asked her to kindly quit my home immediately, for I did not feel well and would surely fall asleep at any minute. She expressed concern, and after checking my temperature with the back of her hand and inspecting my colour, satisfied herself that I was simply in need of a good rest. She said goodbye and thanked me for my kind hospitality. I would not see her again until her funeral many months later, at which I was the only soul in attendance.

§

When the widow Dunsmire took her leave, I sat for the majority of the night in my study, perplexed and frightened. Frightened not at the fact that I had seen the cat speak, or mimic its lips in that fashion, but more so *why* I had seen such a thing. I was not an old man, but an aging one. I did not anticipate the slipping of my mind for at least another decade or so. My senses, I had previously understood, were sharp as ever. I had full quality of sight, hearing, and cognitive skills, had experienced no ailments whatsoever (with the exception of my troublesome knee, the result of a farming accident as a boy). I took the greatest pleasure in my studies and lived my life quite fully and happily in my small wooded home. I could not resolve any rational explanation for what had happened, nor did I desire to investigate it any more. After much contemplation, and conducting some simple tests on myself borrowed from a medical book, I determined to understand myself completely sane and sound of mind.

My thoughts turned to another explanation: perhaps that cat *had* told me to go to hell. By some strange rift of evolutionary progress, it had attained intelligence and awareness. I would have laughed at the thought had it not been so frighteningly real for me. I have never been one to succumb to such fantasies, and considered myself a rational and well-educated man. Not a skeptic, but a realist. I dismissed the possibility after some contemplation. There would have been no rest for me on that night had I not come to the conclusion that perhaps I had eaten or drunk something harmful. The well from which I drew my water had always been dependable, but perhaps some rodent had fallen down and drowned in it, and its decomposing fluids had caused a hallucination upon entering my bloodstream. Had I detected a strange metallic taste upon my last glass of water? Surely I had, but passed it off too quickly to take note of it. There it was, settled and done, my peace of mind.

And so, retiring to bed with the comfort that I had been accidentally poisoned, I decided to dredge the well the very next morning and ease my mind of this terrible mess. Despite my certainties though, my sleep was choppy as an angry sea, and I awoke in fever with a terrible foreboding in my chest.

Rising groggily, bones stiffer than usual, my mind abruptly turned to my experience of the previous evening. I thought of the well and decided I would advance the task directly after breakfast. After toast, tea, and some fresh apple slices, my condition was much improved. I embarked on my task, collecting all the necessary tools from the shed, and began to dredge the well.

As I pulled the rope slowly, I turned my eyes to the sky. It was a marvelous autumn day, clear and crisp. I breathed the fresh air into my lungs with satisfaction. Finally, the dredge platform reached the top, but—to my dismay—it was vacant. I stared at it dumbly for a moment, and then was so shocked by a sudden sight that I let go the rope and it plummeted all the way back down.

It was Wellington, perched upon the lip of the well, looking coyly at me. I had not seen him approach, nor had I heard the crunching of leaves below his paws as he advanced. It seemed as though he simply appeared.

Stricken, I had the sudden urge to give the animal a blow and knock it right down to the bottom of the well and to its death. Recalling the widow Dunsmire's high spirits the previous evening though, I could not lower myself to do such a thing. The kitten stared at me, then down at the dark maw of the well, and then back to me. It seemed to be amused.

"Go away," I whispered, "Shoo."

It stood its ground. Then, to my absolute horror, it opened its mouth and an awful grumbling sound came out. The kitten seemed highly concentrated on its queer endeavour, and strained in every inch of its face.

"*Fiiiind whit you werrrrrrre looking forrrrr?*" The voice was demonic, like nothing my ears had ever heard.

And at that moment, I lost my footing, falling to the ground in a fury of weakness and fear. I opened my eyes when I felt a small weight on my chest and found myself face to face with the creature. I could not move; paralyzed to my very core, I was at the mercy of the ill thing. It sniffed my face a moment then raised a paw, bringing it down across my cheek with surprising strength. Then it leapt from my body and raced back to its home. After I settled onto my legs again and brushed the dirt from my coat, I touched the spot where the kitten had scratched me and my hand reappeared with blood.

I saw Wellington on three more occasions before the widow Dunsmire's funeral. I was facing my kitchen window one day in the midst of washing my dishes, and the cat's striped face appeared on the other side of the glass. I paused in the middle of my scrubbing when I noticed his presence. He did not speak, but skulked about the ledge a pace or two, then turned round so that his back end was facing me. Then, the dreadful thing lifted its tail and pressed its naked extremities to the window, after which it abruptly jumped down and disappeared into the wood.

The second occurrence was on Christmas day. I exited my home in order to breathe in some fresh air, for the air is never as refreshing as it is on Christmas morning. There on my front step, I found a nasty gift from Wellington. I scraped it off with my cane in disgust, and as I turned to go back inside, I saw Wellington skirt out from under the step and disappear back into the yard of

~ Undercurrents ~

his benefactress.

I grew accustomed to avoiding the outside yard. I became fraught with paranoia each unbearable minute of my life. I feared that one more instance of seeing that evil creature speak would surely be too much for my heart, and I would perish. There were times when I could not avoid leaving the house however, as when I needed more fire wood.

I was chopping one morning in the spring, as quickly as I could so that I could return to the safety of my home. I raised my axe and on the downswing there was Wellington, sitting on the chopping block. I was so startled that I led the axe away and injured my back quite seriously. After I fell to the ground in pain, Wellington leaped down and ran across the lawn and back to his home.

I pondered this occurrence deeply, thinking that perhaps the cat wished to be dead. After all, he had put himself directly on the block where he knew the blade would come down and surely obliterate him. I dismissed this because I thought it out of character for him. He somehow knew that I would not follow through with my swing, and would therefore injure myself in the act. He was very clever, and very evil as well.

I told not a soul of my strange stories of the cat, for who would believe such a tale? They would surely lock me away for speaking such nonsense in all seriousness. I was forced to continue on with my dreary secret, day after day, restless night after restless night. I would wake at drastic hours in a cold sweat, thinking that I heard a scratching at the door, or saw a shadow that did not belong. But it was all my imagination, for the cat was nowhere to be found. I thought of visiting the widow Dunsmire and inquiring if she had experienced anything strange about the cat, but never did. The idea of seeing the thing again proved a risk that I was unwilling to take. When I heard news of her death, I knew that it somehow had something to do with the cat, and I felt unrelenting guilt that I had been able to do something about it, but did not out of my own cowardice.

So on a cold, grey day with the frozen February wind scaling the land, I dressed in my suit and attended the funeral of the widow Dunsmire.

§

~ *Undercurrents* ~

A sad event it was for me, being the only one at the funeral. After the service, and the viewing of the poor dead woman's body, I was approached by the executor of her will. He was a short fellow with a neat mustache, and called himself Helmsley.

"Mr. W. Charles Cobbit?" he asked hesitantly.

"Yes," I replied, "I am he."

Helmsley then offered his condolences for my loss, which made me increasingly uncomfortable due to my acquaintance with the woman being so mild, and my neglect of her so strong in the last months of life. He then proceeded to offer me a copy of her last will and testament. I held it with quivering hands as I read the words.

> *I, Willow Loretta Dunsmire, being of sound mind and body, hereby request that upon my death my home and property be sold, and the profits acquired be given to St. Joseph's Parish, as well as the remaining money in my bank account. All furniture inside my home shall be discarded, as it is old and may not be of much use to anyone. I bequeath my collection of bone china to my kind and loyal neighbor Mr. W. Charles Cobbit, who has been of much assistance to me. I also bequeath to this man my wedding band, which may be of some profit to him. Lastly, I bequeath to him the object of very much happiness and affection to me, my darling cat, Wellington. I know he will take good care of him.*

As I read the words, I felt my face go pale. Helmsley must have noted this and mistook it for a sudden wave of grief over the death of the widow, for he put a hand upon my shoulder and said that she was in a better place now, and that God would give her a comfortable spot in his heaven. I started to explain to the man that I could not take the cat, but my tongue stuck in its place. He left me with a humble bow and said that the bone china, wedding band and the cat would be delivered to my house that very evening.

You may appreciate the absolute terror I felt at seeing the cat wandering around my home, sniffing here and there and casting me the odd glance. It came into my mind to kill the thing, but after reflecting on the words in the widow Dunsmire's will, I could not bring myself to do it. Perhaps the cat *had* been very kind to her, and it was only me that it disliked. The widow Dunsmire was far too sweet to conjure a disliking from any creature, man or animal. For she was a woman of God, a good woman, and Wellington had surely known this; I hadn't realized it during her time of living, but she had been a dear friend to me. I felt obliged to take care of Wellington, at least for the time being. I would feed him, water him, and provide a warm place by the fire to sleep until I could find someone willing to adopt him.

Wellington did not speak to me on the first evening; he played a very clever game by acting like a normal animal. He ate the food I presented to him, and slept soundly on the mat beside the fire. I kept a keen eye on him, never for a moment forgetting his aggravated behavior towards me in the past months. He was no longer a kitten, but nearly a full grown cat, which frightened me even more. I knew what he was capable of, I had seen the atrocities of his being, and would not be misled by his present behavior into thinking him cured of his evil.

I kept my bedroom door tightly locked that first night, but even this was of no consolation. I slept very little and listened cautiously for any sign of wrongdoing out in the front room. All was silent though, as any other night. I finally nodded off before the sun came up, hoping that perhaps the cat had returned to its natural state, and the strange spirit that had seized him was now gone. Perhaps a peace had settled within him with the passing of the widow.

I was awakened by the distinct feeling of a presence beside me. Upon opening my eyes, I saw the cat's face directly in front of mine. I could not move or utter a breath. I had no clue as to how he got in, but assumed he had used some sort of voodoo to jimmy the lock. He spoke to me then, as a voice in my head. I was terrified, but somewhat relieved that I did not have to endure the awful sight of him using his strange vocal chords to make words.

You will obey me, it said in a man's voice. *You will serve me three meals a day of my liking, and warm milk in the evening. The mat you've provided me for sleep is unacceptable. You will give me a pillow instead from your bed. You will not give me away or offer me to another home, because if you do, I will punish you. You will adjust, and perhaps we may become friends. It is up to you,*

~ Undercurrents ~

Cobbit.

Then the cat leapt from the bed and returned to the front room. And to my own shame, I began to weep. I felt completely helpless in the situation and knew that I would have to obey the cat, for I believed he could put a curse on me, or do me some other unimaginable harm. He had the upper hand now. After ten minutes of emptying my sorrows into my pillow, I gained the courage to rise from bed and enter the kitchen.

Wellington looked at me with pitiless judgement; he thought me awfully silly for my dramatics. *Let me out,* said the voice in my head. Wellington sat by the front door, staring firmly and impatiently at me. I opened the door and let him out. I debated locking the door and quickly hanging myself by the neck on the eave in the front room, but then decided against it. I did not want to suffer the afterlife that accompanied such a death, and my line of rope was outside in the shed anyway.

I peered through the window sheepishly and watched as Wellington skirted about the yard, chose a place, and relieved himself. As he was doing so, he cast a glance back at me, at which time I ducked out of his view. After a few minutes, he came and scratched at the door and I let him in. He demanded that he eat his meals at the table with me, perched on a chair. He also demanded tea with all his meals. We sat, silently, man and cat, eating breakfast. Wellington then broke the silence.

I saw you watching me, he said, *and I don't appreciate that. If you think me fancy, then you are entirely wrong sir. I am very much disinterested in the attentions of men. If you are fancy, it is none of my concern, unless you look to me for such attentions. Then I will be very concerned. Know this, and know that you may not watch me in my personal business out in the yard. This is the only time we will discuss this.*

I debated standing up for myself, and expressing my disgust at such an accusation (a cat of all things!) but then decided against it. I gave him a solemn nod and kept my eyes on my breakfast, for which I could not muster any kind of appetite.

§

For eight years, Wellington and I lived together. I gave him a pillow to sleep on as requested, and served him three meals a day, and warm milk at night. I did not watch him conducting his personal business in the yard. Continuing my studies, I also began to keep a journal of our strange companionship and how it had begun. I grew used to the strange presence of the cat. He seemed not to notice me at all, but went about his daily schedule of naps and outings as if he were completely alone in the house. In general, he only spoke to give me orders, or to express his dissatisfaction with something. He always spoke in my head. On occasion, we would engage in conversation. I would give him the recent news of politics and happenings, and we would discuss it civilly.

It happened that Wellington, like me, enjoyed his solitude. It was like this that we co-existed; he did not interfere with my studies, and I did not interfere with his routines. I dare say I grew accustomed to his presence; Wellington was not all venom. While his nature could not prohibit him from insulting me every so often, he exhibited enough respect that we did become distant companions. On certain summer evenings, we would sit on the porch together, silently absorbing the purple sunsets, in the silence we both preferred. The insults came less and less frequently as we adjusted to the presence of one another, and eventually I found it hard to remember a time when I was not with Wellington. My years of solitude only seemed lonely after I experienced the years of his company.

Wellington's kindness did not manifest often; he was, for the most part, quite crotchety. On reflection, I supposed that I would be crotchety as well, if I could not wear trousers or sit upright. But I did occasionally see kindness in Wellington.

One winter I became sick. The air, which flew in like a brute from the dervish ocean to the north, abused my lungs incredibly and as a result I remained in bed for nearly a week. Wellington did not resent me for being unable to continue on, but tried to appease me as well as he could. He sacrificed his nightly warm milk for a large bowl of water which he could drink from as he saw fit, and ate canned food of convenience.

It was near the end of the bout that Wellington entered my room in the early afternoon. He said nothing, thinking I was asleep, and hopped onto the bed and began kneading my pillows with his paws. He did this for my comfort, I suspected. As he walked towards the door to leave me, I beckoned him back.

~ Undercurrents ~

"Wellington," I said, "please come here."

He looked over his shoulder hesitantly, and then obeyed.

"Up onto the bed," I said, "I want to see you."

Wellington sat beside me and regarded me with a firm expression.

"How have you come to be, Wellington?"

Wellington frowned, and then looked to the window. *Tell me about your studies, Cobbit*, he replied.

I could see that I would get no response to my question. With a wave of my hand, I dismissed him. "Perhaps we'll talk another time," I said, and Wellington took his leave.

Eight years for an aged man are very different from eight years for a young man. I weakened, and my knee worsened. I was always a strong man, but I knew that I could not stand against the power of passing years. It is such a strange thing to age; the progress is slow and sluggish at first, barely noticeable. But then one day, everything seems to collide. The years, like heavy layers upon one's bones, exert their presence with malevolent force, the colours of the world seem to dim with the fading pigment of hair and skin, and even the most mundane tasks become difficult. It is all accompanied with a deep, deep sadness that sits permanently in the mind.

It was almost springtime when I knew that I would soon die; I felt it in my heart and in my mind. My life was nearly over, and I took to spending the majority of my days lying in bed. I rose only to make meals for Wellington and myself, and I neglected my studies altogether, although at times I scribbled in my journal. Wellington noted the change in me; he regarded me curiously when we sat together at the table, and would sometimes poke his head inside my bedroom door when he thought I was sleeping.

The night that I died, I called for Wellington to come into my room.

The last threads of winter were fighting the approaching spring bloom, and the battling seasons resulted in a terrific rainstorm that crashed about the house. It was unusually vicious on this particular night. The shadows of tree limbs held their shaking profiles in the window, and the sky flashed brightly, illuminating me in chagrined repose on my death bed. I could feel my fate struggling and seizing within each nerve; it pulsed mercilessly and it was all I could do to bear it, let alone fight.

~ Undercurrents ~

Wellington hopped up on the bed and began to talk to me. His face remained a dark impression, save for when the lightning struck, at which time every delicate whisker and stripe became exposed. He looked very grave—for the years had aged him as well—but calm nonetheless.

You are going to die soon, he said, and I nodded. *You want me to tell you how I have come to be.*

I nodded.

Well, Mr. Cobbit, I must ask you a question first.

I shook my head to let him know that I did not want to answer his questions.

Cobbit, what is it that you labour upon? What are your studies?

I pursed my lips and remained silent, for in all truth I did not know.

I had many books, and knew that I had read them, but I did not know what I had been working on. My eyes began to water as the realization came upon me. I was committed to my studies, and spent hours in my library in dedication to them. But what was it that I had been doing? Had I merely been sitting idly, in the grip of some inexplicable trance from which I would emerge with a false sense of accomplishment?

Wellington's question filled me with defeat. Some ruthless truth was at hand, and I wanted no part of it. Just then, I hated Wellington more than ever, and I know he felt it.

Yet he continued without mercy. *Cobbit, how did you injure your knee?*

I felt a flicker of hope, for I could respond to this, I knew the words well. "It was a farming accident," I said through clenched teeth, "As a boy!" I felt that I might win yet.

Tell me the details.

Details? I stammered and puffed, but there were no details. I had no memory to accommodate the words, but I knew the words, I trusted the words—Oh, how I trusted the words! I remembered nothing of my life!

Cobbit, what was the name of your father? What did your mother's face look like? Do you know anything about yourself?

I was helplessly silent.

Neither do I. I know nothing of how I've come to be. The only thing I know is the loop. I am stuck in it, and so are you. Cobbit,

~ Undercurrents ~

what does the 'W" stand for in your name?

Recognition. It came to me suddenly and sharply; we had been here before. I cried out in a rasp, sputtering the answer with a heavy, uncooperative tongue, "Wellington!" I shouted finally, "My name is Wellington Charles Cobbit." A hiccoughing sob followed the words, and I tasted blood at the back of my throat.

Wellington took a deep breath and tightened his face. I recalled such a preparation. He was about to speak through his mouth.

With great strain, the grumbling began, and then words emerged from the noise.

"*Weee are one and the sssssssame.*"

The sight of it, and the shock of it took immediate toll and my heart began to seize. Wellington advanced, bringing his face closer as if to kiss me, but instead drew a great breath from my lungs, and then the world went black. The inky oblivion was familiar. I had been here before. It was a cruel loop, and I was a part of it. I did not know why, but I was a slave to it.

And thus the loop folded in on itself, its self-consumptive nature manifesting yet again. It was now Wellington's turn, my turn, our turn, to switch.

§

I came to in the woods, confused and cold. Something felt very different but I could not identify it. I looked around, and noticed directly that I was in familiar territory. There was a great oak tree to my right, which I recognized immediately as the tree which stood to the east of my property. I got onto my feet, which didn't feel right at all, and began walking in the direction of my house, although it seemed abnormally far away.

I entered the yard of the widow Dunsmire and decided that I would go to her door, for I felt that I needed assistance quickly and she represented the nearest help. Memory was slowly returning, settling like coal dust into the mines of my fate. Next door, a man sat in his study with a single candle burning. I was incredibly jealous of this man, and was already concocting the tricks that I could play on him.

Later, after we had met, he would begin to keep a journal. He might not finish it during this twist of the loop, but I would remember, I would hold these moments until my turn came around again. One day, between us, we would finish the tale. Would it free us? Would anything? I could not know.

In the towns, the company stores were being built, and the angular company houses were being raised. The people looked forward with hopeful eyes. None of that concerned me. I trotted up the steps, raised a paw, and began to scratch.

Born in Cape Breton, Nova Scotia, Seanah Roper is a poetess, fiction writer, and budding activist. She holds a degree in contemporary English literature from Thompson Rivers University in Kamloops, BC, and enjoys delving into the strange and bizarre with her writing. She is known to blend genres and experiment with historical narratives in her work, and pays loving attention and detail to the Canadian landscape, both physical and cultural. She now resides deep in the north of British Columbia where she works as gallery coordinator at the Phoenix Theatre in Fort Nelson.

NetWorld

Three steps from the auditorium door, searing pain spreads outward from the middle of my chest. I stagger from the blow. The wall is just beyond my reach. *Won't last long. Hold on.*

Firm hands grip my upper arms from behind, all but lifting me forward. Someone speaks into my ear. "Sorry Deni, that one was mine. Move your feet, gal."

Bent from the pain, I see a man's dilapidated work boots behind my sneakers. The pain is fading, but my body hasn't recovered enough to speak. I do as I am told.

We come to a door which the man unlocks. He enters, pulls me into a small, dark room and closes the door. My heart leaps in panic. "Wait! Where—?"

"Control booth for the stage," he says, as he switches on a bright light. He nods toward a large window. Beyond it sprawls the school's filled-to-capacity auditorium where my six-year-old granddaughter, Tessa, will soon take the stage as Queen of the Fairies.

I turn back to the man. He looks like an anorexic with insomnia. At the same time, kindness and good humour are apparent in his face. But it's the hundreds of shimmering threads streaming from him that cause my pulse to speed up again. There are more than I've ever seen coming from one person.

"I'm Pat," he says. His plangent voice calms me. "I'm the first one you've ever met, aren't I?"

§

It was Tessa who arranged my meeting with Pat. Over a month earlier, she had come home with news about the play.

The computer hummed reliably, the only sound in the house, as I made the day's final adjustments to NetWorld. The people on the screen—as familiar to me as family—moved through their paces as I tested each change.

The stair tread gave way to the underworld when stepped on. The hat perched on a picket fence transformed the wearer into a mage. The peach rose became a rideable flamingo when touched.

Pushing my back against the desk chair with a stretchy sigh and rolling my head in circles to work out the kinks, I clicked the low sun in NetWorld. 4:45 p.m. Almost time for my daughter, Jace, and Tessa to come home.

I'd developed NetWorld over the years of my adult life as a retreat, a kind of cushion for my own sanity. When the Internet blossomed, NetWorld was perfectly positioned to become one of the first multi-user, role-playing games. It became my livelihood and gave me what I most wanted, the ability to work in isolation from home.

Jace's car crunched up the long gravel drive. Reluctantly, I put my computer to sleep.

Soon Tessa was running over. "GranDeni," she said, breathlessly, "I'm the Fairy Queen in the play! Can you believe it? Will you come see me?" She danced around the room. "Mama's making me wings."

Jace smiled at her unaccountably-frilly daughter. As soon as Tessa twirled out of the room, however, Jace pointed an accusing finger at me and said, "You aren't getting out of this one. You have to come."

I avoided her gaze, staring at a worn spot on the hardwood floor. This was all too familiar. "Jace...I can't promise. You don't understand why I don't go out—why I can't be around a lot of people. I don't blame you. There's no way you could understand it. I just—"

"You just won't stretch yourself even for the 'amazing' Tessa!"

"Jace, stop. I have 'stretched' for my whole life."

Jace straightened her shoulders and took a deep breath. With this slight pause in the action, my vision focused on what I usually attempt to ignore: the threads connecting us. Silvery flickers pulsed along the cords as if our emotions were alternating electrical currents.

I shook my head to clear the image. "I was a disappointment

as a mother, so of course I'm going to be a disappointment as a grandmother. I don't like being a hermit, you know. I certainly didn't choose it!"

"That's highly debatable. What? It's an uncontrollable illness? You're allergic to strangers? I became a psychologist to figure you out, Mom. I still haven't come up with a proper diagnosis. Some weird composite of personality disorders with agoraphobia."

When Jace goes into analysis mode, I have no defense.

The truth is, I don't like to be alone. That's why I weaseled my way into living with Jace and Tessa. Three years ago, when the world's largest Internet conglomerate, Surf! approached me with an offer to buy NetWorld, I was ready to let someone else take over the operation. The fact that my baby went for three million dollars wasn't too shabby either, though I couldn't give it up completely. I successfully negotiated on-going creative input.

But what to do with all that money? I decided to make Jace an offer of land and a great house along with the one, tiny condition that I live with her and Tessa for the rest of my life. Negotiations with Jace proved dicier than the corporate sale.

It's worked out okay. She's a single mother with a demanding career and I'm pretty convenient to have around as a sitter. The drawback is that I have to listen to Jace's lectures about my sanity.

"Why won't you get treatment?" Jace continued. "Take medication? People do overcome things, you know."

I envisioned the scene at the psychiatrist's office. *Hey doc, gimme the best medicine you have for a disorder that doesn't exist.* No. I would never let myself be doped up with anti-psychotics for hallucinations.

"Do you think I'd ask if it weren't important?" Jace said, finishing her diatribe.

But that was just it. She hadn't asked. As usual, she demanded.

§

"GranDeni, want to hear my song?" A week had passed and all we heard from Tessa was the play, the play, the play.

"I'd love to have a private showing."

Tessa's freckled nose wrinkled. Her hair, the colour of new

copper and always tangled, swished as she shook her head. "That won't work. The other kids have to say their parts!"

"I could do their parts."

"No. You'll come see it—won't you, GranDeni?"

"I didn't promise, Tessa. I said I'd try."

"Okay!" Tessa answered brightly, waving away my heavy tone as if it were a dust mote in the sunshine. "Sit down. I'll do my best part. Then, I'll sing."

I watched her perform. As Tessa moved, the silvery strands rose and fell and tugged on me, but with my granddaughter, this pulling was never painful. I didn't know why.

This could be my epitaph: *Deni didn't know why.*

Afterwards, Tessa climbed up on the couch, sitting so her body touched mine. She seemed to need a moment of closeness. Her thin legs stretched out, bare feet in mid-air past the edge of the cushion, toenails painted a plummy red.

I leaned down and whispered, "It sometimes feels odd when we show off what we can do, doesn't it?"

Tessa nodded, continuing to look straight ahead.

"We can end up feeling that we did something wrong even when everyone tells us we're good."

Tessa looked up, her hazel eyes huge. "You understand," she said, "because we're alike."

This response surprised, pleased, and disturbed me all at once. My ears grew warm. The moment passed with Tessa humming. After a minute, she said, "I want you to meet someone after the play."

"A friend?"

"Kind of."

"It's important to you that I come, huh?"

Tessa nodded, concentrating on a flaky scab on her elbow.

I knew better than to go. I also knew that sometimes life encircles you, leaving only one way out.

But it was Tessa's comment about our being alike that dominated my thoughts. I lay awake that night worrying, not for the first time, that I had passed on to my granddaughter more than an ability to sing on key. Before I fell asleep, I also admitted that Tessa had effortlessly persuaded me to do what Jace's demands never could have accomplished.

§

The night of the play, Tessa takes me aside and says, "GranDeni, don't forget. You have to meet Pat. He's the reason I'm making you come."

"Pat's the friend you mentioned?"

Tessa looks over her shoulder before answering. "It's a man. He works at my school. He told me to bring you."

"Tessa, I don't understand. Who is this? A teacher?"

Just then Jace walks into the room and Tessa whispers, "He's okay. It's important. Don't tell." She covertly points a finger back in the direction of her mother.

Driving to the school, I ponder the mysterious Pat. I've always been careful to conceal my identity as NetWorld's creator, but game players can be highly resourceful. This fellow is probably a fan who wants an autograph or—more likely—an insider's tip. The good news is that the mystery of Tessa's "friend" has distracted me from the daunting and imminent prospect of dealing with the real-world Net; the one only I can see and feel.

As I walk across the parking lot, a wave of nausea swamps me. My muscles tense. *Don't focus on the threads.* But that's the reason crowds are so difficult; the silvery connections are everywhere. Dozens of strands streak from each person, going in all directions, intersecting with others.

A flash of silver in my peripheral vision provides the only, ineffectual warning as a sudden pain—like a fish hook through a rib—lands close to my heart. My pace slows. Sweat prickles my skin. Just as the heart-tug lessens, a hard yank zings my right pelvic bone, stealing my breath. I put a firm hand over the spot and gingerly back off the pavement, attempting to blend into the greenery of a large rhododendron, waiting for the pain to pass.

Glistening threads tangle and untangle before me as the excited families file into the school. Families show an abundance of ample, intricate, inter-connecting strands, most of which leave me alone.

But then, there are the rogue threads. Thin and stiff and unattached. These are the ones that hurt me. They move fast, come from people I don't know and there's no way to predict them. These first two herald many to follow tonight.

An auditorium full of strangers. My nightmare.

~ Undercurrents ~

The pathway into the school begins to clear. I set out at a determined pace, hoping to get into the back of the room before being hit again.

Three steps from the auditorium, searing pain radiates from my sternum. I stagger, almost falling to the ground.

Firm hands lift me forward. "Sorry Deni, that one was mine. Move your feet, gal."

When we are in the control booth, Pat introduces himself and asks the most important question I'll ever hear, "I'm the first one you've ever met, aren't I?"

The question baffles me. I stall. "One—of what?" Then, I know. Pat is talking about the Net.

"Whoo-ee," he whistles, "a virgin of sorts. At your age!"

Anxiety gives way to irritation. "Watch it, bud. Just who are you?"

"I'm the janitor here. I know Tessa because she's one of us. We're all NetSensitives. There aren't a lot of us, but once you know what to look for, you begin to realize we aren't exactly rare either. Are you okay?"

My head is down. I'm raking my scalp with fingernails bitten to the quick. "No, I'm very much not okay." In a moment, I look up. "Tessa?"

He nods. "She said you've never talked about it."

"She talked to *you* about *this*? Oh God, it's my worst fear! Tessa has this...this curse? Why didn't I know?"

"Listen, Deni. I'll explain. But right now, let's watch the play." He points to the window. "Look, it's starting. You're okay in here, right?"

The muscles in my face soften when Tessa comes on stage with the other kids. I nod, realizing that I am all right—compared to being in that auditorium.

"Pat, how can Tessa be out there with all those people? Does it hurt her?"

He shakes his head. "Think back, Deni. Did the threads hurt when you were her age?"

Pat's right. The pain started much later.

He flips a switch and the sounds of children's voices fill the tiny room.

§

~ *Undercurrents* ~

The crowd is still applauding, as Pat escorts me to my truck. I jot down my phone number and offer it to him. "Will you come to the house some day when Jace and Tessa aren't home?"

"Of course," Pat agrees. "I was hoping to talk more."

No more painful Net encounters mar the drive home, but I'm far from calm. My life's been shuffled. Pat's simple existence is monumental. He's like me and yet functions in the world. And Tessa...Tessa is like me after all. We're both "NetSensitives."

Grateful thoughts such as, *I have a name,* and *There are others,* fight with frightened ones like, *Tessa's going to have to deal with this her whole life.*

I come down on the side of gratitude. At least Tessa won't have to do it alone. I'll be there for her. We'll figure it out together.

§

When Jace and Tessa come home, I'm at the computer. It has been, as usual, numbing comfort to be in a cyber-world full of others without the secret and pain of the Net.

Seeing Tessa's face snaps me back to reality. The room's dark and as the child comes up to my desk, the light from the computer screen glows on her face.

"Did you talk to Pat, GranDeni?" she whispers. I nod, tears coming to my eyes. But Tessa flashes a big grin and says more loudly, "Did you like the play? How'd I do?"

Jace comes in and switches on the light.

"You were so great, Tessa!" Finding my enthusiasm, I pick her up, swing her around several times and end the swirl with a big hug. We touch foreheads and I wink. Tessa winks back, squeezing both eyes shut and then opening them wide.

Jace says, "Time for your bath, fairy-girl. Let me unzip you. Run on and get undressed. I'll be there in a sec."

After Tessa leaves the room, Jace says, "I saved you a seat but you never came."

Her brittle tone startles me. "I told you I'd stand at the back."

"You didn't. I looked. I never saw you. You weren't there."

"Jace, stop."

"We've had our problems, Mom, but you've never been a liar."

"Jace! I saw the play. Tessa was wonderful."

~ Undercurrents ~

"You wouldn't have had to see it to know that."

"I did come. I found the control booth at the back of the room and sat there."

Jace's eyebrows rise, then lower forming a deep crease.

"Late in the second act, the toadstool fell and nearly rolled off the stage." I huff off to give Tessa her bath, defiantly keeping her up way past her bedtime.

§

"But the pain's real!"

Pat and I are sitting on the front porch of Jace's house. It runs the length of the log-cabin home and is populated by several rocking chairs, a porch swing, and an old cot for taking naps. Tessa's riding toys are stacked at one end.

"Wait," Pat says. "I never said it wasn't real. I feel it, too. I only said it's worse when we isolate ourselves."

"We isolate ourselves because it hurts!"

Pat sits back and looks out over the woods around Jace's house. He tells me he's thirty-seven, but he looks older. His skin is rugged and lined. There's a subtle persistent tug in his voice, like an undertow, that belies his easy-going banter.

"Deni, listen to me. I've done it both ways."

"Okay, I'll listen. I want to know everything. First of all, how can you work in a school?" An involuntary shudder moves through me. "I hurt just thinking about being around all those strangers."

He gives me a sideways look. It continues for longer than is polite. It makes me uncomfortable. "Say something."

"What's a stranger, Deni?"

I roll my eyes. He's treating me like a child. "A stranger is someone you don't know."

He still says nothing. He turns and looks at me straight-on, now, waiting.

"All right, I guess I get your point. You know all the kids. And the teachers. And the administrators. They aren't strangers, so they don't hurt you."

"Bingo."

I get up and start pacing. One of the wide boards of the porch creaks repeatedly under my feet. "Uh-uh. No, Pat. That doesn't work. What about when you didn't know them? If I walked into that school and interviewed for a job, I'd be under the table writhing in pain!"

"True. But you aren't being hurt by me now, are you?"

The memory of the thread that doubled me over in the corridor comes back. Pat still has a huge number of threads scrolling out from his body, but it's true, none of them are zapping me. "It's because you aren't a stranger anymore, right?"

"Exactly. We made a fast connection. The more easily you take in the strands, the less painful they'll be. NetSensitives must receive *and* give, Deni. Let them come and go through you. I should tell you...both my parents were NetSensitives."

"Wow, that's unimaginable. It must have seemed normal."

"In a way, but of course they taught me early on that we were different. I had to learn to keep my mouth shut. I grew up knowing that being NetSensitive is neither good nor bad; like everything else, it depends on what we do with it."

"Hmm. Like being an opinionated broad can be bad, but adaptive in certain situations. Like negotiating contracts, for example."

"Yeah," he smiles, "like any trait we have."

"So what's the good part of being NetSensitive? I mean, what's the point?"

"You have to answer that question for yourself. I was taught that we're lucky because we can—literally—never lose sight of the fact that we're all connected. My dad joked, calling it 'con*NET*edness.' I was probably fourteen-years-old before I knew the proper word had another 'c' in it."

As soon as this memory's been spoken, I see him pull away.

"Your parents?"

"Both gone," he responds, his eyes on the landscape. He jerks his head back to look at me. "The other thing is that you've spent a long time in isolation. You've had no practice. It's like trying to ride a bicycle up a mountain with no preparation. Of course it's going to hurt."

"Damn it, Pat, I thought you were going to help me. All you have to offer is the prospect of going out there and being zapped to the point of collapse in order to get over this!"

He smiles at me. "Take it easy, girl. I'm not telling you that you have to do anything you don't want to."

~ *Undercurrents* ~

"I have another big question. How did Tessa know that we're both NetSensitives when I didn't?"

He grins sheepishly and says, "I told her."

"Huh?"

"I saw you picking her up from school one day."

"You can tell just by looking?"

"There's a different quality to the threads. Look at mine," he tells me.

My immediate and overwhelming aversion makes me turn away. "I, um, I try not to focus on them."

"You have to get over that."

I glance at his threads, then look away. "You have so many!"

"All adult NetSensitives, including you, have more than most people. We seem to attract them."

"So I noticed."

"What else?" he prompts.

Still feeling inner resistance, I make myself study Pat's strings. "They...well, I'm not sure. They seem to...damn, I never noticed that. They seem to go through you...sort of disappear into you. With other people, the threads stop at the body, but your skin looks almost invisible where the threads touch you, as if each one has dissolved your tissue. Or maybe it's more like a glow. It's really hard to describe."

He nods. "I know. Hard to put into words. But you got it. That's how you identify another one of 'us.' Check out Tessa's later. Have you and Tessa talked?"

"A little. I'm still very hesitant."

"Because...?"

"Because I don't have a freakin' clue how! And then...there's Jace to consider."

"Jace should be told. I'll help you. I'll tell her you aren't crazy."

My face must have reacted, because he laughed.

"I know that's what you're scared of. Lucky for you, they don't put people away anymore—at least, not for long." He smiles. "Anyway, it seems you've done all right for yourself." He expands his hands to indicate the house and the surrounding woods.

"Yeah, thank God for the Internet."

We grin at each other over the obvious ironies of my life.

~ Undercurrents ~

§

"Where are you two going?" Jace asks. She's just come onto the porch holding a large bowl of popcorn.

Tessa jumps up from her toys with a "whoo-hoo!" and grabs a handful.

"Oh man, Jace, you should have told us you were going to do that," Pat says. "We have to go now when the town will be almost deserted. I'm taking your mom off to practice."

"Practice?"

"Being. Out. In. Public," I answer, grimly. Pat and I are already half-way to the driveway.

"Pat," Jace shouts, "how great are you? I've never known anyone who could make her do something she didn't want to do. And she obviously—," Jace pauses for effect, "does not want to do this."

Pat gives Jace a big shrug in lieu of an answer. As we drive off, I turn back to look at the house. "She's still there, grinning from ear-to-ear."

"She loves you. She just wants you to have a normal life."

"Humph."

"Okay, groucho, let's have an attitude change," Pat says. "You asked me to help. Remember?"

"Oh God. Yes. I did. What was I thinking?"

"You know, Jace has to be told."

"Could you *please* give me a little time to adjust to all this? Too much change all at once!"

"It's been over a month. What are you waiting for?"

"I—it's hard." I lean back and close my eyes. "She's not open to new things. She assumes too much. She knows all the labels for people and thinks they are sufficient to explain human behaviour."

"You aren't that open to new things yourself."

We drive the rest of the way in silence. When he's parked, I get out, slamming the door behind me. "I'm here, aren't I?"

We begin to cross the grassy tract of the town commons. It's damp, chilly and late in the day. We've planned it so that I'll encounter a few people, but not too many.

"Have you ever done yoga?" Pat asks.

"Yes."

~ Undercurrents ~

"Good. Pretend you are doing postures. Keep your breath in mind as you move."

"Okay, that's helpful."

So far, there's no one around.

"Close your eyes."

"No."

"Deni—"

"Okay, okay." He leads me by the wrist and I realize that for all my grumbling, I do trust Pat. He's reassured me that the pain will lessen once I learn to relax. Learn to *receive the connection*, as he says, *then give it away*. Whatever that means.

Concentrating on my breathing as we walk, I allow him to guide my movements. After about five minutes he whispers, "Keep your eyes closed. You're doing great. Did you just feel anything?"

"What should I have felt?"

"Gawd, woman! I told you not to open your eyes!"

My lids snap shut. "A little tug in my abdomen. Toward the left. I thought it was gas."

Pat laughs. He pulls on my wrist to turn me toward him. "Now open your eyes." I do, and find that he's grinning. "Look back," he says, tossing his head in the direction we'd come from.

A man is walking away from us, his bulldog ranging at the end of a leash.

I gape at him. "That man was my gas pain? It didn't really hurt. Why?"

Pat lifts his shoulders. "You weren't tense. It passed through you."

There's a bench nearby and we sit down. "Pat, I just don't get one basic thing. Why does this happen?"

"The best analogy I've come up with is that we seem to act as lightning rods for any unconnected strands."

"Lightning rods? We're the shortest route to...?"

He shrugs again, smiling. "There *are* one or two things I haven't figured out yet. But I do know that you can't fight it. Be a willing conduit and threads will go through you without pain."

"Well...I'm encouraged. I'm usually so tense I make it worse, right? That's okay. I can admit that. It makes sense. I've always been an uptight bitch."

Pat looks at me with a searching, amused expression. "I

never know what's going to come out of your mouth!"

"I know. Me neither. God, where are all the people? I need practice!"

We stay in the park until dark. I keep my eyes open and I learn.

§

When I get back to the house, Jace wants to know all about it. I inwardly kick myself for not having prepared answers. I'm not ready to tell her everything.

"It was good, Jace. I'm learning."

"You'll try it again?" she asks.

"Yes, I will. I made progress."

"Want a drink?"

"Sure, I'll have a beer." I sit down on a bar stool across the kitchen island and watch her.

"Pat," Jace says to herself as she gets our drinks. "The amazing Pat. Medicine Man. Grand Shaman. Wizard. Are you screwing him?"

"Jace!"

She laughs. "No? Really, I can't figure out anything but new love that can make someone totally change behaviour so suddenly. So, not love...or lust?"

"He's years younger than me. Besides, I'm not interested."

"No. I didn't really think so."

"You?"

Jace laughs again, choking on her wine. "No. Well, I don't know. I never thought about it. He's your friend."

"Yes. Deni has a friend. Imagine that." I'm pleased that the conversation has strayed away from what happened at the park.

"Tell me about him," Jace says.

"Hmm. He doesn't talk about himself." Guilt oozes in on me as I realize how little I know about Pat. It's all been about me and my problems. "No children or wife...I don't think. His parents are dead. I think he lives alone."

"You *think* he lives alone?"

My face flushes. "I guess I need practice at having a friend, too. I'll find out everything I can the next time I see him, okay?"

Jace smiles and says, "Good. I want all the details!"

~ Undercurrents ~

She's relaxed. Jace's relaxed, because I'm trying. That's all she really needed from me.

§

At first, when I can't reach Pat, I assume his cell is out of range, or his voice mail's full. After a week with no answer I ask Tessa, but she can't remember having seen him at school.

I begin to worry.

Another week goes by with no word, so I speak to Jace. "Could you ask about him at the school?"

"Sure," Jace says, "I can do that. But people change cell phone numbers all the time. You're worried about him?"

"Silly, right? He did tell me that day in the park that he was going to be out of touch for a little while. He said...gosh, it sounds odd now that I think of it, but at the time I thought he was just joking about other things we discussed."

"What?" Jace asks.

"He said, 'Our connection might be interrupted.' "

"Well, there you go. He probably couldn't pay his phone bill."

I'm distracted by my memories of that day.

Jace pats the top of my head. "I'll ask at the school. Stop worrying."

§

The pain fills me, eradicating my vision, stealing my breath, extinguishing all thoughts. I might have heard screams before my mind stopped registering anything but the agony.

I'm up late as usual; the house is quiet and dark except for the light from the computer. The pain pushes me forward in my chair. Moments pass and as the worst of it begins to subside, I slide onto the floor. On my hands and knees, I gasp, tears seeping from the corners of my eyes. Sweat forms between my breasts and legs. The overwhelming pain is gone, but instead of recovering, my body, my mind, my senses are traumatized to the point of inertia.

A vision appears.

The Net. Only, this Net is the size of the universe. Silver-white on a backdrop of black, it's unlike the one I see everyday;

the one that constantly changes, slithering and rearranging itself between people. There are no people and this Net is predictable and regular like a well-kept fishing net—except for one spot.

That's where my pain came from. The thought arrives in my mind from somewhere else, a clear drizzle of an idea.

My vision zooms to the broken connection. The threads dangle. Ripped. Jagged-edged. The broken ends are hurting, tender, lost. I'm startled to realize that the Net, the space—all of it —is *aware*. The vacant spot, where the threads should have been connected, is palpably—consciously—empty. And, I know why.

"No!"

"Mom! Mom!" Jace's hand is on my shoulder. "Mom, what's happening? Tessa woke up screaming. Are you sick? Did someone break in? What's going on?"

Jace, her sleep-marked face distraught, holds Tessa in her arms. Tessa, sobbing, reaches out to me.

We hold each other as close as we can.

"Mom. God! What's happening?" Jace pleads.

But I'm crying too hard to talk. Tessa and I cling to each other, rocking back and forth. Jace kneels down and I reach for her hand, squeezing it.

After a few minutes, I pull back from Tessa. "You saw it too?"

Tessa's chest shudders. She nods and then turns to her mother. "It's Pat," she explains between renewed sobs. "He's gone."

§

The next day Jace makes calls and confirms what Tessa and I already know. Pat committed suicide.

It is time. I tell Jace everything, explaining as best I can about the Net. I tell her about Pat and NetSensitives. I tell her that Tessa is one of us. Maybe Jace thinks I'm crazy, but I don't much care anymore. Pat, my hope for the future, is gone.

Jace asks Tessa a lot of questions. I learn of many ways in which Pat helped her.

"He showed me how to tell things about people by how their strings are acting," Tessa says. "And he said it's okay to talk about, but not to anyone who isn't one of us."

"No problem there," says Jace. "You managed to keep it from

~ Undercurrents ~

me. Your mother."

"Kept it from me, too."

"I thought you knew, GranDeni," says Tessa indignantly. "I thought it was like when there's farts in the room and no one talks about it because it's not polite."

Jace and I smile. "Farts," I reply. "Exactly right." I turn to Jace. "Pat repeatedly urged me to tell you but I didn't know how. I'm sorry it took this to make it happen."

"I'm just worried," says Tessa.

Jace flashes me a concerned look.

"About what, Tess?" she asks.

The little girl focusses her large eyes on me. "Who's going to do Pat's job?"

"At the school?" her mom asks.

Tessa doesn't take her eyes from me. "No. Not that. I mean his NetSensitive work. He said people like us get lonely, GranDeni, and that he looked for them in malls and stuff...to let them know there are more of us and that it's okay."

My eyes fill with tears. "I don't know, Tessa. I am so sorry, but I can't answer your questions right now."

After Tessa goes to bed, I ask Jace what she's thinking.

"I definitely understand why you kept it from me, Mom. I wouldn't have believed you. I would have thought you were hallucinating and tried even harder to get you on meds. It's bizarre."

Jace is at the other end of the couch, her feet tucked beneath her the way she always sat as a little girl. She's deep in thought, chewing on her thumbnail; it's a bad habit we share.

She looks up. "I think, Mom...because of the way you changed when Pat came into the picture, I understand it differently than I would have without him. I mean...I don't understand it. I don't know what it is, or why, or anything else. But you and Tessa wouldn't lie to me so, for now, I just have to live with my questions."

"Welcome to the damned club."

The weight of Pat's death is so heavy that I begin to sink into my computer-realities with unprecedented obsessiveness. When Jace comes around, my mantra is always the same; "Leave me alone."

§

Weeks go by. On a summer's day when Tessa has gone to a friend's house, Jace asks me to take a walk in the woods. As usual, I decline. It'll only be another of her lectures.

But she refuses to go away. "I have new information you need to hear. I promise I won't fuss at you."

I finally relent just to get her off my back.

We go down the back steps and into the yard. The sky's china blue and the clouds, glaringly white. The trees, clad in vivid, full-summer green, sway dramatically. Thousands of leaves rustle, sounding like the applause of a distant crowd. I stop just as we reach the path into the woods and turn back.

Jace catches my arm. "No. Come with me."

"Can't. Look at me! I'm crying! I come outside and this day—" Turning back around, I sweep my arm in a wide arc to indicate everything around us, "—this place, this world! Oh God, it's beautiful. Okay? Happy? I see it. I smell it. I know it's good, Jace, but it all just hurts."

"Shouldn't it—couldn't it—be more precious?"

The back of my hand slaps at wet eyes. "I wish to God I felt that. But it's all...unavailable to me."

Jace takes my arm and gently pulls me down the path. "Tell me," she urges.

"I feel so betrayed! This man barges into my life so unexpectedly. He immediately tries to change me, to show me life can be better. Tells me I can live a full life. And then," I snap my fingers, "then he just offs himself with no warning, no thought of anyone else."

"Suicide is always selfish."

"Damn right it is!"

"Never understandable."

"No."

"What else?" Jace prompts.

"He acted like he had it all worked out! He made me believe that people like us could be happy! Shit, Jace, he was hiding his pain. It was all a facade, and for what? Hell, if he'd told me he was miserable we could have shared war stories! But no, he hid it, didn't he? I hate him for making me feel hope!"

"And now that he's killed himself, there is no hope."

~ Undercurrents ~

"Right."

"You let him, this man you barely knew, have that kind of power over you?"

"Yeah, yeah. I get it, Jace. I'm so independent; no one has power over me. But you're missing the point. It's not what he said, but who he was. He walked freely in the world where I've felt like a prisoner. Only now, I know his life was a lie, so I can't believe in what he represented. It was false."

"I've been finding out about Pat, Mom."

I stop walking. "What? How?"

"I finally thought to talk to Tessa's principal. They had a heck of a time with some of the kids. She said Pat was wonderful with them. It wasn't only Tessa who liked him."

A tidal wave of self-disgust submerges me. *I'm not the only one grieving. I haven't even been thinking about Tessa.*

Jace continues, "The principal suggested I talk to Pat's cousin who lives nearby. She's Pat's only living relative."

I'm so sad.

It's a stunning realization, how strenuously I've been avoiding that simple fact. Avoiding thinking about Pat the same way I always avoided looking at the Net. As if somehow that would make the pain go away. Pat taught me better than that.

"It's not a happy story," Jace says. "Pat's mom died of cancer when he was a teenager. The dad didn't cope well. Always a drinker, he became an alcoholic. Pat got into heavy drugs, though it seems he pulled himself out of his addiction. Then, when Pat was in his 20's, his dad committed suicide. He took pills, like Pat eventually did. The cousin told me there were other suicides in the family. She spoke of it as a family trait."

"Suicide runs in families?"

"Yeah, it can recur over generations. Almost as if becomes...permissible, because it's happened before. Maybe it's genetic. We don't know."

"I never asked him about his life."

"Don't beat yourself up. The principal told me he was not open to talking about himself."

"Oh God. I could see the sadness in him, Jace. Talking to him on the porch right after we met, I sensed something below the surface. An undercurrent tugging on him, pulling him down."

"I didn't pick up on it. Is this part of what Tessa was talking about? That NetSensitives discern people's problems?"

"Does that sound like me? Not likely!"

"Don't be so sure, Mom. Didn't you tell me that one of your coping mechanisms was to not focus on the connections between people?"

"Damned right." My voice is rough with emotion.

"So that's my point," Jace says. "Maybe you can do it, if you stop avoiding what's in front of your eyes."

I look away and start walking again. It's as if my daughter sees right through me. And the word "avoidance" has become an irritating, animated banner that draws my attention over and over and over. Inexplicably, at the same moment I feel so exposed, I am aware of a subtle lightening in my chest.

We stroll slowly back to the house. Jace spots an owl sitting high overhead. "There must be a nest somewhere around here. I've heard them at night," I tell her. "It's the mates calling to each other as they hunt. They sound more like bobcats than birds."

Jace grasps my forearm. "It's like this, Mom: you take a step outside the house and you feel better. If it's only for the few minutes that you're out, then okay, at least you've had that. Next time, your peace of mind might last longer. You need to try. Try taking fledgling steps. You need to. I need you to. Tessa really needs you. Can you do that for us?"

For once, Jace is asking, not demanding. I'm afraid to say anything, but "leave me alone" is the farthest thing from my mind.

§

There's a cold snap on the first day of school. After Jace leaves to take Tessa, I put on my fleece vest and set out for my walk.

I walk everyday now and have started a journal to chronicle my progress—and my set-backs. Last week, I went to town and walked through the park. It hurt—in more ways than one—but I did it anyway. I've set a goal to repeat the feat each week until I feel somewhat normal, until I begin to lose my fear of the threads. I often think of bicycling up a mountain.

I stride briskly down the pathway that Jace and I took the day she told me about Pat's life. That was a turning point and I've come to accept that Pat killed himself because he was dealt a bad hand. Because suicide was in his family, his genes. Because it was an undertow he couldn't resist. Because—unlike mine—his pain never got better, even when he practiced. Being a NetSensitive was only a small portion of who Pat was.

The stunning red-orange-yellow leaves drift around me as I walk. I continue to regret not learning more about Pat, but my anger has vanished. Pat did the best he could and so must I. I have a future to think about. There will be more school plays. A graduation. Perhaps a wedding...or two. More than anything, there is Tessa who has the right to expect her grandmother's good advice about being NetSensitive.

I increase my pace. There's another motivation for the future as well. It's my solution to that nagging question Tessa asked right after Pat's suicide. *Who's going to do Pat's job?*

It had bothered me for weeks, but on finding my energy again, I also found the answer. Last night at dinner I shared it with Tessa and Jace. "I have an idea of a way to help other NetSensitives. I can't take over Pat's job the way he did it. I'm not confident enough in the real world. But I thought we could use the Internet to do the same thing."

"You mean an Internet group for NetSensitives?" Jace asked.

"Right! I even came up with a name. Pat once told me that his father made up the word 'conneted' to describe NetSensitives. So our group will be called: Co-Net-Ed. I've already bought up coneted.com, .net, and .org!"

Tessa's eyes lit up. "Oh GranDeni! Can I be in the group?"

"Definitely, Tess. We're going to be partners in this."

As I power up a hill, strategies for helping NetSensitives find our new group running through my brain, my lungs suddenly feel robbed of oxygen. For an instant my vision blanks out and in the blackness, I see the Net as I witnessed it the night Pat died. Recovery or not, this is not a memory I want. Leaning my backside up against an old maple, gasping air, I wait for it to pass. But the Net is still there in the blackness behind my lids.

"I do not want to see this." My voice sounds as weak as my argument. I know now about avoidance. It only makes things worse. Consciously, my breathing slows as I make myself look.

The Net floats—suspended in the vast...*somethingness*...of the cosmos—undulating, fluid, orderly. As my now-calm mind's eye travels over and around this Net, I see broken places. I sense, but don't feel, the pain in each one of these gaps.

I can see what is. I have the privilege of visualizing and experiencing our connectedness while others can only vaguely sense it or utterly deny it or live without ever contemplating it at all. My job is simple. I receive each strand that comes and let it pass through me.

I finally understand.

I, Deni, am a bridge between gaps. I am a link.

And this, to my Internet-sensitive brain, makes perfect sense.

Back home, I settle at my desk. I login to NetWorld, click Menu, then, New Character. A form opens and I start typing.

Name: Pat

Role: Wizard

I hesitate and then backspace over the letters and type in "Healer." I delete it again and type, "Teacher."

I sit for a moment, looking at the blinking cursor. And then, with fondness for all Pat was and all he might have been, I fill out his character.

In my world, friend, you shall live forever.

❦

Nancy S.M. Waldman is a Texan who moved around until she finally found Cape Breton. She has a great deal of education/experience in nursing, counseling, painting, textile arts, and photography. Never having made much money in any of these fields, Nancy now continues this tradition by writing fiction. Her stories vary in length, subject, and genre but are always concerned with complexity of relationships and their resultant emotions. Threads woven throughout reveal her interests in politics, education, ethics, spirituality, J. Edgar Hoover, string theory, and the Wankel engine. She writes for and manages several websites devoted to creative arts and charity. In her spare time, Nancy designs fashions for Second Life.

Ghouls

Although he could walk the decks of a coast guard ship in a swell without losing his step, the shunting motion of trains played havoc with Duncan's balance, producing a lumbering gait as he navigated the long aisles, his hands blessing the headrests of every seat he passed.

A lanky young man already occupied the bottom bunk when he entered the sleeper. The compartment reeked of beer and a fit of snores exploded from the kid's open mouth. One arm dangled over the side of the bunk and Duncan picked up the ticket that had fallen to the floor. Like himself, his drunken cabin mate was travelling to Berlin. Duncan tucked the ticket into the folds of the knapsack behind the kid's head, a hand-painted Swedish flag adorning the strap. Tossing his own overnight bag on the top bunk, Duncan headed to the lounge on the train for his appointment with Herr Schmidt.

In the coach before the lounge car, the air was frigid, a sharp contrast to the fusty atmosphere in the other cars. The half dozen passengers sat somnolent, sedated by the strong ammonia fumes emanating from the vinyl flooring, obviously scrubbed just before departure. As Duncan passed the lethargic travellers, they glanced slowly in his direction with impassive expressions, gaunt-faced and dressed in the pudding-coloured fashions of Eastern Europe before the fall of the Berlin Wall. No one spoke or acknowledged his occasional nod as he passed them. If there was such a thing as *peasant class* on a train, this was it, Duncan thought, shuddering from the cold, and hastened his step to reach the exit.

In contrast, the lounge car was warm and full of passengers, which suited Duncan, as he did not enjoy the isolation of train travel. And to his relief, the air exchange unit was working in the car. Spying two vacant booths, he chose the one with a window and ordered a large draft. Passing his hand under his chin, he discovered it had erupted in fresh stubble. Every muscle in his body ached. Los Angeles, New York, Oslo, Helsinki, Stockholm, and Copenhagen—all in ten days, delivering his stellar lectures on hypothermia to deep-pocketed search and rescue organizations around the globe. The overnight train to Berlin would allow him to catch up on his sleep after all the flights, and even if the kid back in the cabin puked up his guts through the night, Duncan, a heavy sleeper, would be dead to the world.

As Duncan gazed out the window, the reflected image of a man suddenly appeared at his shoulder. Shaken, he tipped over his almost-empty glass.

"I startled you," the stranger offered, wiping up the remains of Duncan's beer with a black silk handkerchief.

Duncan rose and presented his hand in greeting.

"Jetlag," he offered as an excuse for his clumsiness. "I'm on my last nerve." He waited with outstretched hand while the man meticulously folded the sodden handkerchief and replaced it in his rumpled sports jacket. He slid into the booth without shaking hands.

"Please, sit," he said.

Duncan sat down, peeved by the abruptness in the pudgy man sitting opposite him, charcoal shadows below eyes peppered with dozens of small cysts. Duncan felt like a *guest* at his own table.

His companion stared at Duncan for a long moment.

"My name is Karl Schmidt," he said finally, extending his hand across the table.

The hell with it, Duncan thought, maybe it was a German custom to shake hands only after you sat down. He extended his own hand and accepted the limp handshake.

Schmidt was not what Duncan had expected. Flat nose, broken in the past. A thick stumpy neck. Fingernails bitten down to the quick. Schmidt looked like a felon, not the officious German businessman he had anticipated. And the teeth, poorly fitted dentures revealing excessive scar tissue on every gum.

"You're smiling," Schmidt said.

Duncan immediately suppressed his grin. He was about to

accept contraband data that could land both of them in jail for years. Jesus Christ, he was actually one of two crooks at the table.

Wiping his mind of judgemental musings, Duncan concentrated on the prize that awaited him and his analytic detachment took over. History had presented him with a unique opportunity to continue his research. He had no moral twinges. Besides, the Germans should have taken care of this business sixty years ago.

The prize, other than the contraband data, was a lucrative research scholarship at the Heidelberg Institute, surely guaranteed once he crunched the data the German was about to hand over. After that, he could start charging six figures for his lectures.

Schmidt had ordered a Scotch and soda.

"This is what you call a clandestine meeting, no?" he asked.

"Hardly, we'd be meeting in a dark alley if it were."

"Perhaps as it should be," Schmidt said, followed by a long sigh. "Perhaps I leave now? Before it is too late?"

Duncan didn't flinch. Herr Schmidt suddenly looked thoughtful and smiled. "Fine."

"I have an envelope for you," Duncan said. "Would you like it now?"

"By all means, it must be now."

Duncan slid the envelope across the table. Schmidt placed the untouched glass of Scotch on top of it while he detached a USB flash drive from a keychain, passing it to Duncan.

"Feed the statistics into your computer," Schmidt said. "Oh yes, you must have the PIN code."

"What is it?" Duncan asked.

"Dachau."

"D-A-C-H-U-A?"

"D-A-C-H-A-U," Schmidt corrected, with a tinge of disgust.

"Listen, Herr Schmidt, I don't want to have to use this data, but it will save lives."

"'Truth, even when spoken by sinners, is from God.' No? St. Augustine." Schmidt downed the Scotch in one gulp.

Duncan rose from the table.

"Where are you going?"

"I'm going to bed."

"Indulge me for a few moments. Tell me about your work," Schmidt said.

Reluctantly, Duncan sat.

"I design cold-water survival suits."

"Is it true that most fishermen do not know how to swim?"

"Possibly."

"But surely that is important, to know everything about your subject?"

"When they hit the water they don't think about swimming. They go into shock."

"And how long can they survive?"

"It depends. They can survive thirty-six hours until rescue if they're wearing the suit and make it to a life raft."

"And if they are not wearing your suit?"

"A few hours, maybe more, depending on health, constitution."

"And you are there to witness the rewards?"

"I've been on a couple rescue missions, yes."

"And when they have no suits, victims of hypothermia, have you seen their bodies?"

"Yes."

"Are you there when they hit the water?"

"I don't hang around on vessels waiting for a storm to take a man over the side."

"What about your laboratory. Do you use rats?"

"Yes."

"But rats are not people."

"No, we don't use people."

"And yet this data I have given to you, it is based on human rats. Under clinical conditions, of course." Herr Schmidt inflated his cheeks, exhaled, and motioned the bartender for a refill.

"I know what you're driving at, Herr Schmidt. I don't put faces to data. When I was in university, a cadaver was just that. Nobody thinks about histological sections as being part of the body."

"In the great America, you do not murder people and put them under a microscope. Here in Germany, prominent universities utilize tissue samples, even the body parts of concentration camp victims. You should go and see Doctor Hallervorden's collection of brains that he extracted from over seven hundred murdered psychiatric patients. His comment at the end of the war: 'I accepted the brains, of course. Where they came from and how they came to me was really none of my business.' "

"I am aware of Hallervorden's past. And I'm sure that you are well aware the Hallervorden-Spatz disease was named after him. Some good did come from his questionable tactics."

"You, who can't even spell Dachau. When you study your data try not to imagine the prisoners plunged naked into ice water until they were dead." Schmidt dove after an ice cube and placed it between his teeth, biting it in two. "You had better return to your cabin. They will be inspecting passports. You can come back later. I am an insomniac and prefer to sit here all night. We can continue this feisty discourse."

Duncan took a deep breath and walked briskly through the coach, the odour of ammonia as oppressive as his first sweep through the car and the air even icier than earlier. He could feel the eyes of the passengers following him again and he hastened back to the sleeper, slipping into the bathroom in the corridor to relieve his bladder. He faced himself in the mirror. His skin was pale and his eyes bloodshot, his black hair lay flat on his head. He washed his face with cold water and felt his skin tighten. He rinsed his nostrils to rid them of the lingering ammonia he had carried with him from the coach.

He bounced along the wall of the corridor and found his berth. The bottom bunk where he had left the sleeping Swede was empty, the bed freshly made-up. A quick glance to his overnight bag on the bunk above confirmed that he was in the right berth. All of the Swede's belongings were gone. He looked around for a sign of his having been there. Everything was tidy. He picked up his overnight case and emptied the contents onto his bunk. Nothing was missing. He repacked it and sat on the edge of the Swede's bunk.

There was a light rap on the door. He opened it, expecting to see the Swede. Instead, a customs officer stood outside.

"*Pas*," the officer demanded.

Duncan reached into his suit coat pocket and withdrew his passport. The officer switched on a small flashlight and inspected the document. He shined his light into Duncan's face and back at the passport.

~ *Undercurrents* ~

"Purpose of visit to Germany?" he asked, backing out of the cabin.

"Tourist."

"No business?"

"No."

The officer lingered for a moment before tipping his hat and moving down the corridor to the next berth.

The train pulled into a station and Duncan stepped into the corridor to watch the action on the platform outside the train. A couple dozen people waited to board, their shoulders hunched against the cold sting of the wind that whipped along the tunnel created by the train and another across the platform. A trolley filled with the baggage of passengers disembarking clogged the narrow corridor leading to the exit. A woman strode toward it and without stopping scooped up a knapsack emblazoned with a Swedish flag. Duncan looked up and down the platform. There was no sign of the Swede. After the second whistle, Duncan headed for the lounge car.

Most of the passengers Duncan spied on the platform had settled in the coach car, joining the half dozen or so other travellers he had encountered earlier. They appeared oblivious to the chill of the car despite shivering moments before on the platform. Several of the windows in the car oozed condensation, milky pearls that reminded Duncan of the beads of sweat that hived on the top of his old fridge on humid summer days. These were families, some with toddlers, and even though the hour was late, the children were all awake; their eyes following his passage like the others had earlier, their clothes as drab as the adults seated beside them wore. There was no chatter, no hushed whispers, none of them slept. They simply sat; their only activity was the anesthetised adventure of watching Duncan walk along the aisle.

The syrupy odour that had pervaded the car earlier was stronger than before, mixed with the stench of unwashed bodies. Gypsies, Duncan concluded, surprising himself with his bigoted pondering. If so, where were the colourful costumes he had seen in the pages of National Geographic? Where were the guitars and festivity he associated with the Roma nomads? Once again, he quickened his step, following his reflection in the windows of the car, a beacon to lead him to the exit at the other end, bobbing above the sea of dull eyes that watched him.

The lounge car was empty now except for Schmidt; the bartender slouched on a stool behind the counter. He exchanged a glance with Schmidt as Duncan approached the booth and Schmidt nodded back.

"Are you also an insomniac?" Schmidt asked.

The bartender arrived at the table with a beer and removed two empty Scotch glasses, setting a fresh drink in front of Schmidt.

Duncan noticed that Schmidt's face appeared slimmer, taut. He wore a proper suit now, navy blue with matching tie and white silk shirt. A wedding band and sapphire stone adorned his right hand. The stubble was gone from the face.

"I have meetings in Berlin when we arrive," Schmidt said, amused at Duncan's reaction to his change of clothes. He shrugged his shoulders. "I am a man who sets the table for breakfast before I go to sleep. So what if the suit is wrinkled when we eventually arrive in Berlin? I will be prepared. And you will kindly stop staring at the toupee."

Duncan took a long swig of the beer.

Two middle-aged men entered the car. The bartender raced down the aisle, shooing them out with his hands.

"*Wir haben geschlossen,*" he shouted. "We're closed."

"You seem uncomfortable, Herr Scientist. You twitch. Perhaps our German beer doesn't agree with you?"

"Did you see a tall skinny Swede while you've been sitting here?" Duncan asked.

"No."

"He was sharing my berth. He was sleeping when I boarded the train. When I returned to the berth, he was gone. There was no trace of him."

"Perhaps he got off at the stop."

"No, he was travelling to Berlin."

"He told you this?"

"I didn't speak to him. His ticket had fallen on the floor, his destination was Berlin," Duncan said, taking the moment to assess Schmidt's eyes.

"He must have taken another berth," Schmidt said dismissively, "perhaps the porter discovered that he had chosen incorrectly in the first place."

~ Undercurrents ~

Duncan did not like the smugness in Schmidt's voice.

Schmidt exchanged a few words with the bartender, who pulled down a metal grate to lock away the liquor bottles.

"*Gute Nacht*," he said, and left the car.

"You are overtired, Herr Scientist. Our unsavoury business has unsettled you."

"There is nothing unsavoury about our business. You had data for sale and I bought it."

"That is an understatement." Schmidt contemplated his glass of Scotch. "Tell me, Herr Scientist, what if there was more data, more recent, in fact. What would you say to this?"

"I would say that you are finally revealing yourself. Why wouldn't there be more? Why sell off everything at once for one price?"

"Is this how you would conduct yourself if you were the entrepreneur? Sad."

"If there is more data, I want it," Duncan blurted.

"You are greedy."

"I'm ambitious."

"*Cupidus.*"

"I'm sorry?"

"Ambition. Greed. They both share the Latin root. *Cupidus.* Perhaps you would be so kind as to meet me at my compartment. Car seven, berth nine." He rose from the booth. Duncan listened as the door slid open and then shut. He guzzled the last of his beer and decided to follow. Cupidus, be dammed, he thought, preferring to follow the promise of another Latin term, *opportunus.*

Preoccupied and giddy with the prospect of additional contraband data, Duncan was halfway through the coach car when a sudden lurch of the train bumped him to the side. Grasping the nearest headrest for support, he steadied himself. The seat was empty and as he sought the door at the other end of the car with his eyes, his heart skipped a beat. The entire car was empty. Turning back, he headed toward the lounge car, assuming he had passed through the *peasant class* coach without noticing. But when he peered through the window in the door, he could see that the coach was coupled to the lounge. He was in the peasant coach. Impossible. The train hadn't stopped during his brief visit with Schmidt in the lounge. Or had his delight at discovering that more data existed, and his mounting jetlag, wiped out any sensory clue to a stop and uncoupling of the coach car?

He had to find Schmidt.

He noticed footprints on the vinyl. And the vinyl was wet. Bending down he touched the floor, gingerly passing his fingers under his nostrils. Ammonia. No. Ammonia wasn't sweet. This was something else, something familiar but detested.

Formaldehyde.

The gag response he had long ago learned to suppress returned. Covering his nose with his jacket sleeve, he headed for Schmidt's compartment. *Car seven. Berth nine.*

Schmidt occupied a double cabin. He produced a flask of cognac and poured a large drink for both of them. Duncan eagerly inhaled the bouquet, finally clearing his nostrils of the formaldehyde from the coach car. He swallowed the drink in one quaff and poured himself a second.

Schmidt, if he noticed anything in Duncan's fevered state, did not let on.

"There is more data available to you, Herr Scientist. First, you must show me that you want it. We will start with your interest in this roommate of yours. Tell me about him."

"What's there to tell?" Duncan had already forgotten the Swede. Now if he could only forget the image of dozens of eyes boring into his brain every time he blinked.

"Describe him for me."

Concentrate.

"Swedish. Early twenties. Thin. That's all I remember."

"In other words, he made no impression on you?"

"No."

"Now that he has gone missing, you are very interested. Why?"

Better to answer the German. Forget about the vanished passengers.

"Because I don't think he's on the train."

"You are about to make an assumption. Come now, it is your turn to reveal yourself."

"I saw someone, not him, walk away from the last station with his knapsack."

"I have one last question regarding the young man. Did you have occasion to touch him?"

"Touch him?"

"A simple act of bodily contact can often lead to identification when it is required later on. When they pulled the corpses out of the mass graves, the survivors had an uncanny ability to recognize their kin by simple touch, even when little was left to be recognized." Schmidt reclined against the back of the seat. His gaze was neutral, almost bored.

"When I was in Copenhagen yesterday, I visited Tivoli, the most beautiful park in the world," he said. "There was an exhibition in a museum outside the gates. Bodies. Preserved using a method called polymer preservation."

Duncan suppressed a yawn.

"I've seen thousands of cadavers," Schmidt continued, "these looked like hardened silicone rubber. The muscles dyed in various colours. Pretty. But a waste of scientific opportunity."

I saw that exhibition, Duncan thought. Trumped up as a stunning display of human anatomy. Was it possible Schmidt had attended it at the same time?

"A freak show," Schmidt said.

"Yes, a freak show."

"Yet, there was one display that intrigued me. They had injected the blood vessels leading from the shoulder to the tips of the fingers with a hardening agent and dye, and then dissolved all the surrounding muscle and bone mass, the remains a perfect red silhouette of the arm and hand sealed between glass. The young woman beside me thought it was pretty too, telling her boyfriend that she hoped she could buy one just like it at the gift shop. It reminded her of her coral collection and wondered if she could put one in her aquarium."

"My mother kept her gall stones in a jar," Duncan said curtly, trivializing the German's moral narrative. He wanted Schmidt to name a price, not tell tourist tales.

Distracted by the sudden judder of the train, Duncan realized they had pulled into yet another station. His temples throbbed; he needed to sleep. Outside, the platform filled with a fresh crop of passengers, once again meeting his insipid gaze, the same collective gawping he had encountered among the passengers who had vanished from the icy coach car.

Schmidt looked out the window, seemingly oblivious to the crowd. "As you have said, the first thing one must learn is to disassociate oneself from the specimen. One must not show the slightest interest in character, personality, even in what the face looks like. The specimen must be approached clinically."

"What in the hell are you talking about?"

"Histology. That is your profession, no?" He looked again at Duncan. "I am retiring from my profession, Herr Scientist and I would like to entrust you with *all* of my data. You will spend the next ten days with me. An apprenticeship. We will arrange deliveries during the internship."

"You're drunk and you're pathetic. You don't have anything else to sell. I'm not your conscience." Duncan stood up.

"Sit down or I will kill you." Schmidt pointed a pistol equipped with a silencer at Duncan.

"You can't kill me."

"But I am the one with the gun."

"There's a platform filled with witnesses outside the goddamn window."

"I beg to differ, Herr Scientist. The only thing I see when I look out the window is your reflection."

Duncan pounded his fists against the window but there was no response from the crowd outside. The thudding of his palms released a fresh wave of thumping in his temples. He slumped heavily down into his seat.

"What do you want, Schmidt? More money?" His words were breathy; he was panting.

"You are overwrought, Herr Scientist. Calm yourself and pay attention." Schmidt waited, as the rapid rise and fall of Duncan's chest ebbed. He reached over and wiped away the perspiration on Duncan's forehead with his handkerchief.

"That is much better, Herr Scientist." Duncan wanted to grab Schmidt's hand and twist the wrist, snapping it in two, but he couldn't even muster the strength to raise his arms.

"Clinical detachment is a desirable quality in your mind. No? However, it has consequences. You would not stop to aid a stranger experiencing a heart attack because it is not you feeling the pain. You have no empathy."

Duncan's focus alternated between the crumpled hand-kerchief in Schmidt's one hand and the gun in the other. His eyes were pendulums, swaying from one hand to the other, hypnotic, his eyelids heavy.

~ *Undercurrents* ~

"You are a single man," Schmidt said, "no family, no wife or children, no girlfriend."

"Who are you?"

Schmidt chuckled. "Isn't it obvious, I'm a ghoul. Correction, we are both ghouls, harvesting flesh. Me for the money and you for the fame and then the money. But I am retiring."

"You're an extortionist." Duncan's head rolled from side to side against the headrest.

"I am offering you a job."

"Who are you?"

"You are repeating yourself, Herr Scientist. My father died before the war. My mother sensed what was to come and shipped me abroad to wait it out. I returned to Germany in 1955, seventeen years old, tracing my mother. She had been a prisoner at Treblinka.

"What did I expect to discover about my mother? That she was gassed? Executed? No. She was an experiment. A patient of the Nazi doctors, diagnosed as a schizophrenic. They operated on her brain many times. But they were careless when the records were destroyed; they overlooked her, perhaps deciding case number 778D4—my mother—was legitimate because she was not a Jew. I found her remains floating in a jar of formaldehyde at the Max Planck Institute. I petitioned the authorities for the return of her remains. Her brain floated in that jar for years until DNA testing finally proved that she was my mother.

"They were expensive years, Herr Scientist. Lawyers, court challenges, appeals. For years, I couldn't give away the data I had collected on other experiments, hundreds and hundreds of case studies. But I could *sell* it. Have been selling it for years to upstanding young scientists like yourself.

"But now I am old. I will have an heir. You will inherit my data and discover that the appetite for such things is insatiable."

"I already got what I wanted," Duncan said.

"You are whispering, Herr Scientist. Speak so I can hear you."

"I don't want anything from you."

"But you are greedy. That is why you followed me back to my cabin."

"It was a mistake."

"Tell me, Herr Scientist, what is it about the data I gave you that is so appealing? Much of it is available today. You could have obtained it under legitimate circumstances."

"I was told that it was relevant."

"Relevant? What an interesting euphemism. Me, I am of the old school. Plain spoken. By relevant you mean recent. No?"

Duncan blinked several times to remove the blur from his vision. All of his senses were compromised, except for his hearing, amplifying every word Schmidt said.

"The Nazis were clever, Herr Scientist. They did destroy almost all of the records. I sold most of what survived in the first years after my return to Germany. But there were all those bills. Lawyers. Petitions. There were more bills than data. I needed fresh material. Relevant materials as you say. Of course, you know all this and that the experiments were and are continued elsewhere."

Schmidt reached across to Duncan and felt the pocket of his suit jacket, removing his passport, the other hand steadily holding the gun. He flipped through the pages.

"You are a globetrotter, Herr Scientist. South America, Asia, Africa. The stamps in your passport are very colourful. I have colleagues in all those countries, did you know that?"

"They led me to you."

"They have no manners, these men. They lack the hospitality I have bestowed upon you this evening."

Duncan wanted to be angry. Instead he quietly laughed. "You're telling me that you're morally superior to them?" His nervous tittering punctuated every word. "You're nothing but a self-righteous son of a bitch. An arrogant Kraut."

"I resisted their overtures, Herr Scientist. I want you to know that. These are not nice men. Very persuasive." Schmidt clacked his teeth like a snapping turtle. "They extracted a tooth for every day I resisted. When I ran out of teeth, I ran out of courage. I will retire, Herr Scientist, but I must recruit an heir. It's in the contract."

"And the Swede? Was that a warning? Has his corpse been whisked away to a lab for dissection?"

Schmidt chuckled, the gun bobbing in his hand. "What good is a corpse? What would you learn about hypothermia by dropping a dead body into the frigid waters of the North Atlantic? Come, come, Herr Scientist, our Swedish friend is a living specimen."

"But he will die."

"If you do not accept my offer, yes, he will die. And by then he will have been dead a long, long time. Born 1918 and deceased in 1942. A previously undiscovered victim of the Dachau atrocities."

Schmidt placed the gun on the table between them.

"Do you accept my offer?"

"Kill the damn Swede. I don't want your job." Duncan rose. He needed air. Feebly, his fingernails scratched at the windowsill, seeking to unlatch the window, attempting to raise it to allow a fresh breeze into the compartment.

"It would have been so much simpler if you wanted the job, Herr Scientist."

Duncan struggled with the clasp but his fingers were numb.

"I drugged your cognac, Herr Scientist. When we arrive in Berlin, I will accompany you off the train. Just another American tourist. Drunk on strong German beer and needing a steady shoulder to lean on."

Duncan could no longer place the voice speaking to him.

"I will have an heir, Herr Scientist. First, you will watch the Swede die. Then, for every day that you continue to resist, you will lose a tooth. I will retire, Herr Scientist. It will be a pity if I have to remove every digit on your body before you agree."

"I won't agree."

"We will see."

"No," Duncan said. As he gazed at his reflection in the window, he felt the stretch of muscles around his mouth form a weak but insistent smile. His reflection stared at him from deep within the crowd on the platform as he shunted those around him to make space for himself.

D ouglas Arthur Brown is the author of two novels, a collection of short stories, and two children's books. *Quintet*, his most recent novel, received rave reviews, including The Globe and Mail, Quill & Quire and The Halifax Herald. *The Magic Compass* is part of the Nova Scotia Department of Education's Atlantic Collection, which placed a copy of the title in every elementary school in Nova Scotia. For six years he was publisher of the literary magazine *Pottersfield Portfolio*, and his short stories and translations have appeared in magazines and journals in Canada and Denmark. Douglas is past president of WFNS, an active participant in the Writers in the Schools program, and a workshop leader. For the past three years, he has been writer-in-residence at Boularderie Elementary School.

Awake and Alive

Lily pulled her coat closer against the crisp night air. Her cheeks stung, the skin tight from the cold.

Many people would feel uneasy walking alone after midnight down these streets. Lily did not. She knew her hometown well, and when her insomnia kept her awake, she hit the streets. After two years of these late-night walks, she felt comfortable walking alone.

But tonight Lily was not at ease. Something didn't feel right.

She stopped under the awning of an antique shop and assessed her surroundings. The street lights hummed with a life of their own. A stray black cat pawed through a dumpster nearby for morsels of discarded fish or meat. In the distance a car engine whined on the deserted roads. Nothing out of the ordinary.

Lily continued to walk past the shops, nerves now jangling. Her cell phone was a comforting weight in her pocket. Unfortunately, her pepper spray was still at home, sitting on her bedroom dresser. She had never needed it before, but...she straightened and picked up her pace. Better get home.

Her apartment building was just ahead. As she hurried past an alleyway, the sound of a groan stopped her. She held her breath and waited, straining to listen. She took another step and heard a strangled cry of pain.

Somebody was hurt. She stood still, her legs feeling weak. She couldn't leave, couldn't turn her back on someone who needed help.

Lily peeked around the corner. The alley seemed empty, except for an open dumpster and battered boxes strewn around it. She was beginning to doubt what she'd heard, until something moved in the debris on the ground. It looked like a bloodied hand.

The moan erupted again, more agonized. Someone was hurt badly.

Call 9-1-1 from here, she thought. She flicked her phone open. *Damn.* The battery was dead. Should she leave to call for help? Lily's concern kept her where she was. She had to check first.

Lily stepped into the alley.

"Are you okay?" she called out. "I heard you from the street. You sound pretty bad. My apartment is nearby. I'll run there and call an ambulance."

"No," a male voice growled.

No? The man was clearly in agony. His hand was slick with blood. She edged closer and nudged an empty box aside with her toe.

"Holy shit."

Thick chains wrapped around him. The stranger must have had just enough strength to pull his arm free. She found an end of the coil and frantically began unwrapping him. It wasn't easy. He was tall and the heavy chains encircled most of his body. As she worked, she was almost overcome by a nauseating stench. It took her a minute to realize that it was the smell of burning flesh. The chains had seared into the man's skin, though they were cool now to her touch.

She pushed the coil aside and knelt down beside the man. He held himself rigid, fighting the pain.

"I'm going to my apartment to call 9-1-1," Lily told him. "You need help. I promise to come right back." As Lily stood up, the stranger grabbed her wrist. He was incredibly strong for a man who looked like he had been hit by a truck.

"No, you can't do that," he said. His voice was deep and laced with pain. "I'll be fine now that those chains are gone."

Lily wondered if he was mentally ill as she surveyed his visible wounds. Fragments of his shirt hung in tatters. His bare torso was riddled with burns and his face was bruised and swollen. The blood she had seen earlier came from a slash across his bicep.

"Dude, you are seriously hurt. I can't just let you stay here like this. You need help."

"I'll be fine," he insisted.

"Typical male," she snapped. "You're a tough guy, huh? You

can live with third degree burns just fine, not to mention a few other injuries? Is pride getting in the way, or are you in some kind of trouble and the police are after you?" She looked down at him.

He stared back at her stubbornly. "You don't understand. Look." He released her wrist and pointed at his chest.

Lily watched in disbelief as the burns disappeared, leaving unmarked flesh behind. As she looked at his gash, it closed smoothly. Aside from the blood there was soon only a tracery of white scars left as evidence of his injuries. Shocked, she studied his face again. The bruises and swollen lip had faded.

He was by far the most gorgeous man she'd ever laid eyes on.

"But...how...is that possible?" she finally managed to ask.

"I got the help I needed when you unraveled those silver chains. As you can see, I'm fine now. Thanks. I owe you. What's your name?"

"Lily," she said. She stood up, knees shaking beneath her, stunned by what she had seen. He rose and took her hand.

"Go home, Lily. It's too late for a young woman to be out. There are things that go bump in the night, you know. Take care." He turned, walked down the alley and vanished around the corner, leaving Lily dumbfounded.

Ten minutes later she crawled into bed. The encounter had left her confused and exhausted. She expected to lie awake, but she retreated into her blankets and fell asleep instantly.

After a rare good night's sleep, Lily woke to the sounds of the city. The autumn sun brightened her bedroom. The city hummed its everyday tune. Life was normal again.

She lay in bed, debating whether or not to get up. Staying up late took its toll on her, even if she had a good sleep afterwards. She glanced at her clock. She had been asleep for seven hours, a rarity for her in the two years since her mother had died. Lily still couldn't seem to move on.

The memories came back in painful flashes. *Her mother visiting. Lily in the kitchen fixing a snack, the sudden crash from her living room. Her mother on the floor, clutching her chest. Lily had held her mother tightly while she called an ambulance, but she was gone before help arrived.*

Then, images from the night before rose. Lily curled deeper into the blankets. She could clearly see the man on the ground,

~ Undercurrents ~

covered in burns and blood. It sent shivers up her spine. And, even more unsettling, his skin healing and closing over so smoothly.

She caught a glimpse of her nightstand. Her current Stephen King novel sat on the edge. "Must have been a bad dream," she said aloud. "I was reading last night and when I fell asleep I had a nightmare. A damn vivid one, but just a nightmare." There. She felt better.

Tiny paws crossed her bedroom floor, and Duke jumped up beside her. The orange tabby cat had been in a dumpster when she found him last spring. He sported battle marks and an attitude, and she'd thought "Duke" was a tough enough name for him.

"Feeding time," she said as she got out of bed. She put on her blue fuzzy slippers and headed out to the kitchen, Duke following like a puppy.

She fed the fat tabby and frowned at the growing pile of take-out cartons on the counter. Lily hated her own cooking, but did she really eat out that much?

She began throwing the empty cartons into the trash and thought again of the sexy stranger. Too bad it had all been a crazy dream. She would love to see him again, and it had been months since she had been on a date. But it had been a dream; no real-life man could be as perfect. She sighed and bagged up the trash.

As crazy as she was feeling, sighing over imaginary men, she needed to see her best friend. She picked up her phone and dialed Stephanie's number. Lily had a standing date with Stephanie for Sunday breakfast at Joe's Diner.

"Hello?" a groggy voice said after several rings.

"Oh sorry, I didn't mean to wake you. You're usually up by now."

"That's okay, Lil. I was up late last night watching movies with Todd."

"Oh...I see. And is Todd still there?" Lily asked, teasing.

Stephanie sighed. "No, if he was I wouldn't have answered the phone. What's up?"

"Are we still on for this morning?" Lily could almost taste the diner's special brewed coffee. Caffeine would clear her head.

"Of course. I'll meet you down there in a half hour. Are you okay? You sound a little funny."

"Yeah, I'm fine. Just a rough night." An image of a bloodied body on the ground flashed before her. "See you soon!" She headed to her bedroom, threw on some clothes, and left the apartment.

The air was cool but crisp and refreshing. She took in a deep breath and closed her eyes. Peaceful everyday sounds surrounded her. Dogs barking, children playing in the park, and the odd car here and there. Sunday mornings weren't too busy. It was her favorite day of the week.

She realized she was following the same path as the night before. The alley from her nightmare was coming up. She almost stopped, but shook her head and continued on. "Stupid dream," she mumbled.

As she passed the alley, she glanced inside. Nothing there. Then again, what did she expect to see? It was like any other dirty alleyway. Dumpster, stray cats, garbage, a gleaming pile of metal...

Her breath caught in her throat. Beside the dumpster the sun glinted off something metallic. She inched closer for a better look. Silver chains. She picked up some of the coil, and could clearly see where traces of dried blood darkened the links. The chains slipped from her shaking hands and clattered to the ground, waking a homeless man farther down the alleyway.

"Sorry," she gasped. She practically ran back to the street. She needed to get to Joe's and get some solid food.

She walked to the diner in a daze and looked around for Stephanie. Not here yet. The early morning rush was over, and Lily slid into a booth. The lingering smell of bacon made her stomach growl.

A moment later Susie, the waitress, walked over. "Girl, you look like hell."

"Gee, thanks, Susie."

"Sorry, I'm just saying. You see a ghost or something?"

Lily hugged herself. "Something like that." She took another deep breath, trying to calm herself. *I'm not going crazy.*

Stephanie arrived and Lily was glad of the distraction of ordering breakfast.

"You look horrible, Lily. Didn't sleep well last night?"

Susie poured them coffee before heading to another table.

~ Undercurrents ~

Lily drank some of the hot brew before answering. She felt like crying.

"I had this horrible dream—at least I thought it was—and then this morning—well, I found out it couldn't have been a dream," Lily rambled.

"Wait, wait, explain from the start," Stephanie ordered.

Lily began with the insomnia the night before and her late-night walk. Then, quietly, she told Stephanie everything that happened at the end of the walk. "I thought it was just a vivid dream until just a little while ago."

Stephanie stared at her for a long moment, frowning. Then she shook her head. "Well, of course it was just a nightmare. Nothing like that could actually happen."

"You don't get it, Stephanie," she snapped. "It wasn't a dream."

"What do you mean?"

Their breakfast came and they fell silent while Susie deposited plates. Lily found she'd lost her appetite. Pictures of the battered man and the blood-stained chains kept surfacing.

Once Susie left, Stephanie raised her eyebrows at Lily.

She sighed. "On my way here I found the damn chains in the alley, and they were coated with dried blood. And that was in broad daylight, after I slept like a baby for seven hours. Explain that. No way was that a figment of my imagination."

Stephanie sat in silence, chewing on her toast.

Don't tell me I'm a lunatic, Lily pleaded silently.

Finally, Stephanie met her eyes. "I don't know, Lily, I just don't know." She looked down at her plate and toyed with her food. "Something weird is going on, and I just want you to be careful."

Lily stared out the window. If it hadn't been a dream, what the hell was it? And where was the mysterious stranger now?

§

Quinn Carter opened his eyes to the comforting darkness. He stretched his limbs to work out the kinks. This wasn't the most comfortable lair he'd ever had, but the knots were a small price to pay. It kept him safe, from humans and the sun.

He emerged from the hole in the floor of the abandoned

~ Undercurrents ~

building, a single street light outside a dirty window providing the bit of light he needed. He surveyed his naked torso and arms. He had continued to heal during the day, and now not a trace of the burn marks or scars remained. He shuddered. The touch of the silver had been...horrible.

He dressed quickly. Time to hit the streets. He had work to do, starting with his heroine from the night before. He wanted to know who she was, and more importantly, if she had gone to the authorities. He had practically told her his secret. Hell, he had healed in front of her. She must have been freaked out.

Besides, it gave him a reason to see her again. There was something about her...an elusive something. She was beautiful, but it was more than that. He ignited when she touched him. Then again, he thought with a wry grin, if she hadn't, he would have quite literally caught on fire.

Quinn left the building through a door in the back, easily vaulted over an old chain link fence and strode through a thicket of trees. The crisp autumn air tingled on his skin. The moon was full and the sky was clear, millions of stars twinkling in the night. It was a good night to be alive. Or, in his case, undead.

He crept down an alleyway that led into town. Once he was on the darkened street, he relaxed. He couldn't risk his hiding place being found.

It was Sunday evening, so the streets were quiet. The few pedestrians were bundled in warm sweaters or jackets, hurrying to their destinations. In the shadows a drug addict and a dealer held a swift conversation. Quinn liked having a lair near places like this. He fed from the people society swept under the rug.

He stayed alert and sniffed the air as he walked. Last night had been embarrassing. It was the first time anyone or anything had gotten the best of him. He clenched a fist reflexively. It was even more embarrassing that it was Creighton who had bested him.

Creighton had a reputation in the vampire world. There had been other slayers, but not many lasted long. Creighton was an old dog, hunting for twenty years now; he'd been on Quinn's scent for the last five. Last night he'd managed to corner Quinn in the alley, taking him by surprise with the silver chains. Creighton's face had twisted with pure hatred as he'd beaten the vampire.

~ Undercurrents ~

Since Creighton had found him, Quinn had only one option. He had to go to Dimitri, his long time friend and the head vamp for their region, and ask for help. The slayer wouldn't quit when he'd come so close.

Quinn knew where to look for Dimitri. As he walked briskly down the street, something caught his eye. Actually, it was someone. There she was, just up ahead. The woman who had saved his life. Lily.

§

Lily had decided to go for a walk a little earlier than usual. She had tried staying home, but once the sun went down and her apartment grew dark, anxiety flooded her. The memories of her mother's death would not leave her alone.

I'll be home before it gets too late. She was still freaked out about the night before. The memory of the encounter hadn't left her mind all day. She still had no answers.

She was almost home again when she caught sight of him. The man from her "dream" was heading her way. She glanced around. The streets were empty now. *Okay, I knew it wasn't a dream!* Her heart pounded in her chest. She didn't think he would hurt her, because he could have done that the night before. But her fingers still instinctively tightened around the can of pepper spray in her jeans pocket.

Even though nerves made her belly squirm, she couldn't help running her eyes over him. He was tall, over six feet, towering over her in a leather jacket, black jeans and cowboy boots. Shaggy, light brown hair, no longer matted with blood and dirt, fell over one eye. There was no sign of last night's trauma.

She couldn't move; she could barely breathe. She wanted to dash into her apartment, but her body was frozen in place, immobilized by an invisible force.

"Hello, Lily. I didn't think I'd see you again so soon. How are you?"

She stood staring for what was only seconds, but felt like an hour. Was he real?

"I...I'm fine," she stuttered.

"Don't worry, I won't hurt you." He smiled a grin that would make any woman want to fall into his arms. "I owe you one. I'm sure you have lots of questions about last night."

He seemed so confident, staring down at her with his warm brown eyes. Lily felt a hot flash of anger. All the fear and paranoia boiled to the surface.

"Yeah, you could say that," she snapped. "What the hell was that, anyway? I woke up this morning and convinced myself it had all been a bad dream! And now here you are, larger than life. You scared the crap out of me." Lily's eyes welled with tears, but she couldn't stop. "I thought you were a dead man, and the next thing I know, your wounds are healing and everything's just fine. And by the way, you don't owe me anything. I would have done it for anybody else." She was panting now, tears rolling down her face.

His face softened. "I'm sorry. I really am. Last night...last night I made a mistake that nearly cost me my life. And yes, I'm in your debt."

"Maybe an explanation, then?"

"You'd never believe me."

"Try me," she said.

He paused, as if trying to decide what to say. After a moment he put his hand out to her.

"Take my hand," he said. "I won't hurt you. Please, trust me."

Lily hesitated, thinking that she should just run inside. But she needed to know the truth. Cautiously, she lifted her hand and placed it in his. It was cold as ice. He moved closer and put his other hand on her forehead. She felt a sudden shock, like a jolt of electricity. It lasted only a few seconds and then Quinn released her.

"What did you do to me?" she demanded, shaken. She let go of his hand and pulled her coat in closer, hugging herself.

"I have...special abilities. I needed to find out what kind of person you are. I can trust you," he said. "I'll tell you what you want to know. The reason I healed so fast is that I'm a vampire."

Before she could react, a male voice interrupted them.

"Quinn, there you are."

So, the stranger had a name. Quinn.

"Dimitri. I was looking for you."

Dimitri looked over at Lily and back to Quinn.

"Oh, I'm sure you were," he said with smirk.

"I was. I just had something to take care of first," Quinn said

~ Undercurrents ~

and glanced at Lily. "Just give me a few minutes."

Dimitri smiled. "I'll be over this way," he said and walked off into the shadows.

"I'm sorry," she began. "I don't sleep too well and it must be affecting my hearing because I would have sworn I heard you say 'vampire'."

"No, you heard right. I'm putting my life at risk telling you this, but when I looked into your mind I discovered that I can trust you. You're a rare human, Lily." He grinned. "And now you have your explanation."

He started to walk away, but she didn't want him to go. Not yet.

"Wait!" she cried. He turned around to look at her. All she could manage was, "Will I ever see you again?"

He smiled and said, "I hope so" before disappearing into the shadows, leaving Lily alone again.

§

"Creighton is near," Dimitri told Quinn after they sat down at a corner booth in a local bar.

"I know. He attacked me last night. I would have been dead if Lily hadn't come along." Quinn filled him in on the night before.

Dimitri gave his old friend a sly grin. "I can't believe that a *girl* rescued the big bad Quinn." He laughed.

"By the time she got there, Creighton had gone and I was writhing in an alley, literally frying." Quinn stared down at clenched fists, remembering. "If he hadn't had those chains, I would have killed him." Quinn remembered the look of panic on Creighton's face when the police cars drove by. He'd run then, leaving Quinn to suffer in the alley.

Dimitri's laugh faded and a grim look replaced it. "Nobody ever said that Creighton would play fair. You have the right to a piece of him, but I want to make him suffer and pay for what he did to my beloved. Understand?"

Quinn nodded. "Of course."

He knew Dimitri's history. Creighton had murdered Dimitri's wife and he wanted revenge. The one time Dimitri had his chance, the two had beaten each other to a pulp. Just before Dimitri went to make the killing strike, Creighton blew silver powder in Dimitri's face, allowing himself the opportunity to escape. Creighton had been too weakened himself to kill Dimitri.

"Good. I hear he's been hiding in an abandoned motel outside the city. I say we hit him tonight, before he has the chance to come after one of us again."

§

Lily fretted restlessly in her bed. She fluffed her pillows and straightened her bedsheets before closing her eyes again and trying to settle down.

Tonight it was more than her insomnia at work. She couldn't get Quinn off her mind. It wasn't just him, it was what he had told her. If it was true, it could explain how quickly he had healed. But vampires were fiction, just creatures from books and movies, weren't they?

She opened her eyes and looked at her digital clock, the red numbers glowing 1:46. Great. She couldn't stay in bed any longer, and she didn't think she could make herself go outside for a walk. Instead, she got up and went into her small living room and picked up a book.

Just as she sat down in her plush leather sofa, a knock sounded at her door.

This late? She reached under the sofa for the baseball bat she kept handy, just in case.

"Who is it?" She held her bat at the ready and stood just inches from the door frame.

"Officer Morris, Miss. I just have a few questions for you about a crime that took place outside a short while ago. I need to question any possible witnesses."

Lily looked out the peephole. A middle-aged man in a police officer's uniform was smiling into her line of vision.

"I know this is a hassle, but it won't take long." He took out a badge and held it up for her to see. Lily opened the door cautiously.

"Thank you, Miss. This will just take a minute." He took a notepad from his pocket.

"Did you see a young white man outside earlier? He's about six foot three inches, brown shaggy hair. Possibly wearing a leather jacket and cowboy boots."

Lily felt ill. Her gut had been right. She should have called the police after she helped Quinn. *What had he done?*

"Um...um, yes, I did. But only for a minute," she stammered.

He grinned, not pleasantly. It sent shivers up her body.

"Just as I thought," he snarled. "You're going to have to come with me."

Lily swung the baseball bat wildly. He grabbed it before it could make contact.

She turned and ran to her kitchen, yanking open the sink drawer in the dark. Just as she grabbed the cleaver, he was on her.

"Let me go!" she screamed. He held both her wrists with just one hand. His other arm held Lily against him.

"Now, now. Play nice, little lady." Lily tried to free herself from his grasp but he was too strong. "You'll pay," he said to her. "And so will they." He slid one hand up to her throat and squeezed. She gasped and struggled, but stars flashed in her vision and faded into blackness.

§

Lily had no idea how much time had passed when she opened her eyes. At first her vision was blurry. Eventually her eyesight cleared, but it wasn't much of a help. She was in a shadowy mostly empty room.

Her hands and feet were bound, hands cuffed above her head to the wall, feet tied together with rope. The concrete floor was freezing under her bare feet. It reminded her of a movie she had once seen where prisoners were kept and tortured.

The door in the far corner opened and the phony cop walked in, no longer in uniform. He took off his black trench coat and put it on a table. Lily watched as he picked up a belt and fastened it on. The light caught something and she felt herself go rigid. A long knife hung from the belt. Objects clinked and clanged as he worked at the mysterious items. She didn't want to know what they were.

After what seemed an eternity, he flipped a light switch. A single dim bulb began to glow, but didn't do much to illuminate the room. He turned and walked toward her.

"Don't come any closer!" she yelled.

~ *Undercurrents* ~

He let out a howl of laughter.

"And what do you think you can do about it? I have you completely immobilized. Even if you weren't, you couldn't hurt me. You're just a pathetic female."

He shoved a dirty rag in her mouth, tying the cloth in a tight knot behind her head. She winced.

The friendly "officer" who had knocked on her door had disappeared entirely. His eyes now danced with evil in the dim light.

He unsheathed the long knife and fingered the blade. Lily tried to scream, but it was muffled by the gag.

"Oh, shut up. I'm not going to kill you." He started to pace in front of her, fingering the blade of the knife. "However, your vampire friends, those heathens, will." He lifted the knife and came closer to her. "You will be the perfect bait. They have your scent now, and when they know you're here, they will come to your rescue. But when they catch the scent of your blood, that will all change."

He reached out with the knife and delicately sliced the skin around her throat and shoulders. Lily screamed again as the blade pierced her flesh, leaving long wounds. Tears ran down her face from the excruciating pain. Creighton smiled. He cut her exposed arms, too, running the blade down the length of her forearm. "And one more for good measure," he said, slicing the blade across her stomach. He did it easily, as if she were a piece of meat, not a person. Lily kept screaming, the pain unbearable, but the gag stifled her cries.

"I don't know what Quinn told you, but it was all lies, I'm sure." He wiped the blade, almost lovingly. "When they smell your blood, when they see it dripping off you, they won't be able to stop themselves. And while they're busy with you, I'm going to kill them." He moved aside and Lily saw a gun on each hip. The knife slid back in place, beside one of the guns.

He took out one of his revolvers and opened the chamber to show her. It was fully loaded.

"Silver. One clean shot though the heart. It's the only way to kill 'em. I used to do it with stakes, but that's old school. Lot more fun this way. Less mess, too. And of course, there are the chains. It weakens them and burns their flesh. Almost thought I'd lost them. I had to pose as a homeless man during the day. It

was the only way I could get them back without being caught."
He holstered the gun again and walked back towards the door.

The smell of her own blood thickened the air around Lily. It
made her want to be sick, but she held back. Rivulets flowed
hotly down her arms and neck and dripped down her chest.

"I won't be far away, darlin'. See, I can't be here when they
arrive. They'll kill me if I am. I need them to start feeding on you
first." And with that, he was gone.

§

"You sure this is it?" Quinn asked. He looked around the
deserted building. It wasn't like any other place Creighton had
hidden before.

"I'm positive. I had someone staking out the place. They've
seen him here for the last few nights."

The two vampires approached slowly, hoping to take the
slayer by surprise. Vampires were usually very quick, but there
were times it was a better advantage to take their time.

As they approached the basement entrance, Quinn caught a
mingling of scents. Blood, for sure. But it didn't belong to
Creighton. Creighton's scent was strong and vile. The smell of the
blood was teasingly familiar, but Quinn couldn't place it.

They reached the side of the building and listened.

"Did you hear that?" Quinn asked.

Dimitri nodded. "Two hearts beating. One in the basement
and one in the main level. But Creighton works alone. Who the
hell is with him?"

Suddenly Quinn knew. He knew who the scent belonged to. It
radiated off her in waves whenever he had been near her.

"Lily. He's got Lily. He must have seen her with me. He's
using her as bait." Quinn felt a ball of anger and hatred explode
inside him. His fangs slid out to their full length, glinting white in
the moonlight.

Dimitri put a hand on his arm. "We'll get her. Now we know
what he's up to. As long as he doesn't get the chance to use silver
against us, we'll get him. And remember what I told you. I make
the move that drains his life." Quinn nodded and his fangs
retracted.

Dimitri tore the handle off the back door and they entered the

~ Undercurrents ~

dark building. The hallway was empty except for several old mattresses leaning against a wall. Once-elegant wall sconces lined the hallway and a threadbare carpet led into the rest of the building.

The heartbeat was close by, racing. It had to be Lily. The second heart beat fast as well, but not with the same urgency. It still radiated from the main level, but closer this time.

They moved down the hallway, all senses on the alert. Quinn sniffed the air when they reached another empty room.

"She's close by. Her scent is stronger here. There's blood, too." Quinn licked his lips. "Let's go that way." Quinn turned and passed an old supply room, and led them deeper into the building, Dimitri right behind him.

Quinn followed the scent to where it grew strongest, just outside the room in the corner. The door was open. Quinn looked in and saw Lily hanging up against a wall, blood running down her body in sluggish red streams.

§

Lily shivered with cold as her own hot blood poured down her body. She was growing weaker. The pain Creighton inflicted on her so casually made her nauseated. *I can't die yet,* she thought.

She had tried to wriggle free her hands and feet, but they were bound too tightly. In desperation, she had started to chew at the rag Creighton had used to gag her.

She thought she might be loosening it when a shadow caught her attention. The knot in her stomach tightened when she looked up and saw two figures standing just outside the door.

"You're going to be fine," one said in a low voice. She was sure it was Quinn, he sounded so calm and sure of himself. Surely he wouldn't really drink from her blood? She gnawed at the gag furiously, trying to free her mouth. She had to warn him about Creighton's trap.

They stood in the doorway, whispering, for what felt like hours. *Why didn't Quinn free her?* Her teeth and mouth ached from the gag, and she felt her resolve starting to break. They were blood-sucking vampires, after all. What were Quinn and Dimitri—she was sure it must be him—whispering about? She strained to hear them, but couldn't make out what they were saying. Finally, they entered the room where she was kept captive.

"Why has he done this to her, Dimitri?" Quinn shouted. "Why did he have to bring her into it? She's gagged and hung up like a rag doll. And..." Quinn trailed off.

"Creighton diced her and sliced her," said Dimitri. "Very clever. I never knew him to bait a vampire like that. He must be getting desperate."

They came closer, eyes fixed on her. To her horror, fangs extended from both their mouths as she watched. She tried again to scream and thrashed wildly. The gag loosened around her face, and she shook her head frantically. If she could speak, warn them, maybe Quinn would not kill her. After all, that would be twice she had saved his life.

Now they were mere inches from her face. Their bone-white fangs glistened in the light. She whimpered again when she saw their eyes fixed on the blood that dripped from her wounds.

"I'll bet her blood's not poisoned. It smells too sweet," said Dimitri.

Lily cringed as he leaned in and smelled her.

"I thought you liked her because she saved your sorry ass. I wonder if she tastes as good as she smells." He bent his head down and licked her neck. Lily sobbed helplessly. "Yeah, she does, Quinn. Have a taste. You know you want to."

As the vampires drew closer, Lily looked past them. Creighton stood in the doorway, revolvers pointed towards Quinn and Dimitri. Lily locked eyes with Quinn. She finally managed to spit the rag out and whispered, "He's behind you."

The two vampires spun around and seemed to vanish, reappearing next to the slayer. The two guns dropped to the floor with an echoing clatter. Quinn pinned Creighton's arms behind him. Dimitri plucked Creighton's blade from its sheath and buried it in the man's chest. Creighton gasped for air. Lily heard a snap and a blood-curdling scream as Quinn broke both Creighton's arms. Quinn picked him up by his jacket collar and threw him against the wall. Creighton hit with a crunch and slid to the floor.

"You can have him," Quinn said to his friend. Dimitri smiled. He walked over to the crumpled form.

"I've been waiting a long time for this, Creighton." Dimitri dragged him out of the room.

~ Undercurrents ~

Quinn went to Lily and pulled the rest of the tattered gag from her mouth and neck. "I'm getting you down from there." She could only nod in response. He quickly freed her from the cuffs and rope that bound her. Lily was so weak that her knees buckled and she slumped into his arms when she was finally free.

§

"It's going to be okay," Quinn crooned as he held Lily close. Her breath came in gasps against his chest. Quinn knew she had lost too much blood, but he didn't know how to help her.

Dimitri entered the room, his face a mask of gore.

"How is she?"

Quinn glanced down at Lily. Her eyes were closed and her body shook from shock. "She's lost a lot of blood."

Dimitri narrowed his eyes at his friend. "There's only one thing you can do. One way to save her."

Quinn looked at Dimitri. He understood immediately. But would she do it? Quinn picked Lily up and crossed the room to sit on a table. She stayed on his lap, her face hidden in his shirt like a scared child. "You'll be okay now," he whispered to her. She began sobbing hysterically. Quinn rubbed her back, trying to calm her.

"Lily, you're growing weaker with each minute. I can save you, but you have to let me." He cupped her face in his hand and looked at her. "Trust me."

He took out a pocket knife and rolled up a sleeve, then made a small slice on his exposed wrist. Blood dripped down his arm.

"Drink," he commanded.

Lily shook her head. "No! I can't!"

"You have to, Lily. It's the only way to help you."

"I don't want to be one of you."

"It doesn't work like that. This will make you stronger and help you heal. I don't want you to die here tonight. Drink my blood, and you will be fine. I promise it won't turn you." He stared at her intently, hoping she would accept his help.

§

Lily hesitated for another minute, hardly believing what he was asking her to do, but she had no options. She was too weak, her body felt like a dead weight. Slowly, she took his arm in her hands and began to drink. She gagged at first, but forced the dead blood down her throat. Her stomach churned. Somehow she managed not to vomit. Eventually Quinn pulled his arm from her and wiped her mouth clean with the hem of his shirt. His wrist was already closing.

"I'll take you home," he said.

"And I'll see you later," Dimitri said. "I think tonight calls for a celebration. Creighton is no longer a threat. I'll dispose of the body."

Quinn nodded to his friend. "Thanks."

Dimitri grinned. "Thank you. I'll be in touch. You know, I had planned for so long to draw out his torture. It didn't go exactly as planned, but it was good. Real good." His face sent shivers up Lily's spine.

"Th-thank you," Lily managed to say. Dimitri had been one of her rescuers, and she was grateful, but he scared the hell out of her.

"It was my pleasure," he said. Then, like a shadow, Dimitri was gone.

She looked at the slices on her arms. They were already beginning to heal. She shivered at the sight and tried to put it out of her mind.

Lily looked up at Quinn. "I thought you were going to kill me back there. Drink every last drop of my blood," she whispered. Her head rolled back and she closed her eyes. He brushed stray hair from her face.

"Never. Our plan was to kill Creighton tonight. We didn't think we'd find bait laid out for us. I'm sorry Creighton brought you into this." Quinn stopped.

Lily looked up at him and could tell he was upset.

"When we realized you were here, we knew Creighton was close by. We had to make it look good, or he'd have never come out of hiding. We wouldn't have hurt you. No matter how tempting you were." He smiled down at her. "We're not all murderous creatures like humans think."

"If I could move, I'd hit you right now. I thought I was a goner."

~ Undercurrents ~

Quinn smiled. "Not as long as I can help it," he whispered. "Let's get you home. You've had more than enough for one night."

§

Lily woke, her head throbbing. She looked at her bedside clock. It was seven in the evening. The sun had dropped below the buildings and the street lights shone brightly. She had slept the day away. She had gotten up once or twice, but had been too tired to stay up.

It took her a minute to realize the heartbeat in her ears didn't belong to her. She looked at Duke, curled at the foot of her bed. She moved towards him, and the closer she got the louder the heartbeat became.

That is some messed-up shit! She couldn't bear the sound, so she left the cat in the bedroom and headed for her kitchen. She needed coffee—even her own awful coffee—and lots of it. By the time the coffee was brewed she felt calmer. Someone knocked on the door.

"Who's there?" she asked, although before the words were even out, she knew. She could sense him.

"It's me," Quinn said quietly.

She thought of telling him to go away and leave her alone, but she pushed that thought aside. After all, he did save her. She opened the door.

"Can I come in?" he asked.

She nodded, stepping back and holding the door wide. She couldn't help drinking him in with her eyes as he walked past her. He looked spectacular in his denim jeans and the black t-shirt that clung to his chest like a second skin.

"How are you feeling?" he asked. "You don't look as pale now. And your heartbeat seems fine."

"How do you know about my heartbeat?"

"It's something we vampires can sense."

"I didn't know that. Then again, up until a few days ago I didn't think vampires existed," she said, her voice sharp.

"There's a lot you don't know. The night holds many secrets."

"Then I don't want to know any more of them," she said. *Well, maybe some of them*, she thought as she looked at Quinn. Maybe there were a few things worth knowing. "I'm fine, by the way.

~ Undercurrents ~

Thanks. I just got up a few minutes ago."

She motioned him to follow her and they went into the living room. She sat in her recliner and he sat across from her on the sofa. Duke hissed at him and jumped into Lily's lap.

"I get that a lot," Quinn said.

"So. I drank your blood. I was able to hear Duke's heartbeat when I woke up. And I knew it was you at the door. What else is in store for me?"

He shrugged. "For a month or two you'll feel pretty good. You'll have more energy and you'll be stronger. But that will pass. What won't pass is that we'll have a connection to each other. If you're near I'll be able to feel your presence, your mood. And you will feel the same of me. That connection will last as long as you live."

"Oh, great! That's something I need in my life now, isn't it? I'll always be wondering if you're 'tuned in' to me," she growled. She looked over at Quinn and felt slightly guilty. He saved her life the only way he knew how. And maybe the idea was a little bit exciting. Just a little bit.

She smiled. "I'm sorry. I guess it could be worse. After all, you could have turned me into a vampire."

Quinn chuckled. "I think Dimitri would have liked that. I have it on good authority he wouldn't have minded keeping you at his side for a century or two."

Lily shivered. "Well, I'm glad that didn't happen."

"I can see your arms and neck have healed. Those scars will be gone in a day or two."

Lily looked down at herself. Thin pink lines etched her skin where the blade had cut into her. The pain the knife had caused left shortly after drinking Quinn's blood.

Quinn stood up. "I just wanted to check on you, see how you were. I'd better go."

Lily stood up and followed him to the door. "Wait!"

From the moment she had first met him, she had wanted to get to know him. *Heck*, she thought, *I might even come to terms with the fact that he's technically dead.*

Before she knew what she was doing, Lily stood on her tip-toes and kissed Quinn softly on the lips. "I never properly thanked you for saving my life," she said.

Quinn smiled. "That's the best thanks I've ever gotten." He

~ Undercurrents ~

tucked a stray hair behind her ear.

"Am I ever going to see you again?" she asked. She could feel something warm radiating from him. It was...happiness. *Maybe this connection we have won't be too bad after all.*

"You can bet your life on it." He turned and walked out the door. Lily ran to the window, and looked outside. Quinn was nowhere to be seen. She tried using their bond to sense him, but he was gone.

"Drop by anytime," she said into the darkness. "I stay awake most nights."

⁂

Kerry Anne Fudge is proud to have been born and raised in Cape Breton. As a child, she loved to tell stories to her big brothers, and began to put those imaginative tales on paper as she got older. In high school, her short story, "The Fire" was published in *Kimberlins*, an anthology of Nova Scotia student writing.

Knowing that writing probably wouldn't make her rich and famous, she became an esthetician at the age of nineteen and continues to work in the field. When Kerry's not curled up with a good book or spending time with loved ones, she's usually cooking something up for her next dark romance.

Winter Bewitched

We were six days out of Salabad when we crossed the sudden border into winter. One moment the air was warm and dry blowing down from the steppes, and then a frigid breeze sprang up, a rime of frost appeared on the trail ahead, and the sky darkened to the colour of yesterday's gruel.

I reined in the mare to slip my warm Surcyian cloak over my head, and Gemmin scampered ahead. When his paws hit the frost he turned back, a look of unmistakable dismay on his feline face. Three leaps took him from the ground to my shoulder. He kneaded his long toes into the collar of my cloak as a lock of my hair blew over the crown of his head, giving him a comical auburn topknot.

Enchantments, Jalia, he nuzzled into my ear, in a tongue few mortals would have understood. Gemmin was most comfortable conversing in the words he'd taught me, the language of the strange, inaccessible place of his birth.

I nodded. "A witch, a curse, the usual sort of thing," I told him. "If you can believe tavern tales told by a half-drunk barkeep." We were still in the steppes, and at least another fortnight's travel from the higher altitudes where snow might normally be expected.

Jalia wrote it down? Gemmin asked.

"Of course I did. What kind of scribe lets a good tale go to waste? At any rate, a frosty ground means we'll have to find lodgings for tonight, whether we can afford it or not. I doubt we're still being pursued. It was only the price of a meal, after all."

Jalia beckons trouble always, Gemmin chided me, his whiskers and hot breath tickling my ear.

"I do not," I retorted, trying to nudge him off my shoulder

without taking my hands from the reins. "You know what happened wasn't my fault." I sighed and shrugged, but Gemmin would not dislodge.

Instead, Gemmin snorted delicately. I knew what he was thinking. No matter how hard I tried, I couldn't seem to get ahead. I called it bad luck; Gemmin ascribed it to bad planning. I twitched the cloak tighter around my shoulders and we rode in silence until the glow of street torches gleamed through the trees ahead. It was none too soon. The further we advanced into the eerie, unending winter of Aleram, the colder the wind nipped.

It seemed the weather was keeping folks at home, and the inn had rooms open. Curious about the curse, I ate with little attention to the thin, lumpy stew and unblushingly sent Gemmin to eavesdrop on the nearby conversations. He's a great talent at pretending to do inconsequential, catlike things while he's really on a more complicated mission, and few folk notice that—while he is certainly catlike—he is most certainly not a cat.

Spoke of the witch, he told me later, when we were ensconced in a great featherbed under arching whitewashed beams, he curled up on the pillow beside me. *How to bring the end of the winter.*

"Are they hatching a plan?" I asked, because I wasn't certain I'd want to be in town when a pack of local oafs confronted a witch who had the power to control the weather. "Why hasn't the Keliph done anything?"

Gemmin yawned widely, the sides of his rough pink tongue curling past dagger-sharp teeth. I hoped he'd retain his cat-form tonight. Gemmin never meant to frighten me, but sometimes his dreams caused an involuntary shapeshift. I didn't enjoy waking to the companionship of a giant spider or many-toothed, otherworldly beast.

No plan. Empty talk. Keliph's fault, but too proud to admit it. So folk think.

They were probably right. Back home in Minstoke he would have been called "Duke," but in any language the peerage wasn't noted for its humbleness.

Gemmin blinked sleepily and dropped his head down to nestle on his paws. *Keliph's offered reward*, he added.

"Really? How much?"

Not enough.

~ *Undercurrents* ~

"Humph. Since when are you in charge of the purse strings?"

Magic involved. Jalia is no sorceress. Jalia should do what Jalia does best. He closed his eyes, ending the conversation.

I said nothing more, since Gemmin is more likely to keep to his comfortable form when he's not agitated. He'd transformed into some terrifying things since we'd met. Fortunately, I could tell it was still Gemmin by looking to his eyes. *Eyes are intrinsic, unchanging,* he'd told me once to reassure me. *Forms alter, eyes remain.* I shivered despite the press of woolen blankets. It unnerved me when he shifted, whatever the circumstance.

There in the dark after Gemmin's breathing had settled into the steady rhythm of sleep, the idea of assisting the Keliph rattled around in my brain for a time. True, I was no sorceress, had no magical power to command, but I did have Gemmin.

Exactly what Gemmin is I'm not certain. I suspect he belongs to a cadre of supposedly mythical creatures called *cawnnin.* He has the shapeshifter's gift, and a few others besides. I hadn't guessed, the day I found him near death and used my meagre healing skills to save him, how much I would come to value his companionship. The business of the day, however, was to find out more about the Keliph, the witch, and the perpetual winter she'd called down. I pondered what might persuade her to change her mind. If a winter could be witched, after all, it could be unwitched. And I'm a great believer in persuasion.

In the chill morning we set off for an audience with the Keliph.

The Kcliph's house was a grand three-storey affair, but the drooping silk trees that flanked the entry, their leaves curled tight against the cold weather, lent it a forlorn look. The Keliph received me after only a brief wait.

"Well-met, Scribe Jalia," he said in a voice like flawed silk. He offered a florid hand. It was chill to the touch, which wasn't a wonder as the whole mansion was cold. He had unpleasant eyes, yellowish and bulging, like ripe berries on a bead tree, but his manner was warm. He glanced once at Gemmin, who sat like a stone carving at my feet, only the tip of his twitching tail revealing any life. "I fear I have no scribing work for you at this time."

I smiled. "It's not scribing I've come about," I said. "I'm enquiring about your misunderstanding with a certain witch."

He lowered himself heavily into a brocaded divan and drew

his brows together under his turban. "Looking to write the tale down, are you? I'm not keen to have this story recounted about the countryside."

"Not at all, your Grace," I replied. "I'm not only a scribe. I've solved more than one difficulty for payment in coin; whether by quill or by blade, it makes little difference to me."

"Ah." He crossed his arms over his chest and tilted his head to consider me. "A common mercenary, then. You don't look the part, if I may say so."

"That," I said, crossing my own arms in mimicry, "is because I am not so common as you might expect—and neither are my methods. You have heard, perhaps, of Lady Serling of Dow's missing sapphire necklace?"

His eyes widened at that. "You retrieved it from that—that was you?"

I smiled slowly. "Would you care to tell me about your difficulty with the witch?"

"I'd hear your price first," he countered.

"What would you think fair to rid your land of winter's curse?"

He thought for a moment, taking his time. "Twenty gold Surcins," he said finally. "Thirty if you can expel the witch from Aleram for good."

It was a rich sum, but I kept a serene face. "Five in my hand before I leave today, on the undertaking that I will make my best attempt," I suggested. "Whether I meet with failure or success. If I succeed, the five may be counted toward the total fee."

"Done."

I settled more comfortably in my chair. "And now, your Grace, please tell me the tale from start to finish."

Alas, it was not as interesting as I'd hoped, and in only one respect original. The Keliph's nephew (who was also his ward) was enamoured of, and wished to marry, a maiden of the middle class. The Keliph forbade it; the boy rebelled. The Keliph put him in confinement. Then came the twist in the tale. The maiden in question turned out to be a witch, threw a curse of perpetual winter over the entire country of Aleram in retaliation, and retreated in high dudgeon to a cottage in the nearby foothills. Now the Keliph's citizens were near to an uprising and faced the spectre of starvation if they couldn't put in crops soon.

~ Undercurrents ~

When he finished, I raised an eyebrow. "If you'll pardon my frankness, your Grace, you are in a pickle."

Gemmin made a sound that could have been a sneeze, but to my practiced ears was a laugh.

The Keliph sighed and tapped two fists together distractedly. "I know."

"You won't consent to the marriage?" I pressed.

The Keliph leaned forward and stared at me earnestly, the whites of his eyes as transparent as half-cooked egg. "I would, now. Danzeyn's useless. But I won't appear to have been forced into it. When an elephant is down, even a frog will kick him. Every knight with ambition would be raising an army to try and take my seat. For a bent copper piece, I'd send a troop of men-at-arms to slay the hag." He sighed. "But even if they succeeded, that would likely bring down the wrath of any number of her coven sisters, and we'd be worse off than before. I've had dealings enough with witches to know they stand together." He sat back slowly, shaking his head. "Oh, no, whatever's to be done must be by subterfuge."

The door to the room opened and a blonde woman stepped inside. She was finely dressed in an emerald velvet cloak, her head circled by a matching green silk rolled scarf. A double strand of pearls hung from the sides of the scarf in a graceful curve below her chin. "I'm off to the noon market, Feydin," she said, then caught sight of me. "Oh, good day. I apologize, I did not realize you had a...guest."

"My wife," the Keliph said stiffly, "Emeraude, Keliphas of Veliyor. The Scribe Jalia."

She nodded, barely registering my face, I could tell.

Giggles wafted in through the open door, and a shrill of "Emmy? Are you coming? All the best silks will be picked over by the time we get there."

"Good day, then," Emeraude said to the room in general, and followed her friends. She didn't close the door behind her.

The Keliph's lips were pressed together in a thin white line, so I asked, "May I consult with your nephew?" I wanted those twenty gold coins. They would see us comfortably through the next few months. Of course, thirty would be even better, but I had to know more before I'd feel at ease engineering the witch's exile.

The Keliph shook himself, then sighed. "I suppose. He's quite well, I assure you. Simply sulking."

I hastened to reassure him. "Oh, I suspect no maltreatment. I should like to question him about his personal knowledge of the witch when they were...close."

"Very well, then." He pulled a long braided cord and a servant appeared in the doorway. "Take Scribe Jalia to see young Danzeyn," the Keliph commanded. He nodded to me. "I'll instruct my bursar to pay you the five Surcins before you leave," he said. "And I trust I'll hear from you soon."

I followed the servant down a long corridor hung with varicoloured silks, carrying Gemmin to keep his insatiable curiosity in check. Our path led up a double flight of stairs. It wasn't exactly a tower, but it was the topmost floor.

The servant unlocked one of the heavy oaken doors with a silvery key. "Scribe Jalia to see you, Master Danzeyn, at the request of your uncle." He stepped back to let me pass.

The shades were drawn, throwing the room into murky shadow. The mournful echo of a lute hung in the air, as if a song in progress had been beheaded when the door opened. A heavy sigh followed.

"If you've come to write down my songs, it won't do you any good," a quiet voice said from the depths of a shadowy corner. "They're for one set of ears alone, and if she can never hear them, no-one else shall, either."

"Songs, Master Danzeyn? No, I haven't come about your songs. I've come about the mess you're in, and how we're going to get you out of it." I allowed Gemmin to leap down from my arms. Then I crossed to one of the windows and threw open the curtains. Dust snowed down around my head, but I ignored it, looking around instead for my quarry.

He sat blinking on the floor, slouched back against the wall with the lute cradled on his lap. Not a bad-looking lad, if you discounted the face as mournful as a cow's and the shaggy hair that begged for a good barber. His clothing, while not as dusty as the draperies, was bedraggled and wrinkled. I settled myself in a worn velveteen chair near enough to him that we could speak in low tones. Gemmin sniffed tentatively at Danzeyn's boots.

"So, Danzeyn." I regarded him for a moment. "I had no idea you were a bard. Your uncle was remiss in not mentioning it."

He pulled a face. "My uncle discounts my talents. He thinks I should be learning the running of his estate, as befits his heir. He is childless, as you may know." He turned his face to one of the windows and squinted into the chill grey sky. "I have no interest in such things. I appreciate my uncle's generosity, but I believe I would die being tied to a plot of land. I long to be free, to take my words to the folk of this land and others. Shirina understood that."

I nodded sympathetically while my mind raced. I'd had no idea Danzeyn was a possible heir to the Keliph's title.

"Tell me about Shirina," I prompted.

He strummed a few notes on his lute in answer, and sang;

Shirina takes the garden
Like a knight upon the field
And her stunning grace and beauty
Are the weapons that she wields
Her lips so soft and red they put
The blushing rose to shame
Her eyes so blue the azure sky
Should bow before her name
Her golden hair outshines
The nodding head of daffodil
But on her iv'ry brow descends
No hubris or ill-will
For she is gracious on the field
As charming as a queen
My heart is vanquished, and my lance
stands awed before her mien.

It was rather dreadful. Danzeyn had a decent singing voice, and his fingers made no missteps on the strings of the lute, but a lengthy apprenticeship to an established bard would do him no end of good.

"It's obvious you love her dearly," I said gently, avoiding critical comment on his composition skills. "It must have been a terrible blow to discover she was a witch."

He leapt up, eyes blazing. The lute tumbled to the floor with a twang of protest. "Shirina is no witch! She has nothing to do with this plague of a winter, and she hasn't a vengeful bone in her body. I've told my uncle so endlessly but he turns a deaf ear! And

~ Undercurrents ~

I've no duty to listen to such accusations from you, whoever you are! Out! I've no more to say to you!"

He stood with a quivering finger pointing to the door, his face suffused with a horrid purple. I nodded and stood to go. Inwardly, I cursed the Keliph. Why hadn't he told me that Danzeyn clung to this belief? Gemmin stalked ahead of me with his tail at a haughty angle. The servant must have been standing close enough to the door to overhear Danzeyn's outburst, as it swung open at my approach.

I stood indecisive in the hallway for a moment. Should I speak further with the Keliph? I thought not. There was little else he could tell me at this point. I should have to go to the source of the problem: the witch, Shirina.

§

Gemmin was angry. *Already Gemmin said, Jalia is no sorceress*, he muttered in my ear that night. *Jalia should do what Jalia does best.*

"I don't think it will be dangerous," I said, "not the first time I go to see her, anyway. Look, she either truly loves Danzeyn, or she wants to marry him for his title. Either way, she's likely to listen to someone who wants to help mend the rift, don't you think?"

Gemmin growled. *Trust not witches.*

"I didn't say I was going to trust her," I said. "I said I was going to talk to her. Anyway, you'll be with me."

He made a snuffling noise that I'd come to recognize as his laughter. *Witches do not fear me. 'Twas a witch who left me as you first found me.*

My heart clenched; that meant bloody, battered, and near death. I shook off the memory and tickled him under the chin, something he tolerates only when the two of us are alone. "Not all witches wield that much power. We're just going to talk to her. All right?"

He turned his back on me and lay down on the quilts. Through his fur, I could see the scars from his last encounter with a witch. I felt a stab of guilt about what I might be asking of him.

~ *Undercurrents* ~

§

I easily obtained directions to the witch's cottage, although I sensed people making warding signs behind my back as I walked away. Gemmin hung back, constantly straying from the path and then catching up to me distractedly. I refused to pick him up and carry him. It was probably exactly what he wanted.

In due course we reached the cottage. It looked pleasant enough—no rotting timbers or walls leaning askew. Just a neat and tidy house, in good repair, with an herb garden nestled inside the gate. I turned to give Gemmin an *I-told-you-so* look, but he'd disappeared into the underbrush again.

There was a gate bell, which I duly rang. The curtains at a front window twitched, and then the door opened to reveal Shirina.

At this distance, I couldn't make a judgement on her beauty, but the golden hair Danzeyn had mentioned was in evidence, twisted in a long plait that hung over one shoulder.

"Yes?" she asked, in a voice that was not at all hag-like.

"My name is Jalia, a scribe," I answered. "I've come to speak, if you will, about Danzeyn."

She frowned. "Do you bring a message from him?"

"Not exactly," I said. "I've been retained to try and find a resolution to this situation, hopefully to the satisfaction of all involved."

Shirina stepped outside the door and closed it behind her. Her full sherwal trousers billowed in the wintry wind, and her long-sleeved crimson tunic curved open in the front to reveal a bright yellow comis beneath. Her feet, below the sherwal, were shod in red silken slippers. It was not exactly winter garb, but she didn't seem to notice.

She folded her arms over her chest. "Can you convince the Keliph to set Danzeyn free and offer his blessing to our marriage?"

"I'm not sure what I can do just yet. That's why I'm here to speak to you."

"Why would the Keliph hire a scribe? Do you plan to write down my tale of woe and profit from it?" Her voice was as cold as the frozen ground beneath my feet.

"I doubt it," I said honestly. "The Keliph would like to see this

~ Undercurrents ~

matter resolved quietly."

She cocked her head to one side. "And without damage to his pride, I'll wager."

I risked a grin. "He did mention something of the sort."

I felt Gemmin rub up against the side of my leg, but Shirina took no apparent notice of him.

"Come inside then, and we'll talk. But I make no promises."

"Fair enough. Neither do I." Gemmin was close at my heels as I followed the witch inside.

The cottage was warm, thanks to a fire that crackled in the hearth. If it was conjured by magic, it cast heat as efficiently as the real thing. I glanced around, curious about the interior of a witch's abode. The walls were cleanly whitewashed and the air pleasantly heavy with the scent of the dried herbs hanging like bats from the ceiling. Shirina seated herself on a chair next to a small wooden table and gestured me to another. A long-haired calico cat appeared from another room and hunkered down in the doorway, its gaze fixed unblinkingly on Gemmin.

I began, "I visited Danzeyn yesterday. He spoke fondly of you."

"How was he?" she asked, but it seemed a perfunctory question.

"Melancholy," I said. Up close, I could discern the beauty that had moved Danzeyn to commit love poetry. Her eyes, though, seemed hard. "He makes no move to leave the rooms to which the Keliph has confined him."

"The Keliph," she spat suddenly, "is interested only in having an heir for his estate, so that his greed can extend even after his death. He cares little who or what he damages to attain that goal."

"Danzeyn seems to have scant interest in the prospect of such an inheritance," I said carefully.

She pressed her lips together as if she regretted her outburst. "Scribe," she said, "I did not invite you in here to dance a verbal *raqs beledi* with you. Do you have an offer from the Keliph?"

I sighed. "Not really. I came to see if you were open to bargaining. The people of Veliyor, in fact all of Aleram, are nearing desperation. Food stores are running low, and it's obvious no crop will grow in this winter."

She smirked. "And the Keliph is concerned for his people?

Concerned for his own hide, more like, if they rebel against him for getting them into this mess." The calico cat leaped up on the table next to her mistress and sat down. Shirina stoked its back with long fingers.

"I don't wish to harm the people of Aleram. The Keliph forced my hand," she said after a moment. "Tell the Keliph that I will consider lifting the winter curse for the sum of five hundred gold Surcins. I will accept them only from your hand, Scribe Jalia, or the Keliph's own."

I sat silent for a moment, because my throat had gone dry at her words. Five hundred gold Surcins! The Keliph would never pay such a price, I thought, even if he had such wealth at his fingertips.

"And what of Danzeyn?" I said finally. "Shall I take any message to him for you?"

She shook her head. "If he doesn't bother to lift finger nor voice to be released from his confinement and come for me, I owe him nothing. Not a message, and certainly not my heart. Five hundred gold from his uncle is all I require now." She and the cat stared at me without emotion, two sets of green eyes equally inscrutable.

"Danzeyn refuses to believe that you are responsible for the winter curse, you know," I said, but if I hoped to shame her into any further response I was disappointed. She merely shrugged.

"Then I shall relay the message," I said, standing. She didn't move to see me out.

At the bottom of the cottage steps I bent and picked Gemmin up, stroking his fur as I walked slowly down the path. Shirina's attitude puzzled me. If she'd been in love with Danzeyn, it hadn't taken much to wither that love. And if she'd only been interested in his prospects, five hundred gold was paltry by comparison.

I shook my head. Men! Hadn't Danzeyn been able to look into those eyes and see the coldness there, colder than the winter that had settled on the land? No, instead he'd written poetry about them—

Her eyes so blue the azure sky should bow before her name.

But Shirina's eyes were green, as green as her calico cat's.

I stopped suddenly, clutching Gemmin, who mewled in protest. When I looked down at him, he winked slyly. So he'd come to the same realization as I. *Eyes are intrinsic, unchanging.*

~ Undercurrents ~

Therefore the green-eyed witch was not, could not be, Shirina. Who was she?

I started walking again, quickly now. I needed time to think.

§

First thing the next morning I went back to see the Keliph. He had travelled into town to meet with the Merchant's Guild, but his wife the Keliphas Emeraude agreed to see me. I was led to a sumptuous apartment overlooking the frost-blackened back garden, where the Keliphas was in the process of having her blonde hair curled with heated tongs by a long-suffering maid. Emeraude regarded me with the ghost of a frown and slightly pursed lips for a moment, and I hastened to assist her.

"We met briefly yesterday, when I was in conference with your husband," I reminded her. "He's retained me to try and convince the witch to lift her winter curse."

"Ah, yes," she said, obviously relieved. "And have you spoken with her? This cold weather is indeed a curse! My poor hands are chapped, and just look at the state of the garden! The jasmine should be blooming now, and this deep frost will be the ruination of the walnut trees."

To say nothing of your people going hungry, I thought. "I did speak with her yesterday, but did not learn much. I came to ask your husband something. He mentioned in passing that he'd had other dealings with witches, and sounded none too pleased about them. Do you know what incidents he meant?"

She did not visibly start at my words, but the colour drained from her cheeks, leaving them pale as the frost on the ground outside. She shook her head.

"I am not privy to all of my husband's dealings," she said evenly. "Witches? I cannot imagine what my husband would have to do with witches." She glanced down with distaste at Gemmin, who was sniffing around the hem of her gown. "Is that all you wanted to ask? I am due at the Lady Miriam's for *tirazi*."

"Yes, that's all. Thank you anyway, your Grace."

I left her brushing at imaginary cat hairs and snapping at her maid about a minuscule spot on her gown. "Either she knew exactly what I was talking about, or she's had her own dealings with witches, Gemmin," I murmured to him when we were out in the frosty air again, "or I'll eat my best quill."

He mewled at my feet and I bent and picked him up.

She smells of witchcraft, he agreed, then went on smugly, *Gemmin always says, Jalia should do what Jalia does best.*

I stopped walking and glared at him, not caring if anyone saw. "Why do you keep saying that? I'll write it all down when we get back to the inn, but I can't do it right here."

Writing is not what Jalia does best, he said, *although she is very good at it.*

I started walking again, holding Gemmin close to let his warm fur keep the chill wind from my hands.

"Then what, may I ask," I said finally, struggling to keep my voice even, "is it that Jalia does best?"

He had the audacity to purr, snuggling up against my chest as I strode towards the inn.

Jalia gets people to talk, he said simply.

It would have given him too much satisfaction if he'd stopped me in my tracks with that, so I kept walking. But his words rang true. People told me things, whether they meant to or not. I thought furiously while I marched back through the town, and by the time we'd reached the inn, I had a plan.

§

Gemmin didn't approve.

She is a witch. She will suspect, he argued.

"She didn't say anything about you when we visited her the other day," I rejoined. "The cat took more notice of you than she did."

She will be angry. All you have is a suspicion.

"I know, but I don't care. We need that gold."

Jalia is suddenly very mercenary.

I sighed. "Oh, all right. If you must know, I can't bear to think of all these people going hungry. And the real Shirina must be in trouble—where is she? I feel like I have to help."

Gemmin climbed up on the small desk in our room and batted at my cheek with a soft paw. *It is not a bad thing to have compassion.*

"Humph. I thought you'd call it a weakness."

If not for your 'weakness,' Gemmin would be dead.

~ Undercurrents ~

I stroked his fur. "I didn't do all that much. Some healing salve, a little care, that was all."

Jalia knows that is not true. He settled on the desk with a very human-sounding sigh, curling his tail around his body like a pashmina. *This is not what Gemmin intended. He meant that the Keliph and the witch should talk,* he said. *But Gemmin will help.*

§

We arrived at the witch's cottage early next morning. Gemmin, riding my mare and looking exactly like the Keliph except for the wrong colour eyes, rode up the trail while I skulked through the surrounding woods. I found a spot where I could see the witch's front door when she came outside to speak to Gemmin.

Gemmin rode the mare into the yard and waited. The door of the cottage opened and the witch stepped outside, smirking.

"So you've come, high and mighty Keliph," she drawled.

"As you say," said Gemmin.

"Come to beg me, or come to pay me my due?"

The horse shifted uneasily, but Gemmin did not dismount. "You told the scribe five hundred gold. Come, Shirina, is that fair? Five hundred gold, and a country ruined, because I wouldn't let Danzeyn marry you?"

The witch was intent on her visitor now. I crept through the trees toward the back of the cottage, and saw exactly what I'd hoped—the sloped hatch that led to a root cellar. I concentrated on moving silently toward it across the frost-hardened ground, but I could still hear the conversation at the front.

"That might be reason enough for some women, Keliph. Although I've never set much store by men myself. No, for me it's a matter of honour."

"Is it honourable to hide behind another's name and face, when in fact your dispute with me has nothing to do with Danzeyn—or the real Shirina?"

I held my breath. This was where Gemmin and I were taking the biggest risk. After a pause, though, the witch answered.

"So you know me, Keliph? Fair enough. Five hundred gold was not our initial bargain, I'll admit. But was your treatment of me fair? I provided you what you asked, in good faith. And you

~ Undercurrents ~

refused to pay my fee. Now you are living with the consequences."

I was easing open the root cellar door now, hoping that the hinges were well-oiled. Still I strained to hear what Gemmin would say. This was the tricky part of the script, because while deduced from what I'd observed and been told, it was still guesswork.

Gemmin lifted his voice in anger. I made a mental note to compliment him later on his acting ability. "I refused to pay, witch, because your magic did not work!"

I couldn't hesitate any longer since I had no idea how long the argument might continue, or when the witch might begin to suspect our deception. I trod carefully down the mouldering earthen steps and into the dank cellar.

It was dark, but some sunlight followed me down the stairs. A glint in a dim corner drew me straight to it, a stray beam of sunlight catching golden hair, and I hurried over. She was dressed in muddied blue sherwal and emerald green tunic, bound hand and foot. She was also gagged and possibly bewitched, because the eyes that turned to look at me were fogged and unfocused.

But they were blue. Blue as an azure sky.

"Shirina?" I whispered.

She nodded slowly.

"I'm going to get you out of here," I said, "but we have to be quiet." I cut the leather straps that bound her feet and hands, and waited until she nodded again before I undid the gag. I didn't want her screaming.

She was unsteady on her feet and leaned on me for support, clutching my cloak as we struggled up the stairs and out into the watery sunlight. I led her as silently as possible toward the nearby copse of trees, listening for the voices of Gemmin and the witch.

"—a fair offer," Gemmin snapped.

"I have little concern now for what you consider fair," the witch answered. "I know I cannot trust you, Keliph of Veliyor. My price is set. It will not change."

The witch turned on her silken heel to end the conversation just as Shirina and I dodged into the trees. Two things happened then.

Shirina caught sight of the witch, still wearing the girl's own face, and gasped, "Oh, she shouldn't wear red with my complexion!" And her blue sherwal trousers, caught by the breeze, billowed like a flag announcing our presence.

The witch screamed with rage. It was followed by a sharp sentence in an arcane tongue, and in an instant the wind pushed up against us with the force of a tide. The air filled with dizzying snow and flailing branches. Shirina gasped and fell, almost dragging me down with her, but I stayed upright and pulled her back to her feet.

Through the snow-filled air I saw Gemmin leap down from the back of my horse and run toward the witch, shifting to a huge furred shape as he ran. The witch, too, changed, letting go of her guise as Shirina. I caught a glimpse of curly brown hair, but couldn't take the time to watch the transformation. I pushed through the trees and the howling wind, pulling Shirina behind me, but we made little headway. I whistled for the horse, trying to move us closer to the trail so the mare would see us.

Then I heard a squeal that stopped me in my tracks. I'd heard the same noise the day I'd first found Gemmin, although the battle was over and everyone else dead or vanished by the time I'd located the source of the sound. I'd hoped never to hear it again, but there it was. Gemmin was in trouble.

I pushed Shirina into the questionable shelter of a tree and fought harder to reach the trail. The mad swirl of snow ahead outlined two figures, one writhing on the ground while the other stood over it. A few steps closer, and I could make out the crackle of golden light surrounding the twisting form of Gemmin, shrunken back to normal cat-size. The witch had him magically pinned to the snow-covered ground.

"Stop!" I commanded, stepping out of the trees and onto the trail. My racing heart felt too big for my chest.

"Why should I?" screeched the witch. She was taller and older than she'd been as Shirina, and more imposing. "You tried to trick me!"

"I tried to level the field by taking that poor girl out of the equation," I shouted above the wind, anger making me bold. "If you and the Keliph have a business disagreement then take it to the magistrate. It would not be in your interest to have Shirina come to harm in your keeping."

"The Keliph!" she spat. "He tried to ruin me, spread the word that my magic was weak."

"And so you were right to wreak vengeance upon every inhabitant of Aleram?"

She turned narrowed eyes on me. The golden beam imprisoning Gemmin did not waver. "What business have you to interfere?"

"The business of anyone who would rather see justice done than the innocent suffer," I said. "You turned the Keliph's personal difficulties to your own purposes."

"He cheated me and threatened violence. Said he'd petition the Emperor to outlaw witchery if I, or my sisters, pressed the matter further. I couldn't do anything openly." Her eyes flicked toward the wood, where a flash of Shirina's sherwals showed through the snow. "I saw a chance and took it."

I shook my head, gaining confidence. Perhaps Gemmin was right, and getting folks to talk truly was what I did best. "But now you're stuck," I said. "Let Gemmin up, and let me help you settle this with the Keliph."

She snorted. "If you had any influence with him, you'd have brought me my five hundred gold."

"No. That was not a fair offer. That was extortion. You could probably imprison the three of us now, but it won't get you any further toward a resolution. Let us go. I can sway the Keliph to meet with us, and settle the debt that started this mess."

The witch glared at me, but she looked tired. "Why? What can you do?"

I risked a grin. "I can do what I do best."

"And what's that?" She didn't look entirely convinced, but she withdrew the energy that had incapacitated Gemmin. Slowly he gathered his paws under him and pushed up to sit, shaking his head.

"Get folk to talk," I said, reaching down to gather him up. He nodded at me and I knew he hadn't been injured. "And write things down."

§

The Keliph may or may not have been surprised by the note I sent round to his house the next morning. I asked an audience with him, his wife, and Danzeyn, and advised that he should have my fee ready.

~ Undercurrents ~

There was a general stir in the air when we arrived, I in my best tunic and cloak, Shirina bathed, rested, and wearing clean clothes, and the witch, whose name I had discovered was Iliasta, keeping close behind me. She still wore her crimson tunic, and I had to agree with Shirina's assessment that it suited her nut-brown hair and tanned complexion better than it had Shirina's guise.

That stir was nothing compared to what happened when we were shown into the Keliph's morning-room. Danzeyn and Shirina leapt into each others' arms like two lodestones. The Keliph's eyes bulged alarmingly at the sight of the witch Iliasta and he let loose an involuntary bark of indignation. The Keliphas Emeraude narrowed her eyes and sat down abruptly on a velvet daybed.

"Keliph, I believe you know my guest. Keliphas Emeraude, Mistress Iliasta."

The Keliph had found his tongue. "Scribe, I don't know what you think you're doing—"

"Pardon me, your Grace, but I am saving your face, your country, and quite possibly your life. If you don't want to sit quietly and listen, perhaps you'd like to read what I have to say instead." From my satchel I pulled a sheaf of parchment. "The whole sorry tale, as I have deduced it, is told here, and I have several more copies that I'm quite certain will bring a fair price in Jiuri and Harberdin, to say nothing of the rest of the Empire. Folk are always in the market for a good story. Especially folk with an abundance of coin and visitors."

He glared at me.

"Ah, yes," I continued, "you wanted this settled quietly. Then here is the crux of the tale. You retained the services of Mistress Iliasta and then refused to pay her fee when you thought she had not fulfilled her part of the bargain. She retaliated by taking advantage of your personal difficulties with Danzeyn and Shirina to force your hand. You were too proud to speak to her, whether you thought she was actually Shirina or knew her real identity. Iliasta has admitted that she acted rashly, and you have let your pride blind your judgement. You are both in the wrong, but the people of Aleram have had to suffer for it."

"I'll not be lectured by a snip of a girl," the Keliph began, but he was interrupted by a shrill question from his wife.

~ Undercurrents ~

"What sort of 'services' did you purchase from this woman, Feydin?"

The Keliph pursed his lips and said nothing.

"I believe he requested her help in begetting an heir," I said bluntly, and all eyes turned to Iliasta. She nodded briefly.

Danzeyn's eyes grew very wide.

"Not that way, you goose," I said. "He purchased a spell, or a charm, or a potion."

"Well, it didn't work," the Keliph retorted. "Unless Emeraude is extremely talented at keeping secrets." He threw a glance at his wife, who flushed.

"That remains to be seen," I said. "I've made inquiries; Iliasta has an excellent reputation for her skills in that particular area. However, there is no evidence that your wife is with child. Which caused me to wonder why."

"My deduction," I continued, setting the parchment sheets down on my lap and smoothing them, "is that the Keliphas has, in fact, no interest in bearing a child. She is quite engrossed in the many interests she indulges with her friends; exploring the latest fashions, visiting the market, taking *tirazi*. I speculate that, to the end of remaining free from maternal encumbrances, she retained the services of another witch."

A glance at Keliphas Emeraude's burning cheeks told me my arrow had flown true. "That is why Iliasta's magic did not work. It was countered by another just as strong. A stalemate, so to speak."

The Keliph turned and glared at his wife with a gaze so heated I would not have been surprised if she had burst into flames. But he was a Keliph after all, and he had his pride. He transferred his gaze to Iliasta.

"How much would you accept to settle our debt," he said, his voice very even, "and to lift the winter curse?"

She hesitated only a moment. "The amount of our original agreement," she said. "Scribe Jalia has helped me see that the curse was...ill-advised. I have retracted it."

"Very well. I will have my bursar settle with you—both of you —before you leave here today. Scribe Jalia," he took a deep breath and pointed to the parchment on my lap. "Will you agree to surrender all copies of that to me? With your undertaking not to create any more?"

~ Undercurrents ~

"Of course, Your Grace," I said. "I believe fifteen gold Surcins is the balance owed, since naturally I am not asking Iliasta to exile herself from Aleram."

He nodded. "And now," he said, flicking his gaze toward his silent wife and then back to me, "If that concludes our business —"

I kept my seat. "One more thing, if I may."

His jaw clenched, but he nodded.

"Those two," I said, tilting my head toward Danzeyn and Shirina, who still stood with arms defiantly about each other. "There won't be any further impediments to their marriage, I assume?" I grinned at the Keliph. "I haven't put their story to paper yet, and I'd like to know whether it's to be a tale of love thwarted or love triumphant. Folk all over the Empire and beyond will clamour for the tale, either way, but I like to be able to keep my tales true—after a fashion. Of course I'll change everyone's names, to protect the...innocent."

The Keliph wasn't ready to return my smile—he still had his wife to deal with—but he managed to give in with good grace. "Oh, you may give them a happy ending, Scribe Jalia," he said. "In fact, you might stay until after their wedding, since I understand Danzeyn wants nothing more than to travel the Empire as a wandering bard. He can do so with my blessing. You'd make a fine travelling companion for a young couple, I'd wager."

"Mmm. We'll see," I said.

§

Wanting no encumbrances of our own, Gemmin and I left Veliyor just after dawn broke the next morning. The rising sun was warm on our backs and the ground beginning to soften, but Gemmin rode on my lap nonetheless. His battle with Iliasta had left him tired.

"Thank you again," I said, taking the reins in one hand so I could stroke his fur with the other.

Gemmin needs no thanks, he said. *Gemmin hasn't saved Jalia's life yet.*

The old curmudgeon. I knew damn well he stayed with me out of more than just a sense of obligation.

~ Undercurrents ~

"Oh, not for that," I said airily. "I knew you'd help me with the witch."

Then what?

"For reminding me what I do best," I said.

He kneaded his paws into my leg, perhaps a little harder than was absolutely necessary, and settled down to nap.

Ahead of us, sunlight dappled the road, and in the distance, I heard birdsong like laughter in the air. The winter, unwitched, had fled, and spring surged to take its place.

❧❧

Sherry D. Ramsey never expected to become an Internet geek. However, after publishing a web magazine for ten years, creating numerous websites, copyediting for the *Internet Review of Science Fiction*, networking with writer's groups online, and becoming part of a writing community in Second Life, she fears it's an inevitable conclusion.

When she's not online, Sherry writes science fiction and fantasy, moderates her local writers' group, and sometimes even spends time with her husband and two children. Every November she disappears into the strange realm of National Novel Writing Month and emerges gasping at the end, clutching something resembling a novel. Sherry is a member of the Writer's Federation of Nova Scotia and SF Canada, and a founding editor of Third Person Press. Her stories have appeared in print, online, and over the airwaves. Visit her at www.sherrydramsey.com

Edgar MacDonald's Last Wish

I sit in a wicker deck chair on my front porch and stare at my fingernails, searching—unsuccessfully, it turns out—for one that has not been bitten down to the quick. I light a cigarette instead and inhale deeply. It's a recently reacquired bad habit. My ex-wife, who two years ago took every stick of furniture with her except for these wicker fashion atrocities, would probably say that I've been drinking too much as well. She would be right.

It rained heavily last night and the coffee mug I left out here yesterday has filled with water. On its surface, the swollen corpse of a honey bee floats in lazy circles, bobbing and swirling with the cool spring breeze. I turn away but I can't stop the image that forces itself into my consciousness—the same image that has invaded my dreams every night for the past two weeks. Edgar MacDonald.

He's standing on the beach near the mouth of the harbour, his flesh blue and bloated, bulging through the torn seams of his orange Maritime Marine jumpsuit. Wet sand clings to a gaping wound in his scalp. Ribbons of desiccated tissue hang from his bony fingers, which appear to be pointing out over the dark calm waters toward the open ocean. Strands of seaweed are tangled in his thick red beard. His eye sockets are vacant holes, the eyeballs eaten by fish or eroded away by sand and salt. He picks up an incongruously beautiful violin from the beach and starts playing a slow mournful tune, a vaguely familiar tune, though I can't name it. The night is clear with a three quarter moon and I can make out the dim outline of a ship in the harbour. A woman screams. This is where I always wake up.

The first time this dream came to me, it was before I knew—before anyone knew, in fact—that Edgar MacDonald had gone over the rail of the Newfoundland Ferry. Just a nightmare, I told myself, nothing to worry about. But when Dr. Jones, the coroner, called with the news the next day, I felt as if the glue that held my world together had dissolved, and nothing but fragments of nonsense remained. I grabbed the side of my desk to prevent myself from falling, the room spinning furiously around me. I willed myself to wake up again—surely this was just an extension of the nightmare.

"An apparent suicide," Dr. Jones said, in his clipped, business-as-usual British accent. "Coast Guard found the body this morning."

I struggled to catch my breath. "Not an accident? You're sure?"

"It was a calm night, Dr. Farrell. It's hard to imagine how he could have fallen in accidentally. You were treating him for depression, is that correct?"

"Yes," I said, not liking where the conversation was going, "but he was doing well—I can't—I just saw him last week."

It didn't matter. The coroner had already made up his mind—and who could argue with his logic? Edgar MacDonald's medical charts read like a case study of the high-risk suicidal patient: male, fifty-five years old, alcoholic, chronic back pain, history of depression, previous suicide attempts. Five years ago Edgar's wife Katherine found him hanging from an extension cord which he had draped over the rafters in the garage. He was already unconscious when she cut him down. She divorced him the following year. At the time of his death, he was taking two anti-depressant medications. He lived alone. He had demons—bad demons, among the worst I'd ever seen—from the past.

"Edgar was not suicidal when I saw him last week," I said, feebly, not even convincing myself. Images of the previous night's dream were imprinted on my brain. The torn flesh, the green ribbons of seaweed.

There would be no inquest into the death of Edgar MacDonald. The obvious conclusion being that I, his psychiatrist of fifteen years, had misjudged, that I had missed the signs.

"I'm sorry," Dr. Jones repeated.

"Just one more thing," I said, struggling to get my thoughts in order. "When they found his body, did Edgar have any... injuries?"

~ Undercurrents ~

There was a pause on the other end of the line. "Beyond what you'd normally expect for a body that's been in the water for a while? As a matter of fact, Dr. Farrell, he did. There was a nasty laceration on the top of his head. Why do you ask?"

I felt my lunch rising up into my throat. "Never mind, it's not important," I said, dropping the phone as I ran for the toilet.

§

I take another puff on my cigarette and pull my jacket tighter around my neck. In the two weeks since the coroner's phone call, my world has become unrecognizable to me. The nightmare comes every night now, and every night the same grotesque scene is repeated—Edgar's distorted corpse standing on the beach, mangled fingers pointing out across the harbour. Is he pointing toward the dark outline of a ship? I can't tell. I always wake up when the woman screams. More than once I have awakened to find *myself* screaming. With each replay of the dream I notice new details: broken teeth, a small wound at the corner of his mouth, salt stains on his lips, the forlorn expression on his eyeless face, the smooth contour of the rocks behind him.

I do everything I can to avoid sleeping, sitting up in front of the television until my head nods forward in exhaustion. My work has suffered. Co-workers at the hospital whisper behind my back —I catch them at it when I come around a corner or walk into a room. Dark shadows have formed under my eyes and my shoulders sag with exhaustion. The sight of food makes me nauseated. My clothes have become loose, hanging off me as if I were a child trying to wear adult clothing. I startle like a skittish pony every time a door slams or a car backfires. Friends avoid me, and I do nothing to discourage this—what would I say to them, anyway? That I'm losing my mind? That I'm haunted by the ghost of a former patient? Two weeks ago, I would have prescribed anti-psychotic medication to anyone making such a claim.

I douse my cigarette in the water-filled coffee mug, the filter temporarily bobbing along with the drowned bee until it swells up and sinks to a watery grave. Once again, I play my last visit with Edgar over in my mind, searching for what I might have missed: Edgar smiling and joking, his bald head catching the reflection from the fluorescent lights; Edgar showing me a picture of his new grandson, talking of his future plans, proudly displaying his six month pin from Alcoholics Anonymous, eyes bright and hopeful. But yes, he is worried about something, too, and he will not tell me what it is.

"It's nothing I can't handle," he says. He is smiling and I don't push him. He seems like a man with a future. He'll tell me in his own time. Is he contemplating his own death? Could that be what is on his mind? Every fibre in my body, every neuron trained to recognize the signs, says no, even if the facts—and the coroner—say otherwise.

I grab my car keys and drive myself to the clinic, even though it will be a full two hours before patients start arriving. I stare at the nameplate on my office door: *James Farrell, M.D., FRCPC, Psychiatrist.* My name, my credentials, but somehow they seem alien to me now, as if they belong to someone else and I'm just a pale imposter. How can I be the same person who sat here so confidently, reducing the meaning of life to the movement of dopamine between brain cells; reducing happiness to the efficient transmission of serotonin? The same man who prescribed chemical cheerfulness, who returned people's thinking to "normal"—a word whose meaning I can no longer even grasp?

A year ago, when I gazed out over the mounds of paper that crowd my desk, I considered myself lucky to have a view of North Sydney Harbour, where I could watch the Maritime Marine Ferries make their way out to sea. The sight of those steel workhorses filled me with a sense of faith—faith in science and engineering, faith in mankind, in the orderliness of things. The rhythm of my day was set by their comings and their goings, and my seasons were marked by their changing schedules—more sailings in the summer, less in the winter. The harbour itself filled me with a sense of calm, the dark water and the smell of salt, the smell of home.

The blinds in my office stay closed now—something my patients find very strange—and I no longer take noon hour walks along Indian Beach. My imagination has become too vivid; my mind plays tricks on me: something red—a Coca-Cola can—but when I look at it I see a pool of blood. Collections of seaweed morph into human hair, a gull bobbing on the surface of the water becomes a hand grasping at the air, waving for help. I am beginning to understand—in a visceral way, not just the intellectual or statistical way I understood it before—what drives people to commit suicide. For the first time in my life, I am suffering that black rot of the soul, that damp smothering hopelessness which my patients have, for so many years, tried to describe to me.

§

At the end of the day—a quiet day, thanks to my secretary's valiant efforts to protect me—Edgar's ex-wife, Katherine, is waiting for me in the reception area. Edgar has been dead exactly fifteen days. My stomach churns. I have failed this woman and her children

"Come in," I say, struggling to maintain eye contact.

She is a slim attractive woman, well-dressed, but with the drawn, haggard appearance of someone who has lost weight too quickly—a look all too familiar to me. Her hair is jet black with streaks of grey. A small white scar transects the middle of her lower lip. I guess her age at about 50 but, since she is not my patient, I don't have a chart in front of me to confirm this.

There is an awkward silence before she speaks.

"I want you to know that Edgar thought very highly of you. He told me that you saved his life. We were still close after the divorce, you know."

I want to cry. I want to hug this woman. I nod.

She continues. "He put his affairs in order before he died." She picks at a piece of lint on her pants, hesitating. "But he didn't want to die. I know it sounds strange, since I'm the one who cut him down from the rafters five years ago, but I will never believe that Edgar killed himself."

"I have a hard time believing that myself," I say. "His mood seemed better than it had been in years. I must have missed something."

"No," she says. "You didn't miss anything. I know this sounds crazy, but I believe Edgar was murdered."

"Murdered?" Strange, but this possibility has not even crossed my mind. "Who would want to kill Edgar?"

"I don't know," she says. "Look, I probably shouldn't be telling this to a psychiatrist, but I think Edgar is trying to show me who did it."

I stare at her, wide-eyed, and say nothing.

She continues. "I have this horrible recurring nightmare with Edgar standing on the shore. His body is all mangled and there's green seaweed in his beard and he's playing—"

I cut her off: "A fiddle?" I ask, trying to calm the panic that is rising in my chest.

She gasps, but then reaches for my hand and squeezes it. "You've been having the same dreams, haven't you?"

My mouth feels like it is full of soda crackers.

"The tune he is playing in the dream—do you recognize it?" she asks.

"It's vaguely familiar," I say, still stunned. "But I can't recall the name."

"Can you hum it for me?" she asks.

I've never been known for my musical abilities, but I do my best.

She nods. "O'Donnell's Lament, same as in *my* dream."

My mind is racing. "But what does it mean?"

She can only shrug. We part with a promise to keep in touch.

I return home, bewildered but strangely calm. A soft rain, barely more than a mist, is falling. My little house is showing signs of neglect in the grey light of the late afternoon. A patch of lichen has taken up residence on the north side. One of the shutters hangs at an angle. The iron hand rails leading up to my front door are rusting. A bachelor's house. It's been almost two years since my wife stripped the house bare, as if she were the aggrieved party, as if it were me who cheated on her and not the other way around.

As I fumble for my keys, clumsy with fatigue, my right foot sinks in something soft and slippery. Seaweed. Green ribbons of it. I scream and throw it as far away from the house as I can. A curtain moves in the window of the house across the street. I have to steady my right hand with my left to get the key in the slot.

I walk into the living room and scream again. My dog, a sturdy little Scottish terrier named Max, is cowering in the corner, trembling visibly. My vinyl record collection is strewn about the room and one album is on the turntable playing. It's one of my original Beatles albums, *The Magical Mystery Tour*, and it's skipping repeatedly over one line—the title line—of one song. *I am the Walrus*, John Lennon croons at top volume, *I am the Walrus, I am the Walrus, I am the Walrus...*

I rip the needle from the record and collapse beside my terrified dog.

"So our ghost likes the Oldies, does he, Max?" It's the closest thing to a joke I've made in weeks. "Did he tell you what he wants from us?"

For a full half hour, I sit on the floor, taking in the destruction, too exhausted to pick up the mess, too exhausted to be afraid. Max sits beside me, still shaking, pushing his muzzle under my hand. I wonder if he has nightmares too.

My life further fragments in the following week. Broken, nightmare-haunted sleep. Bits of seaweed and sand where there should be clean floors. Objects misplaced. And every night when I return from work—*I am the Walrus, I am the Walrus, I am the Walrus...* Max follows me closely, never letting me out of his sight. I start taking him to the office with me.

When I can't take any more, I call Katherine MacDonald. It's two o'clock on a Tuesday morning. She answers on the first ring, wide awake, judging by her voice.

"He's getting worse," I say. "Angrier."

She sighs. "What's he done now?"

I give her a brief synopsis of the past week and ask if we can meet again. She agrees to come to my office at the end of the day.

I suffer through a mercifully light day at the clinic, struggling, rather heroically I think, to keep my mind on my work. I avoid looking at the growing stack of unfinished paperwork—letters to be written, insurance forms to be filled out. Katherine is sitting in the waiting room as the last patient, a chronically depressed hypochondriac named Louise, exits my office. Even the impressively narcissistic Louise has noticed the dark circles under my eyes.

I invite Katherine into my office and fetch two cups of stale but still palatable coffee from the kitchenette. She looks older than the last time I saw her—was it only seven days ago? I suspect she is thinking the same about me. We get right down to business, like two grizzled homicide detectives.

"What do we know?" I ask.

Could it have been murder? Who would want to kill Edgar,

the gentle giant? And, most importantly, what is he trying to tell us? Why can't he rest?

I stare at the coffee in my mug as I stir in a spoonful of sugar, mesmerized by the whirlpool I've created as it pulls the white crystals under. Is this how Edgar went down, I wonder, dragged below by the currents and the weight of his clothing, thinking about the grandchild he would never see again? I shake my head and look at Katherine.

We go through every detail of Edgar's death—middle of the night, no witnesses, nothing out of the ordinary. Katherine can recall only one co-worker at Maritime Marine whom Edgar did not like. Walter something. Walter Beckett? She isn't sure. Nor can she recall why Edgar didn't like him—just that he had warned her and their daughter Kate to stay away from him.

"Edgar had good instincts about people," she says. "Almost a kind of psychic gift. When he touched people—shook their hand or patted their shoulder or something—he would get flashes, images of things. Good things, evil things, painful things—always meaningful things—although he usually didn't know how to make sense of them. I used to wonder if that was half the reason he drank. It upset him so much at times."

I rub a hand over my face. "In fifteen years of psychotherapy, Edgar never mentioned this *gift* to me. Probably proves that he did have good instincts about people because, until a few weeks ago, I would have dismissed such talk as superstitious drivel, if not outright delusion."

My tired brain is having trouble keeping everything straight, so I grab a marker and start making lists on the white board. I write down:

Walter something—bad?
I am the Walrus
Dream: Edgar on the beach—pointing to a ship
Fiddle tune—O'Donnell's Lament

"Anything else?" I ask Katherine.

"National Geographic," she says. "Every day when I come home, one particular issue is sitting on my coffee table. From 2003, I think. Edgar didn't even read National Geographic! I don't get it."

~ Undercurrents ~

I add *National Geographic—2003* to the already puzzling list.

"Okay," I say, trying to think like a detective. "Why O'Donnell's Lament? And what do *I am The Walrus* and National Geographic have to do with it? Was there anything about ships in that issue of the magazine?"

"The Walrus!" Katherine blurts. "There's a walrus on the cover of that issue." Katherine is staring at the white board, her eyes growing wider. "Oh my God," she says, "Walter—the one Edgar didn't like—his nickname is *the Walrus*."

I sit down heavily. "But what does the Walrus have to do with a ship in the harbour and an Irish dirge? And what do we do with this information—go to the police and tell them we're getting cryptic clues from the spirit world?"

"It works on TV," she says.

I stop by the house of an old friend, Jimmy MacKinnon, on the way home. Jimmy has the most extensive collection of traditional Celtic music I've ever seen, and I'm not surprised that he has not one, but three, recordings of O'Donnell's Lament in his collection. I borrow one of them, bring it home and play it several times, and learn absolutely nothing. So I Google it—both the song and the name "O'Donnell." I find nothing until I cross-reference the name "O'Donnell" with "Cape Breton" and find an article that looks interesting. It is a reference to a newspaper story from nine years ago—September 16, 1998.

Port-Aux-Basques Woman Missing

A thirty-one year old woman from Port-Aux-Basques, Patricia Claire O'Donnell, has been reported missing. She was last seen on September 13, walking on to the MV Islander in North Sydney, Nova Scotia. Ms. O'Donnell was reportedly on her way home to Newfoundland to visit family. Her mother, Mary Alice O'Donnell of Port-Aux-Basques, says that Patricia has always stayed in close contact with the family. "It's totally unlike Trish not to call us if she changed her plans," a tearful Mrs. O'Donnell said, "I'm worried that something terrible has happened to her." Police say that foul play cannot be ruled out. They have no leads, and ask that anyone who has information regarding the whereabouts of Patricia Claire O'Donnell contact the local detachment of the RCMP immediately.

There is one more reference to Patricia Claire O'Donnell from about three weeks later: still missing, anyone with any information, no leads, etc. I assume that this means she's never been found. I call a friend at the local RCMP office and she confirms that the O'Donnell case is still an open file.

"Precious few leads, either," she says, "It's as if that woman just vanished off the face of the earth without a trace. Why? Did one of your patients confess to killing her?"

"Not exactly," I say.

I go over my list on the white board and write two names: "Patricia O'Donnell" and "Walter the Walrus—last name?" I call Katherine and tell her about my discovery.

"Maybe he killed her," she says.

"What?"

"This Walrus character—maybe he killed the O'Donnell woman and threw her overboard, and maybe Edgar found out."

My first thought is that Katherine is making a rather large leap to a very tenuous conclusion, but I have an idea.

"I'll call you back," I say.

I call my friend at the RCMP detachment back and ask her to put me through to the detective handling the O'Donnell case. I'm happy to learn that it's Detective James Murdock, another friend I've made on the front lines, in the emergency room.

"I have some information for you about the O'Donnell case, Jim," I say, "but it's, um, sensitive."

"You mean it came from a patient and you're breaking the rules of confidentiality by telling me?"

"Something like that. I think you should look at a guy named Walter, works for Maritime Marine, goes by the nickname of—"

"The Walrus," he says.

"You know this guy?"

"Walter Burkett," he says. "Between you and me, we were looking at him from day one. There was a rumour that he was having an affair with the O'Donnell girl. He was working the night she disappeared, too, but we could never prove anything. Can you tell me anything more?"

"Sorry, that's all I have."

It's only a few hundred metres from the hospital to the Maritime Marine terminal, so I leave my car in the parking lot and walk over. The wind is picking up, but it's a warm afternoon. Whitecaps crash on Indian Beach, where a young family is trying desperately to keep their picnic supplies from blowing away. Celebrating Dad's return from Fort McMurray, perhaps. I envy their simple pleasures.

I ask and am told that Walter Burkett is working in the ticket booth. I wait for the last few cars to trickle through, then approach him. He is a short but solidly built man in his fifties with the beginnings of a paunch protruding over his belt. His face is ruddy and scarred, the product, I assume, of too much alcohol, too many bar fights, maybe a difficult case of chicken pox. A thick moustache covers his upper lip, walrus-like. I notice that there are bits of mashed potato stuck in it.

"Hello Walter," I say.

He stares at me and says nothing for a good ten seconds, his eyes narrowed to suspicious slits. "Do I know you?"

"No, we've never met," I say in my best soothing doctor voice, "but Edgar MacDonald suggested that I talk to you."

The man's face goes from an unhealthy cherry red to an even more unhealthy green, the colour of overcooked cabbage. "Get out," he says, pointing to the gate of the compound, "or I'll have you thrown out."

"Edgar told me to mention Patricia O'Donnell. Is she a friend of yours?"

Beads of sweat are forming on Walter Burkett's pudgy white face and for the briefest moment, I almost feel sorry for him. He looks like he's about to have a heart attack.

"Harvey," he says, his voice little more that a hoarse whisper. "Harvey," he says, louder this time, motioning the security guard over to the ticket booth.

"It's all right Harvey," I say, "I was just leaving."

Harvey, a former patient of mine, nods and smiles. "Have a great day, doc."

I wink at Walter Burkett as I back out of the ticket booth. I feel as if Edgar is standing beside me.

I return to the office, restless and amazed at the audacity of

~ Undercurrents ~

what I've just done. I call Katherine.

"Do you suppose Edgar is visiting Walter in his dreams too?" she asks.

"Judging by the look on the man's face when I mentioned Edgar's name, I'd almost guarantee it."

§

Three days later, the coroner calls. "We've reopened the Edgar MacDonald case," Dr. Jones says, his voice as animated as I've ever heard it. "We were investigating another suicide—another floater—looked like a copycat if you want to know the truth. But this fellow left a note confessing to two murders: Edgar MacDonald and a young woman who disappeared a few years back."

"Patricia O'Donnell," I say.

Dr. Jones pauses. "Is there something you're not telling me?"

"Just a rumour I heard. Thank you for calling, Dr. Jones." What else can I tell him?

In the weeks that follow, my sleep gradually returns to normal. My house becomes my own again. Work goes on. There is never any shortage of human suffering. I am less confident in my craft, but what I have lost in confidence, I have gained in empathy. I am a different psychiatrist, neither better nor worse.

I resume my noon-hour walks along Indian Beach. Katherine MacDonald meets me there most days. Our shared trauma has forged an enduring bond between us, like comrades in arms. Who else could we talk to without sounding like we've lost our minds? Shared walks lead to shared dinners. Max the terrier falls shamelessly in love with the new woman in our lives, ignoring me whenever she is in the room.

Three months to the day after his death, Edgar appears in my dreams once again, this time looking young, rosy-cheeked and very much alive. He is dressed as a priest and stands beside the altar of a church. He takes my bulky right hand and places it in Katherine's delicate white one, looking at our faces as he gives us his blessing. I awake wondering whether this dream is Edgar's gift or the creative work of my own subconscious mind. I can't wait to ask Katherine if she's seen Edgar lately.

~ Undercurrents ~

⚜

Julie Curwin divides her time between Sydney and Boularderie, where she lives with her husband and a variety of furry critters. Her fiction and creative non-fiction has appeared in *The Medical Post, Canadian Medical Association Journal,* and on the web at Coffeehousefiction.com. In 2007, Julie was selected as one of twelve finalists in the Writer's Union of Canada Short Prose Competition for Developing Writers, and in 2008 her short story "World Backwards" was chosen as the overall winner in the Commonwealth Short Story Competition, sponsored by the Commonwealth Broadcasting Association. She works as a psychiatrist. In her spare time she enjoys gardening, riding her bicycle, and staring at her tropical fish when she should be doing housework.

Undercurrents

*Like the stories we tell ourselves, like the deepest
currents that course through the oceans and influence
the climates of distant continents, our myths shape the
nature of our being, buttressing the lies that are often
left unsaid.*

Tales and legends swirled the length of Haunted Depths
River. The river and these stories were part of the reason Joseph
Bright stood with his slender frame leaning against the dirty post
office wall. It was the day of the draw at Cameron's General Store.

His cigarette drooped from his lips as he watched the
townsfolk hurrying in and out of the post office door. Whenever
the door was fully open, he was left staring through its unwashed
glass.

Sixty years old, he thought. Still looking in, looking out.
Extinction means much more than elimination of a species.

His people were the Mi'kmaq and his spot here at the post
office—looking in, looking out—was an appropriate symbol, he
thought, for his people's awareness of their position in the larger
culture. His interior acceptance of this had gradually become as
embedded as a slowly growing cancer.

Joseph Bright had been reclining against his leaning wall
almost every day for a month. He was praying. *Praying without
ceasing, just like it says in their Bible,* he thought. Trying to
connect. Forwarding strong invisible petitions to his ancestors
and to his Creator. Requests that Natalie, his beloved five-year-

old niece, might win the draw for the stuffed cougar in Cameron's General Store window.

Natalie—orphaned as a baby—had been adopted by Joseph's sister. Now his sister was showing signs of becoming unhinged. Joseph knew why. Not long ago, she had sobbingly told her horrendous story of childhood abuse to Joseph. He felt deep compassion for her, but even more fear for his Natalie, who still embodied a lively imagination and abundant faith in the rightness of creation.

The stuffed cougar was eight feet from nose to tail, with eyes that were wild, intelligent and wise. Everyone knew that Robert Cameron, the store's owner, was intrigued by cougars.

So was Joseph Bright. As a member of the cat clan, a day never went by that he didn't think of the cougar, now extinct in Cape Breton. He had powerful empathy for the vanished and beautiful animal who once wandered the dark, densely forested Highland crags and valleys.

Cameron came at his fascination from another direction. His great-grandfather was—by legend—known as the fellow who shot the last cougar in Cape Breton. Stalked her for five days. Tracked her through thick forested Highlands. Mi'kmaw lore had it that the cougar's death scream was heard across the island. The elders also said that when the deed was done, the Haunted Depths River boiled up into such a tantrum that it tore out the local bridge, swallowing it whole.

Some might explain that the deep river's currents are fast and strong, with dangerous eddies capable of carrying people and objects away. Joseph Bright and his ancestors knew more. They knew that evil must go somewhere. Extinction is definitely nefarious and cause for demonstrable anguish by the spirits of land and water.

His niece's desire for Cameron's stuffed cougar had everything to do with the Haunted Depths River's furious and quick temper. Out of pain, and out of the river, had come a gift: a tiny stuffed cougar that Natalie dearly loved.

Last April, the snow and ice had melted into a roar of angry water. A van carrying three white folks had been speeding through the reserve. The vehicle hit the rebuilt bridge wall, flipped over the barrier and plunged into the hungry monster's foaming maw. It was swallowed and spit out past the beach

~ Undercurrents ~

where the water takes a bend. There they found the van, upside down, the front wheel spinning around like a wheel in a hamster cage.

The bodies of two adults and a little boy were taken out of the wreck. The boy was the same age as Natalie. The news said speed killed the family. Many on the reserve agreed with elder Charlie Tuna that their ancestors were angry and demanded a sacrifice.

Didn't their ancestors know that the giant quarry now angrily chewing away at the back edge of Kelly's Mountain was owned by one of Cameron's sons? Cameron and his family had no respect for the sacred home of Glooscap. Joseph Bright and the other people thought it only natural that the Haunted Depths River would be provoked.

The day after the van accident, Joseph walked down the river beach. He had a sense for smelling blood days before and after a tragedy. That day there was too much in the air. He spotted a wee stuffed toy floating amongst the tufts of water plants clinging to the riverside.

It was a cougar.

Joseph Bright cleaned it up and gave it to Natalie, a fitting gift for her to look after since it was their clan's totem.

"When I sleep, my baby cougar is alive, Uncle Joseph," his niece said, months later when they first spotted the huge cougar in Cameron's store. Natalie stood transfixed for a moment and then said, "I must win him so that the little boy's cougar will have a daddy."

Joseph looked at her with wonder.

"Uncle Joseph," she continued, "if God can breathe life into dirt, then I'm going to pray for dreams about my cougars..."

She's already talking as if the large cougar is hers, he thought.

"...because that's when they are alive."

Joseph Bright had a big problem with the fact that Natalie wanted something from Robert Cameron. One of the certainties of his life was that he would never set foot in Cameron's store. He'd always be looking in and never out and he'd go to hell to buy a pair of boots before he'd cast his shadow on Cameron's soiled, wooden floors. And it wasn't only because Cameron's ancestor had killed the last cougar. There were even worse, more personal evils that Cameron's family had performed against his people.

~ Undercurrents ~

Cameron's great-grandfather had desecrated Joseph Bright's ancestors, their bones torn from the burial ground to make way for expansion of his commercial enterprises. Yes, theirs was a long tradition of making money off the misery of others. The bones had been piled in wooden crates and later, laid out on a table in the back room of the store.

Red skeletons at the Last Supper.

Joseph Bright's recollections were disturbed by Robert Cameron's voice.

"How are you today, Joseph boy?" He was walking fast as he usually did, a man comfortable with himself, in control of his world. His greedy eyes bobbled behind tiny lenses in the shadow of his Cameron's General Store cap.

"Pretty good," Joseph responded.

"Just pretty good? My God, you'd think you'd be rested and feeling top notch. You must be working too hard!" Cameron's laugh was like thick, muddy clay.

He went into the post office followed by his wife. Mrs. Cameron was beautiful in a simple way, but sad. Joseph thought that her paleness might come from the dominating ways of her husband and maybe from her faith, too. He had heard that her home—which of course he had never been in—had plenty of pictures of Jesus and religious sayings plastered all over the walls. His white friend told him that they had moved out of the top floor of the store because Mrs. Cameron believed it was cursed. Maybe she felt the pictures protected her.

Just too much righteousness, Joseph thought.

Something powerful had happened the night Cameron's great-grandfather put those bones in the store. They disappeared.

Afterward, the explanations centered on vandalism and other simple, orderly reasons that fit comfortably into the stories that civic and church leaders told themselves, stories that they could believe about their universe. But that wasn't the end of it. Before long a new story unfolded from the town clerk who had been driving by that night.

The lamps were off in the buildings and the moon was waiting on the other side of the mountain. The only light was a pale glow from the clerk's headlights as he passed by the store. Just then a gigantic, dark shape rose in the blackness. The clerk clearly saw a cougar standing on the table with one of the ancestors' bones in his mouth. Almost before the sight could register in his brain, the shape leapt out the window.

"Hogwash," the Camerons and other white folk said. "Superstitions!"

To their minds, the wild universe of spirit and body must be tamed. But to Joseph, neither cougars' nor heathens' bones could be redeemed "by the blood of Jesus."

Joseph Bright's thoughts were interrupted again as Mr. Cameron burst out of the post office with the wife in tow. Talking as he walked, peppering sharp words around like he was at a turkey shoot, Cameron addressed Joseph again.

"You're going to have to get your name into the contest, Joseph boy, if you want to increase your chances of winning the stuffed cougar for your niece. She told me that she's 'going to win.' You should drag yourself over to the store so you can help the poor little waif."

He laughed that clogging laugh again and Joseph Bright's stomach turned over as he thought about all the deals the Camerons had completed with that heavy laugh and heavier handshake.

Mrs. Cameron gave Joseph a sad smile and he was reminded that there is goodness in all people. Humanity was not tied to culture. Sometimes when he looked at non-Natives such as Mrs. Cameron, he could see that many were burdened with something he couldn't touch or know. Joseph knew that non-Natives also had tragic, true stories and thought that maybe they needed their Christ to make themselves feel loved while living in a world that many of their ancestors had so efficiently raped.

The Natives told a different story about the disappearance of the bones from Cameron's store all those years ago. They talked of a great cougar who had been buried with Joseph Bright's ancestors. When Cameron removed the bones, the cougar's spirit had returned to transport the ancestors back to their sacred soil.

Since that day, locals—both native and white—had reported seeing bobbing lights inside the dark store. One recent evening, Joseph had seen luminescence rising from the floor and forming featureless shapes. Orbs of white light glided toward the window. He watched the stuffed cougar absorb the light and its body take on vitality. Saw life in its eyes. Saw that it breathed.

He thought of what Natalie said, "If God can breathe life into dirt, then I'm going to pray for dreams about my cougars. When I sleep, my baby cougar is alive."

Natalie had no qualms about going to Robert Cameron's store. She'd been purchasing whatever her allowance and her uncle's subsidies would allow. The rules stipulated that you had to make a minimum purchase of five dollars for each entry form. Nearly every day Natalie was there, having convinced someone to take her to town so she could buy something.

Last night, the night before the day of the drawing, Joseph had gone to his sister's as he did most nights. He and Natalie settled at the table in the dimly lit kitchen as they had so many nights in the previous weeks, so that Natalie could fill out her entry forms.

She climbed into the cozy, high-backed chair behind the round table. He waited and watched her, while his tea curled steam up to the greasy light fixture. Natalie's raspberry drink perched next to her tiny elbow. Her jet-black hair was done up at the back with a red scarf.

Natalie wrapped her fingers around the thick pencil as if she were hanging onto a precious gem. At first he had helped her fill out the cougar prize forms but by now, she'd become proficient at it and could do it all by herself.

"I'm excited, Uncle Joseph! The draw's tomorrow!" she said.

"I know. Just before closing time at 8 p.m.," he replied.

"Soon, my baby cougar is going to get a father."

She was absorbed in her work and needed no answer. After finishing her form, she said, "God must have a big, strong imagination if he can make everything come alive. Why do people kill when they don't know how to make things be alive?" Then quickly she added, "Except in their dreams."

"I think your imagination is pretty lively," he answered.

"I'm going to pray again tonight that someday my cougars will start to breathe even when I'm awake."

Joseph Bright hoped that his prayers to his ancestors, and Natalie's faith and diligence in accumulating so many contest forms, would do the trick. He worried that if she didn't win the cougar, she would be left with no faith. He had seen how life could destroy imagination and hope.

"Why don't you fill out a form, Uncle Joseph? I don't care if you win. I'd trust you with my baby and daddy cougars. I can dream them to life at your house too, you know."

Joseph laid his hands over his eyes so she couldn't see the tears welling up. He had told her many times that her imagination was stronger than his. What he hadn't told her was that he would piss on Robert Cameron before he'd put his name on anything of his.

Today, the day of the draw, Joseph began leaning against the post office wall at ten a.m. At noon, he walked over to the coffee shop and sat down at his favourite table just behind the glassed entranceway where he could look in and look out. After eating, he walked back to the post office and took his place.

The mountains hovered over the town, their tops lost in clouds. He prayed that their power could be persuasive as he watched the shadows lengthen out from Cameron's store.

"Hello Joseph," his sister said. Her eyes looked drugged. She must have upped her anti-depressants, he thought.

"I put all last night's slips into the aquarium," Natalie said. Her face was red with excitement. "I double-prayed over them, too, and last night I dreamed that the big cougar and my little cougar came to life."

His sister pulled at Natalie's elbow and took her away.

"Aren't we going to stay for the draw?" Natalie asked. But her aunt just kept walking.

Joseph knew that Natalie's optimistic chatter was wearing on his sister's prescription, but also that his sister was hurrying Natalie home because she wanted to prolong the child's excitement and faith. She didn't want Natalie to be there when her name wasn't drawn.

The shadow from Cameron's store had almost reached Joseph's leaning place. He stared at the store and talked to the ancestors he believed were back under the store, covered by the darkness that the Camerons carried with them.

An hour before closing time, Joseph Bright spotted a girl about Natalie's age hanging onto a man's hand. Probably her father. She had short, blonde hair and looked timid and wistful. When they walked by the store window she pulled away so she could look at the prize. Joseph Bright could sense that she really wanted that cougar. They entered the store.

Joseph watched as Cameron handed the little girl a contest slip to fill out. The two men talked as she wrote and when she went to put the ballot in the aquarium, Joseph saw Robert Cameron take the ballot out of her hand and put it into his pocket. He patted her on the head while giving her father a wink, wink.

The long hours of meditation and his constant remembrances of his ancestors had fine-tuned his senses, his intuitiveness. He was filled with the conviction that his niece wasn't going to win the stuffed cougar. The fix was in. Like so many times before.

As he felt his spirit work itself into furious, hungry eddies, the little girl gazed out the store window and locked eyes with Joseph Bright. Did she know? A child's heart is powerful. How much in jeopardy was her faith? Her imagination?

Then she smiled. Joseph Bright had never seen her before and yet he had seen a thousand innocent people like her and he realized that she deserved the cougar just as much as Natalie did.

It was a hard thought.

§

Joseph Bright stayed at his leaning wall right up to the draw. He looked at the expectant crowd of would-be-winners. The little blonde girl in the yellow dress and her father were standing behind Robert Cameron. Joseph could see her excitement.

The sun was setting behind the dark Highlands as Cameron made a big fuss of making the official draw. He rolled up his sleeve, turned his face to the crowd and gave them a big smile. Then his face turned and Joseph, who was lit up by the street lamp, caught his eye. Cameron stopped smiling.

It gave Joseph some pleasure to know that Robert Cameron most certainly did know that Joseph was on to the fix.

Cameron plunged his hand into the aquarium and pretended to stir up names. He pulled his hand out of the heaped papers of hope and Joseph observed his mouth move as he named the winner.

The girl in the yellow dress bounced up and down and Joseph was glad only that Natalie had a few more minutes to live with her hope and faith.

Joseph was getting in his old pickup as Cameron helped the girl's father load the cougar into the back of their big SUV. Joseph drove to the coffee shop. He wanted to stall, to think about what he was going to tell Natalie. He sat as usual in the place where he could see through the glass into the parking lot and through the glass at people entering.

It wasn't long before the winner and her father came in for a cold drink.

"Hey, that's the little girl who won Cameron's cougar," Mrs. Nerburn shouted. "You are a lucky little girl!"

The child smiled shyly, grabbing her father's hand.

"Yes," he said, "She's going to put that stuffed cougar in her playroom with her other toys. Where we will find the room for such a big toy, I don't know."

"I'm going to make a tree fort, Daddy. So that it can be up in the big oak trees. I want it to be able to live just like a real cougar."

The two left quickly. If someone other than Natalie had to win, Joseph Bright was glad it was this child. He wished he knew her name. He sipped his coffee and thought, *At least I can tell Natalie that the winner is a nice little girl. A girl she would like.*

He meant to start home, but when he got in the pickup he found himself heading off toward the Highlands. The sun was now only a faint, shimmering aura behind the forest. It seemed to Joseph that the sun had held onto this side of the world for a longer time than normal. It must be the dense clouds hovering over the heights. *The world can be so mysterious,* he thought.

Joseph drove up the gravel road that took him to the top of the mountain. Here he could see the whole reserve laid out before him. The lights twinkled and he thought about all his friends and family who lived down there. Suddenly loneliness welled up and he wanted to get back to the Reserve to see Natalie.

He was about a mile and a half from Haunted Depths River bridge when he smelled blood. As he drove around a curve and saw flashing lights, his anxiety and the smell grew stronger. There were three police cars and a tow truck.

Kevin, a Native RCMP officer, was directing traffic through the scene.

"What's going on, Kevin?" Joseph asked.

"Keep it to yourself for now, Joseph, but a car's gone in the river. Ontario license plate. Seems like it's Robert Cameron's relatives. A man and his little girl."

Joseph Bright started to shake. He held on tightly to the

steering wheel, picturing the child who had smiled at him from across the street.

Kevin didn't notice Joseph's distress. "Charlie Tuna happened to be driving by. He reported some kind of big animal jumped out in front of the car. When the vehicle swerved, it went into the river. A deer or maybe a moose. You know Charlie Tuna, though. He's going on about it being a cougar."

"Are they...dead?" Joseph asked.

"The father. But the little girl survived. Kind of a miracle. The first on the scene found her hanging onto a huge stuffed animal. It was a crazy thing, they said. She was in the meanest part of the swirling river, hanging onto a big stuffed cougar."

"Saved by a cougar," Joseph said, giving silent thanks to his ancestors. "Charlie Tuna sure about that cougar thing?"

Kevin smirked, saying, "Oh yeah, he was certain that it was a real cougar that saved the girl. Then he was surprised to find out the cougar that 'jumped into the river' turned out to be a stuffed one!"

Joseph said good night and drove on. As he passed by the reserve school he felt the full coolness and calm of the Highland night sitting in the passenger seat next to him.

Didn't it say somewhere in the book that we pray without knowing for what?

Joseph Bright was grateful that he had taken the time to loiter around the post office, looking through dirty glass and communicating with his ancestors.

Better than that, Natalie, his beloved niece, was happy about not winning the cougar. She believed it was a miracle. That God had made the stuffed cougar live to save the nice little girl in the yellow dress.

"Uncle Joseph, maybe when my baby cougar grows up it will save someone too."

Joseph Bright was certain that the tiny stuffed cougar had already saved his niece's imagination, faith and her belief in life.

For Joseph, so used to observing from the outside in or the inside out, it had all played out in a familiar way—though repetition didn't make it any less mysterious. Joseph Bright was still left with one big question. Just who was hoodwinking whom in this great big universe?

L arry A. Gibbons, a graduate of Queen's University and St. Lawrence College, is a former library clerk, photo technologist and veterinary technologist. Known as a book lover, enthusiastic hiker and passionate writer, he spends as much time as he can in Cape Breton, where he has lived on and off for sixteen years. When in Ontario, Larry and his wife live in a cabin in the woods. The Highlands and the woodlands are where Larry feels most at home.

The Canadian Authors Association has recognized one of Larry's stories and he has been published in magazines and newsletters in Nova Scotia, Ontario and America.

Larry's writing often focuses on the spiritual depths hidden and revealed in nature, and in the relationships between Natives and non-Natives.

Sense and Exsanguinations

The letter had lain on the silver tray since Alice had brought it in that morning. Luciana had studiously ignored it, but now, pacing the pale rose parlour alone, she found it impossible to resist any longer. She smoothed her blue linen skirts, trying to steady her trembling hands. Breathing deeply, she picked up the letter and carefully studied the neatly handwritten address, the satiny paper, the thick seal of indigo wax impressed with the Academy's seal. After a moment, in which she listened to be sure that her mother's carriage had truly departed, she broke the seal and unfolded the single sheet of paper.

Dear Miss Morgan,

It is with deep regret that we note we have not received notification of your intention to attend the Academy. Out of respect for your privacy, we will not inquire as to the reasons for your decision. The results of your ability testing indicate that your gifts, left untrained, pose no threat to the health and welfare of the general populace or to the British Empire, and so your attendance at the Academy will not be enforced. We wish you the best for the future, and remind you that any unexpected changes in your abilities must be reported immediately to the National Registry of Thaumaturgists; you may be contacted in the future by the Academy or the Registry for statistical purposes.

Sincerely,
Master Florian Edgewood &
Mistress Linnea Norton,
Registrars, Royal Academy of Arcane Arts

~ Undercurrents ~

Luciana crushed the paper in her delicate fingers, trembling now with anger rather than apprehension. Her mother's presence still radiated from the chair where she had sat that morning, and Luciana found the sensation suddenly intolerable. Clutching the wounded letter, she stomped from the parlour and ascended the stairs, caring little that her mother deplored stomping. She defied another of her mother's rules by slamming the bedchamber door behind her. The sound was quite satisfying, although it would have been more so if her mother were in the house to hear it.

She sank into her burgundy wing-back chair and smoothed the letter against her thigh before scanning it again. Her eyes lingered over the third sentence: "The results of your ability testing indicate that your gifts, left untrained, pose no threat..." For once, she wished that she could make things burst into flames like her cousin Benedict, or influence people's minds like the notorious criminal, Eleanora Greer. Well, perhaps she had wished to have Mrs. Greer's power before—then she could have persuaded her mother to let her attend the Academy.

She gazed at the letter, imagining it bursting into flames in her hands, but her efforts didn't produce so much as a wisp of smoke. She knew, of course, that there was a chance she could learn those skills or others, but not unless her mother miraculously decided that the Academy was a suitable place for young ladies after all.

She sighed. She might as well wish her father were still alive; he would have been proud to see her at the Academy.

There was a rapping at the door downstairs, but she could not stir herself to be interested. No doubt it was one of her mother's friends come to gossip—or even worse, to parade yet another suitor in front of Luciana. She knew she should be grateful that her father had provided for her well—and she was, truly. However, it was exhausting to be courted by every younger son in her mother's acquaintance, especially when she knew that her mother planned to make the decision herself, despite the fact that her father's Will allowed Luciana the final word.

A soft tap sounded at her door. "An Inspector Lawrence Hargrave to see you, Miss. From the Yard," Alice called, surprise warring with politeness in her tone.

Luciana sat for a moment, bewildered, before managing to

answer. "Thank you, Alice. Have Goodwin show him into the parlour, please." She remained in her chair. An inspector, come to see her? Had she, unbeknownst to herself, committed some crime? The line between sanity and madness was fine, but surely she would remember doing something that would draw the attention of Scotland Yard.

Unless...perhaps her magic had flared out, somehow. Perhaps it was not as harmless as the Academy thought! Excitement at that thought propelled her to the door, although she schooled herself to a more ladylike pace before descending the stairs.

She sensed her caller's presence before she reached the parlour. He was certainly no one she had ever met; the sensation reminded her of the first breath of true country air after leaving London, or of the breaking of clouds over Hyde Park after days of rain. He was unmarried; marriage mingled people somehow, and she could detect no threads of another's presence in his. No gloss of Society touched him—none of the requisite veneer of affability —but that was somehow comforting; the veneer was a deception, and even without it there was no stain of menial drudgery or baser feeling on this man. She paused in the hall, adjusted her skirts, and folded her hands demurely before entering the parlour.

The Inspector stood by one of the chairs, his head bent over a notebook as he pencilled something in. He tucked the book away immediately when she entered, raising his head to regard her steadily with dark grey eyes. He was not at all what she had expected—little older than she was, and handsome, though not in a dashing way. There was something serious yet kindly about his face.

"How do you do, Inspector Hargrave?" she inquired politely.

"Very well, thank you. You are Miss Luciana Morgan?"

"I am," she said. He bowed, and she nodded in return. "Please, be seated," she said, gesturing to his chair. He thanked her, but waited until she was seated before sitting himself.

"Would you care for tea?" she asked.

"Yes, thank you," he said. He waited while she rang the bell and spoke to Alice, then addressed her again. "Please forgive me for calling on you in this fashion, Miss Morgan. Believe me, I would never trouble a young lady such as yourself except in the most extreme of circumstances."

"It's no trouble, Inspector," she said, looking him over discreetly. He was tall and lean, and even sitting gave off an air of activity and honest work. His dark suit was clean and of a decent cut, but also very serviceable; it suited him well.

"You may feel otherwise after I explain my reasons for being here," he said, retrieving his notebook.

Alice came with the tea and set the tray down on the low table. Luciana busied herself in pouring out two cups and offering the inspector a biscuit, which he refused.

"Inspector...have I done something wrong?" she asked, glancing up from her teacup to meet his eyes.

"Oh, heavens, no!" he exclaimed. "Miss Morgan, I apologize—I should have set you at ease at once. You have done nothing wrong; rather, I have come to request your assistance in a matter of the gravest importance and, I am afraid, of some danger."

Despite her hopes of some unknown development in her abilities, Luciana was relieved. She did not wish to have caused harm to anyone. She was also intrigued. Why on Earth would the Yard need her assistance? "Pray, continue," she said, attempting to sip her tea with some degree of patience. "I must confess, I don't understand."

"No, I must explain myself fully. I'm so sorry to have frightened you." He regarded her earnestly, his eyes so grave that she was moved to reassure him.

"Inspector, please, I am quite untroubled. Proceed with your explanation."

"Very well," he said, and a brief smile lit his face, quite in contrast to his sober attire and manner. He flipped a few pages in the notebook before finding the one he wanted. "You are the daughter of the late Thomas Morgan?"

"I am," she said.

"And you were recently tested by the Royal Academy of Arcane Arts..." He flipped another page. "You were found to have a gift for sensing and reading people's 'presences.' You showed an ability to learn, but no dangerous innate abilities. Correct?"

Luciana stifled a sigh. "That is correct. Given the results of the tests, I could not be compelled to attend the Academy."

"And you will not be attending?" he asked, making a note in his notebook.

~ Undercurrents ~

"No," she said, trying to keep her anger out of her voice.

He glanced at her quickly, but politeness forbade his question. "These 'presences' you sense...are they what some people would call 'auras?'"

She shook her head. "No. They are quite different, as I understand it. For me, it is a sense, like that of sight or hearing. The sensation of a person's presence is complex; I cannot always tell exactly what it means immediately, although some common traits are easily recognized. Also, from what I have heard, auras can only be seen when one looks upon a person."

"And the sense of this presence remains even when a person is no longer in a room?" he asked, consulting his notes again.

"Yes, for some time—some trace of it even remains on items a person has carried or worn for a time."

"Once you have encountered a person's presence...can you recognize it again?"

"Oh yes," she said. "It's much like recognizing someone's face. There are some that are similar, but I can usually discern some distinguishing features."

He made a few more notes, looking both pleased and apprehensive. "This is all exactly as I had hoped," he said. "However, now I must come to the point of my visit. I am loath to involve a young lady in this, but your ability is a rare one, Miss Morgan. I believe you are the only person in London who can help me."

"I have not considered it a particularly useful ability," she said. "Of course, it gives me some insights into those I associate with, but beyond that..." She shrugged delicately.

He looked surprised. "My dear Miss Morgan," he said. "I would trade fifty of our good constables for one with your ability. Forgive me if this sounds rude, but...well, there are some criminals that even the best hound can't track. But someone like you—you could."

Luciana smiled at him over her tea. "Are you suggesting that I am some sort of tracking dog, Inspector?" she inquired.

He began to protest immediately, but she shook her head. "I am not offended. It's a fascinating idea." *And one of which Mama would heartily disapprove, which makes it all the more interesting,* she added to herself. She set her tea aside and folded her hands in her lap, looking at him squarely. "I think you had better explain how I may help."

He settled back in his chair, his gaze suddenly considering. "Very well, then," he said. "You've heard of the recent crimes in some of the poorer neighborhoods, I trust? The papers have been rather freer with their accounts than we would like."

"I have," she said, shuddering. The string of murders were the talk of London. "The killer is still at large, I understand?"

He nodded grimly. "It is my hope, though, that with your help I may be able to change that."

"What do you propose?"

He leaned forward slightly. "There was another murder last night. I believe that someone with your abilities would be able to track the killer from the crime scene. You see, this man possesses talents of his own; our dogs can't follow him, and he leaves few footprints. The Thaumaturgists have no record of anyone like him."

"Then, I checked with the Registry for anyone possessing ways of tracing people, and you're the only one living, except for a farmer's son in northern Yorkshire. I would have sought his assistance, despite the distance, but the boy is only six years old."

"And so you want me to visit the crime scene with you and see if I can detect a sense of the killer?"

"That was my idea. A group of constables stands ready to accompany us, for safety. I assure you, the unfortunate victim has been removed; there should be nothing there to alarm you."

"Nothing save the presence of a cold-blooded murderer," she said grimly. "It will not be pleasant."

"Miss Morgan, if you do not wish to become involved in this investigation—"

She held up a hand to silence him. "I could not refuse; every subsequent murder would plague my conscience if I knew I might have helped catch the killer."

"In that case, I should speak to your mother. I expect she will want to send a chaperone to accompany you."

"My mother is not at home," said Luciana. *And thank goodness for that!* "I do not expect her to return for some time."

"That...is unfortunate," he said. "It would not be right to take you without her knowledge, but I scarcely dare to wait. The trail grows colder as we speak, and the killer has shown no aversion to killing in the daylight."

She focused on her sense of him again, trying to tease a better understanding from her impressions. He was conscientious about propriety, but more because of his own sense of what was right than because of society's expectations; it was a refreshing change. Her respect for him grew. "Inspector Hargrave, I am ready and willing to accompany you now. I am legally able to marry whom I choose and commit myself into the permanent care of a drunkard or a wastrel; surely I should be able to temporarily place myself under the protection of a Scotland Yard inspector and a troop of constables." It was a daring speech, she knew—but it worked.

He stood decisively, picking up his hat and coat. "I'll send for the boys, then, and notify the driver. We'll go as soon as you're ready."

"Give me a few moments," she said, rising as well and ringing the bell for Alice.

Her stomach swooped and rolled as she hurried up to her room and had Alice help her into more suitable clothes—her dark green serge was quite serviceable and would do nicely, she thought; it was finely cut, but would not draw attention to her or her class. *Although it does make my complexion look quite nice*, she thought, and then wondered that such a thing had crossed her mind. "Alice, if Mama returns…"

"Aren't you off to the shops with some friends, Miss?" Alice asked, her face innocent except for the spark of mischief in her eyes. She was about Luciana's age and had been in the household since she was of an age to work; the two understood each other quite well.

"Yes, that's right. I need…"

"Some new gloves, and perhaps a shawl, Miss."

"Yes, thank you, Alice," Luciana said, flashing a smile. Both knew that her mother approved unquestioningly of shopping expeditions.

Within moments she was being handed into a tidy cab by Inspector Hargrave, who climbed in after, seated himself across from her, and rapped the door to let the cabby know they were ready. They were soon gliding by the stately houses of Belgravia.

Although she and the Inspector had talked easily enough in the parlour, Luciana was at great pains to stop herself from twisting her hands in her lap and saying something ridiculous about the weather now that they were confined to the close quarters of a cab. Apparently, all her social training had not done one whit to prepare her to make small talk with a Scotland Yard inspector while en route to the scene of a murder.

"This is a lovely neighbourhood," Inspector Hargrave said, looking steadily out his own window.

At least I am not the only one at a loss for things to say, Luciana reflected. Saying that Belgravia was a lovely neighbourhood was like saying that Queen Victoria was very respectable. "Yes. The recent rains have done much for the gardens," she said, berating herself for the inane pleasantries that welled inside her.

"I'm afraid we're headed somewhere quite different," he added.

That's better, Luciana thought. *This is an investigation, not a tea party.* "I feel quite equal to it, Inspector, I assure you. We must all serve in whatever capacity we can."

"I suppose so. Still, there are other tasks generally considered more fitting for young women such as yourself."

"Such as pouring tea, decorating sitting rooms, and raising sons for the Empire, you mean?" Luciana's gloved hands tightened on her skirts. She was being impertinent again, and she found she didn't care.

Hargrave gave a startled laugh. "When you put it that way, the crime scene doesn't sound so bad," he said, still chuckling. "You're not quite like other young ladies, are you?"

As his gaze caught hers and held it, her tongue seemed to cleave to the roof of her mouth. The sense of his presence was suddenly overwhelming. *That first patch of blue after a long storm...*

"Forgive me, Miss Morgan; that was inappropriate." He glanced out the window.

"Not at all," she said easily, but the tension between them did not dissipate. After a moment, she said, "Perhaps you should tell me what to expect."

Business-like again, he tilted his head thoughtfully. "The most recent murder took place in an alley, sometime last night. The victim was a poor man; he worked at a blacking warehouse not far from the Yard itself—bit of a slap in the face, really. The body's been removed, as I mentioned, but—I'm afraid there may still be some blood. This murderer...his powers go beyond making himself untrackable. When we find the victims..." He seemed to be searching for a delicate way to say something, and having little luck.

"It's all right, Inspector. The papers have been helpfully indiscreet. I have read that the victims are usually... exsanguinated."

He threw her a grateful look. "Yes, precisely. We've washed the area down, but we wanted to bring you in as soon as possible, and that didn't leave us much time for clean-up."

"I understand; I believe I am up to it."

He smiled, and Luciana found it again most suitable to look out the window. She was amazed at how quickly the beautiful houses of Belgravia were replaced by increasingly shabby-looking dwellings. She had been out of the neighbourhood countless times, of course, but she was quite certain she had never taken the turnings the cab driver followed. Muck and garbage littered the streets. The few people who were about looked downtrodden— their clothes little more than rags, their faces drawn and heavily lined with care.

Luciana drew back and looked down, suddenly acutely conscious of her clean, expensively-made clothes, of the comfortable luncheon she had enjoyed earlier, of her new boots with their shiny black buttons. Inspector Hargrave caught her eye and grimaced.

"Not quite what you're used to," he said.

"Oh no," she said. "It's not that. It's just...my life is so easy." She stopped, collecting herself. She opened up entirely too easily with this young man, she reflected. In one partial afternoon with him, she had revealed more of what she really thought than she had in ten Saturdays spent riding in Rotten Row with the other young people of her set.

Several minutes later, the clopping of the horses' hooves slowed, and they drew up at the mouth of a dingy run between two crooked buildings. Uniformed constables lined the sidewalk and the alley itself. Inspector Hargrave opened the door, stepped down, and helped Luciana to the ground. She could not resist the urge to hold her skirts up away from the ground, although she felt ashamed to do so when so many people clearly lived in such conditions at all times.

~ Undercurrents ~

Hargrave greeted two of the constables, who respectfully tipped their hats to Luciana. He looked at her steadily, offering his arm. "Ready?" he asked.

She nodded, taking his arm, and together they entered the shadows of the alley. The day was warm, but a chill clung to this spot, as though the sunshine declined to warm the air of so foul a place. Several darkish smears marred the crumbling brick walls and the cobbles underfoot, but Luciana firmly directed her mind away from those things. She glanced around at the constables who stood attentively to either side. "Can they wait on the street?" she asked. "I need as little interference as possible."

"Of course." Hargrave bent to speak quietly to one of the constables, and a moment later they were alone in the alley.

With the constables gone, Luciana began sorting out the threads of what she sensed. It was difficult; so many people had been about the crime scene that the remnants they had left behind almost blinded her ability. She walked about slowly, her head on one side as though listening, trying to find some way to distinguish them from one another.

Suddenly she stopped. There was something just on the edge of her perception. She took another step, and the full force of it swept over her, as strong and distinct as if she had entered a room that had been abandoned for years by all but this one person. It was the foulest thing she had ever encountered, and images of oozing sewage, unseemly crawling things, and discarded entrails flickered through her mind in quick succession. It was overwhelming. Her stomach roiled and a dark fog filled her vision, and she flung out a hand in an attempt to catch herself.

Hargrave was there instantly, one hand gripping hers firmly and the other arm strong around her waist. "Miss Morgan! What is it? Are you all right?" He twisted his head towards the mouth of the alley. "Oi! Help here!" he shouted.

Steadied by his strength, she drew deep breaths, slowly straightening. "It's all right," she said. She could feel the grim set of her own mouth, her tongue curling as though she had tasted curdled milk. "Just here. The murder happened just here?"

Several constables had rushed up at Hargrave's call, and stood watching her warily. Hargrave glanced about to get his bearings, then nodded. "You feel something?" At her nod, he asked sharply, "Will you be able to recognize it again? To follow it?"

She glanced at him and saw a new spark in his eyes—the keenness of a dog on a scent. She swallowed. "I should recognize it now in a crowd of a thousand." She drew a deep breath, then strode determinedly to the street. "That way," she said, pointing to the right.

At Hargrave's nod, several of the constables set off down the street, examining the ground and the surrounding buildings carefully. Luciana and Hargrave followed them, the other constables forming a loose box around them. Still touched by the remnants of the criminal's presence, she was grateful for the protection.

As they proceeded down the street, Luciana caught fleeting ripples of what she had sensed in the alley, and was able to guide them through several turnings. Finally, they stood outside a rough shack, its weathered grey wood peppered with rusted nails. The sense hit her again, stronger now, rolling in sickening waves from the shack. She clutched her stomach, trying to settle it as her face grew clammy.

"In there?" Hargrave asked gently.

She nodded. Fear welled in her as she realized that the grey walls before her held a person horrible enough to generate the presence that threatened to overwhelm her. Suddenly she became aware of something else, something beyond the tangled presences of the constables surrounding her. Another presence, this one humble and kindly. She gasped. "There's someone else in there!"

"An accomplice?" Hargrave demanded, his voice sharp again.

She shook her head, horrified at the thought of this gentle presence trapped in that small space with the murderer. "No...oh, hurry!"

Hargrave tucked a hand under her elbow, steering her back behind a line of constables. "Wait here," he said, waving over a few of his men. "Brown and Cooper will stay with you." He strode off, signalling to his men and murmuring orders.

Luciana turned away, pressing her hands tight to her ears. If there had been any way to stop up her magical sense, she would have done that as well. She was desperately glad for the two constables who stood quietly between her and the shack; they were good men both, she could tell, and she tried to distract

~ Undercurrents ~

herself with her sense of them. She was aware of the other constables moving away from her, towards the shack, and was painfully sure that Hargrave was leading the approach.

Unable to bear not knowing what was happening, she turned in time to see Hargrave kick in the door and disappear into the shack with a troop of constables behind him. There were shouts, another crash of splintering wood, and the pounding of feet. Moments later, Hargrave re-emerged from the shack, supporting a stooped, shaking man. Mere feet from the building, the man slumped and Hargrave lowered him carefully. He beckoned to Luciana. "Have you any hartshorn?" he called.

Hurrying towards him, Luciana slipped a hand into her reticule and felt around for the small glass bottle she usually carried. Her fingers finally closed around it, and she thrust it towards Hargrave.

He took the delicate vessel carefully, opened it, and waved it under the nose of the man on the ground. After a moment, the man coughed and sputtered, opening his eyes and looking around wonderingly.

Hargrave recapped the bottle and handed it back to Luciana with a tight smile. "I was afraid you wouldn't have any. You don't seem like the fainting sort."

"I have a close friend who has frequent need of smelling salts," she said, returning his smile. She was about to ask what had happened inside when the reviving man clutched at Hargrave's arm.

"Thank you, Officer," he said.

"Not at all," Hargrave said, helping the man sit up. "Think you can tell us a few things?"

At the man's nod, Hargrave waved Luciana off. "I'll speak with you in a moment, Miss Morgan," he said, nodding to her reassuringly.

Luciana walked back to the waiting constables, tucking her salts back into her reticule. She felt a little put out at being sent away, although she knew it was foolish. She could not expect to be privy to all aspects of the investigation.

Moments later, two constables heaved the man to his feet and escorted him from the scene. Hargrave jotted some notes in his notepad, spoke to a few of his men, and then returned to Luciana.

"I apologize for sending you off like that, Miss Morgan," he said. "I'm still not happy to have involved you in all this—perhaps even less so now. I didn't want you to hear anything that might disturb you; there are enough of us losing sleep over this already." The solicitude in his voice dissolved her annoyance.

"I understand, Inspector," she said. "But what happened? I was certain the murderer was in there."

"You were right," he said. "That poor fellow was terribly shaken, but he was certain about two things; another man had dragged him in there, and that man was planning to kill him. Had him trussed up in a chair, and was tightening the knots just before I broke the door." He frowned. "However, when we went in, there was no one else there."

"Was there a back door?"

"Yes—he must have gotten out that way, but..." He looked away as though trying to sort something out.

"What is it?" Luciana asked.

"Well, I had constables stationed at the other end of the alley to make sure no one came in that way. They made sure no one came in...but no one came out, either. And he clearly didn't come out through the front."

"He's disappeared? How?" A chill prickled Luciana's skin at the thought. *A man so powerful, so horrible, who could disappear at will...*

"I'm hoping you can tell me," said Hargrave. "Can you come into the back alley and see if you can trace him further?"

"Of course," she said. She followed him around the shack, feeling somehow disappointed that he had not offered her his arm again. *I'm just shaken,* she thought. *I'd be glad to take anybody's arm right now.*

The back of the shack resembled the front, although the door looked even more battered, and the wood was shrunken; it hung several inches above the threshold. A few shards of dry wood littered the ground, and the weathered doorframe was cracked. Luciana approached the door, trying to quiet her stomach as her sense of the killer's vile presence intensified. She gingerly touched the old wood—the damage was obviously new. "He broke the door coming out?"

"Actually, I did that," Hargrave said sheepishly. "I knew he must have gone out the back, but the door stuck dreadfully when

I tried to follow."

"Perhaps he was able to jam it somehow? Using magic?" she mused.

"It's possible. We don't know all his capabilities."

She followed the stomach-twisting trail away from the shack, thrusting the stench of filth and images of dark liquid out of her mind. The abominable presence was horribly easy to follow. She found, though, that focusing on Hargrave's presence fought it some, sweeping away the foulness the way clear sun and a fresh breeze sometimes swept the smoky haze from the city.

The trail stopped abruptly and Luciana glanced around. *Where did he go?* She stood in the middle of the alley. Even had he been able to walk through walls, he was not close enough to either wall to have escaped that way. If he had flown, one of the many constables would have seen him. She looked down and saw a rusted grate at her feet, its rough bars clogged with dried leaves and unidentifiable muck. Frowning, Luciana crouched down— and shuddered in disgust as the killer's presence intensified, mingling with the reek rising from the drain.

She understood, suddenly, why the killer was able to disappear so easily, and how someone so depraved could move about the city without being so close to others that the urge to kill would be uncontrollable.

Hargrave had been studying the brick walls of the alley, but when he noticed her bent form he hurried over in alarm. "Miss Morgan? Are you ill?" He crouched beside her, worry creasing his face.

"I am quite well. I have discovered something," she said, rising. At her words, the keen spark flared in his eyes again.

"Something about our quarry?" he asked.

"Yes. He has escaped through there," she said, pointing at the grate. Triumph swelled in her chest, but when she looked at Hargrave, his face was skeptical.

"How is that possible?" he asked. "I doubt the grate would budge; it's rusted shut. And even if it would...a child would scarcely fit down there, and the footprints we've found are certainly those of an adult male."

"I don't believe he had to open the grate. I think he was able to fit through the bars."

Hargrave frowned. "How could a grown man—any human—fit

through so small a space?"

"You said yourself that we don't know what this man can do. What if he can transform himself somehow? Into a rat, a snake, an insect..." She trailed off. Hargrave looked uncomfortable.

"I wish you could be right. However, the ability you speak of is very rare, and is never attained without Academy training." He drew his notebook out of his pocket, flipping through it again. "Here it is; I investigated earlier, when I was trying to discover how he could elude us every time. There are only sixteen people living who are able to transform into anything smaller than a dog, and they are all accounted for."

"I assure you, Inspector, the killer went down this grate. You are quite right that he cannot have done so in his human form, but he has done it in some form or other. If you could sense him as I can, you would find the trail as obvious as an arrow painted in blood." She knew her voice sounded a trifle hysterical, but the killer's presence was exhausting, and Hargrave's reluctance to accept her theory was...unpleasant. Her face grew surprisingly hot.

"Miss Morgan, I should take you home," Hargrave said gently. "This is taxing for you. I should not have involved you, no matter how troublesome this case is."

She scoured his voice for any trace of a patronizing tone, but she could find only warm concern and regret. "Please, Inspector," she said, "you must let me continue to help you. Might I study your notes? There may be something that would help me to understand him better—to make sense of this vileness. I cannot possibly withdraw now that I have felt what he is like. Such a person *must not* be allowed to remain free in the city." Her tone was vehement, and she laid her hand on his arm, gazing at him intently.

He paused in the act of tucking his notebook away. "Very well, then," he said, pressing the book into her outstretched hand. The leather was warm against her palm. "I will take you home now, though; if all remains quiet, I shall call in two days to see if you have found anything."

"Thank you," said Luciana, allowing him to escort her back to the street and the waiting cab.

The ride back to Belgravia was perhaps more silent and uncomfortable than the ride to the crime scene had been.

~ Undercurrents ~

Luciana could not rid herself of a sense of disappointment at his reception of her idea, although she sometimes forgot this when her eyes strayed from the window to steal glances at his folded hands, strong profile, or clean-shaven jaw. It was, on the whole, a relief when he handed her down from the carriage in front of her house—especially as she could see that her mother was still out.

He bowed to her politely. "Thank you again for your assistance, Miss Morgan."

She nodded. "I am glad to help, Inspector. I would feel personally responsible if I did not do what I could in such a situation. It is my hope that the next few days will shed some light on things."

He looked away, towards the house, and shifted his feet. "About your...theory," he said awkwardly. "Perhaps you are right...but I have no way to set guards on every storm drain and cesspit in London."

She knew he was trying to be kind, to make it seem as though the impracticality of her information was the problem, rather than its improbability. Still, it stung a little. "I understand you, Inspector," she said in a chilly voice. "I hope my perusal of your notes will yield something more useful. Good day," she said, and with another nod, she went into the house.

§

That evening, Luciana sat in her room, quietly seething as she tried to focus on the inspector's careful notes. The seed of bad temper that had been planted by her disappointment in Hargrave had grown, watered by her disgust at the noxious presence she had encountered that day and her certainty that she would be much more help if she had been able to hone her ability, and perhaps add others to her repertoire, at the Academy.

Her frustration at her own helplessness had risen to such a pitch by the time her mother got home that she had broached the subject after dinner, and the ensuing row had demolished her last tendrils of composure. She had gone to her room in tears, and had risen from her bed an hour later with the headache and a determination to find *some* shred of information that would bring them closer to capturing the killer.

She turned up the wick of her oil lamp and leaned over the

notepad, willing herself to sort through the information. As she did so, she picked up traces of Hargrave's presence, the sudden sense of clean open air mingling with the warm, honest scent of the worn leather cover; feeling somehow soothed, she began to scan the neatly-pencilled notes.

Hargrave had been thorough. Every idea that occurred to her, every question that arose in her mind, had already been researched and answered. Each crime scene was described in detail, the tone detached and analytical—although she thought the writing was somewhat darker in these sections, as though suppressed emotion had made him press the pencil rather harder than usual. She learned more than even the papers had revealed, although the gruesomeness of the crimes was no surprise to her after her encounter with the presence of the criminal.

Hargrave noted that the killer was moving closer and closer to Scotland Yard, possibly in order to taunt the police force. The next two pages of the notebook were covered in a sketched map of London, on which Hargrave had mapped out the locations of the murders. Glancing over the dates noted next to the crime scenes, Luciana saw that he was right; each killing was closer to the Yard than the last.

She was about to turn to the next page when something made her look again at the murder sites. "There is something about that..." she murmured, frowning at Hargrave's tidy notations. She read the names of the neighbourhoods where the murders had occurred, but could find nothing striking about them except that they all held pockets of poverty.

Taking up her own pen, she began to draw the curve of the Thames on a sheet of paper. With frequent references to Hargrave's map, she marked the sites of the murders, and then connected them. The line they formed swept down towards the Thames in a shallow arc, then hugged the curve of the river tightly. It was unmistakably familiar. Inspired, she took her lamp and crept out of her room and downstairs.

The house was in darkness, her mother and the servants already abed. The warm glow of her lamp lit her way to her father's study, little changed since his death. She pushed open the door and went inside. Leaving her lamp on the broad desk, she took down a large leather-bound volume. Her father had kept many bound collections of newspapers, and this particular

~ Undercurrents ~

volume had once been used in a game of theirs.

As a way to encourage her reading when she was a child, he used to create puzzles using clues found in books. One summer he had created a complex one based entirely on the contents of this particular volume of newspapers, and as a result she had memorized almost the entire volume in the process of working out the puzzle. Now she turned to the middle of the book and flipped several rustling pages before finding what she sought.

"LONDON'S SEWERS TO BE IMPROVED," read the headline. Below it was a story detailing Joseph Bazalgette's plan, with a map showing the major lines that would be connected to the city's myriad drains and sewers. She laid the sketch she had made next to the map; the line she had drawn to connect the murders matched the curve of one of the sewer lines precisely.

Satisfied, Luciana noted the date of the newspaper, returned the book to its shelf, and took her lamp from the desk. As she closed the study door behind her, she was swamped by the salty stench of blood, the drone of insects over rotting flesh, the taste of bile. Her stomach heaved, and she clamped a hand over her mouth—both to keep herself from screaming and from being sick.

The killer was here. In Belgravia. Near—or in—her house.

Trembling, she forced herself to walk down the hall, straining to hear anything out of the ordinary. Could he be a fly in the parlour? A mouse under the floorboards? She walked faster, and the light from her lamp shook around her, throwing the walls and furniture into frightening gold and black shapes, robbing them of familiarity. She tread lightly up the stairs, feeling the presence fade behind her, slipped into her room and closed the door firmly. The presence was gone now, and she made herself relax. Bundling up a robe, she stuffed it tightly against the crack under her door.

Luciana paced her room for many long minutes, but the killer's presence did not return. Finally, she got into bed and blew out her lamp, but it was only after a long interval of studying the shadows that she drifted into a troubled sleep.

§

Luciana awoke with bright sun streaming through her window, and instantly knew something was amiss. Her mother thought that sleeping late was bad for the character, and so Alice generally woke Luciana long before the sun had reached such strength. She got up and rang for Alice, then hurriedly began to wash and dress, recalling what she had sensed in the night.

Alice appeared, pale and red-eyed. "I'm sorry, Miss; Mrs. Morgan says I'm not to speak of what's going on," she said, before Luciana had a chance to ask. "She wants you downstairs." She helped Luciana finish dressing and did her hair up neatly, but her hands trembled.

Luciana went downstairs, apprehension growing with every step. She entered the small dining room where they generally took breakfast and found her mother pacing by the window, a damp handkerchief hanging limp in her hand. "Mama?" she said, pausing by the doorway.

"Oh, Luciana!" her mother cried, crossing the room and embracing her. "It's so horrible!"

Luciana patted her mother's back uncertainly. "Mama, what has happened?"

"There's been...a murder," her mother whispered. "Here, in Belgravia."

Luciana went cold. "The killer from the papers," she said.

"Child, don't think such things! We have no way to know what's happened or who's to blame."

I have, Luciana thought. "Mama...do you know who?"

"A maid at Mrs. Fairlie's. Hester...Harriet...something like that."

"Hannah," Luciana whispered. "She's...she was a friend of Alice's."

That did something to jolt her mother into her normal state of control. "Oh, Luciana. Must you be so familiar with the servants?"

"Mama, is this really the time for that?" She paused, trying to lighten her tone. "I was planning to go out directly after breakfast. I couldn't find the right colour shawl yesterday. Alice can accompany me; it will take her mind off things." *Hargrave will be needing his notebook,* she thought. *Surely I can find him out there.*

"You will do no such thing! Luciana, what are you thinking? Until Scotland Yard declares this business to be resolved, you will go nowhere unnecessarily; it is safest to stay at home."

Gritting her teeth, Luciana sat down at the table and helped

~ Undercurrents ~

herself to breakfast. She would have to find some other way of returning Hargrave's notebook, and of informing him of her discovery.

§

After breakfast, Luciana sat in the parlour alone, pretending to read while trying to contrive a way to get out of the house. Alice came in, bearing a folded paper on the tray. "A message for you, Miss," she said.

Luciana took the letter and reached out to squeeze Alice's hand. "Don't stray too far, Alice. I may need you," she said as the maid went to return the tray to the hall. She turned the letter over. Whoever had sent it had not kept it long, as it held no trace of presence. It was written on plain paper, and sealed with an unmarked blob of red wax. The wax reminded her unpleasantly of recent events, and she shuddered. She broke the seal, unfolded the letter, and read:

> *Clever girl, following me like that. Perhaps if you hadn't been so caught up in the handsome inspector, you'd have noticed me following you, too. He's a clever one, as well—a proper challenge. Who would have dreamed I'd find two people who were better sport than all the rest of Scotland Yard? It's enough to make me break from my original plan—for a few days, at least. I wanted to thank you both for making this all more interesting, so I'm arranging a gift for each of you. I'm sure you've already heard about yours. Just think, if you'd known what I was up to last night—if you'd had the nerve to look into things, or raise the alarm—that chit might still be alive.*
>
> *Time for Hargrave's gift now, I think. I'd like to give him you—after the way he looked at you yesterday, I think that would shake him up properly. This is more fun, though, I think; I'm sure you'll be glad of a reason to scurry off and see him again, won't you? I just know he'll like to see you again. And so will I.*

Luciana struggled not to crush the paper, though her hands

shook. Her face burned; the murderer's insinuations made her feel exposed and vulnerable. His polite tone only magnified the insult. He was right about one thing, though; she had to tell Hargrave what was going on. And she could think of only one thing that would persuade her mother to let her out of the house.

"Alice," she called. When the maid came in, Luciana beckoned for her to come near. "Who brought this letter?"

Alice frowned. "Just a messenger boy. I'm not sure of his name, Miss, but I've seen him about."

No help there, then, thought Luciana. "Alice," she said quietly, "I need you to help me as you did yesterday when I went out."

Alice shook her head. "You mustn't go out today, Miss. It's not safe. And—" Alice glanced towards the hall, making certain they were alone. "The Inspector's not here today to take care of you."

"Please, Alice," Luciana said. "I can't explain—the less you know, the less you have to cover up. But—I don't want this to happen to anyone else, and I must find Inspector Hargrave and speak to him."

Alice's lip trembled. "What do you want me to do?"

"I'll need you to come with me as a chaperone, but Mama mustn't know where we're going."

Alice hesitated, then nodded, and she followed Luciana out of the room. They found Mrs. Morgan still in the breakfast room; she was pacing again, although she composed herself rapidly when they entered.

"Mama, I've had an invitation," Luciana said, trying to sound as excited as her mother would want her to be. "Caroline Burnham is going to see a concert this afternoon, and she has asked me to go with her. Her brother James is going as well. Please, may I go?"

Her mother looked startled, although at the mention of James Burnham her eyes narrowed eagerly. "I suppose a concert would be safe enough, especially if James is there with you. May I read the note she sent? Does she say who will be going as a chaperone?"

"I'm afraid there's no note; one of their servants stopped in with the message. He was being sent on an urgent errand by Mr. Burnham, and Caroline asked him to stop on his way back to ask me, but she had no time to write the invitation out." She strained to make her face the picture of innocence.

Mrs. Morgan's brow creased. "This is somewhat irregular. The Burnhams are generally very conscientious about etiquette."

"I'm certain Mrs. Burnham will have arranged an appropriate chaperone for us, Mama, and Alice could go with me." Luciana smoothed a loose curl behind her ear, trying to look nonchalant. "Master Burnham mentioned this concert to me particularly. He expects it to be quite good."

Her mother smiled. "Oh, very well, then. It is an odd way to deliver an invitation, but I suppose everyone's a bit off today. You may go, so long as Alice goes with you. Will they be calling here in the carriage?"

This was the tricky bit, especially as Luciana could see that her mother very much liked the thought of the Burnham's carriage being seen at their house. "Well, Caroline did offer, but I saw a shawl yesterday that would go perfectly with my lilac watered silk; I haven't worn it yet, and it is so lovely. I thought perhaps we could take the carriage to the Burnham's, and Alice could run in to the shop to get the shawl on the way."

"I'm afraid I shall need the carriage this afternoon to call on Mrs. Crawford."

"Oh," Luciana said, her mind racing. She fought a smile. "That is too bad, but Alice and I could take a cab; it's not far." It was perfect; she would not have to ask Shaw, the driver, to conceal her whereabouts.

She could practically see the war in her mother's mind; it seemed odd to send her out in a cab, and the outing lost some of its social gloss if the Burnhams did not call at the house. However, Luciana knew her mother's desire to have her well turned-out would win, especially when James Burnham was involved.

Mrs. Morgan sighed. "Very well, though it's really not the done thing."

"Thank you, Mama," Luciana said, her heart pounding as she left the room. Now she had only to while away the time until she could leave—and to sort out how she would find Hargrave.

§

"Mmf!" Luciana stifled a grunt as Alice snugged up her stays.

~ Undercurrents ~

"I'm sorry, Miss," Alice said reprovingly. "But you did insist we go immediately after tea."

"I know," Luciana replied between gritted teeth. Alice finished and she sighed, letting go of her bedpost. She eyed the lilac day-dress Alice held ruefully. "I should never have said I'd be wearing that. It would be fine if we were actually going to a concert, but as it is..." She trailed off, holding her arms out resignedly.

Alice helped her into the dress with care, smoothing and tugging the silk until it hung perfectly. "She'd never have let you go without that story you concocted."

"You're right," Luciana said. "This is a small price to pay, if it helps." She picked up her reticule, patting it to make sure Hargrave's notebook and the killer's letter were inside. "I have been wanting to wear this dress, after all," she added. Still, she felt a bit silly to be wearing such an extravagant gown to see Hargrave. What would he think?

A short time after they found themselves safely ensconced in a cab, en route to the shop where Luciana was supposed to have seen a shawl. "I hope they do have one to match," Luciana said fervently. "Mama will be suspicious if I come home without one."

They drew up at the shop and Alice stepped down, returning triumphantly a few moments later with a lilac shawl in hand.

"Oh, Alice, it's perfect," said Luciana, wrapping it around her shoulders. "Now, to find Hargrave." Alice directed the cabby, and they soon halted at the curb near Mrs. Fairlie's.

A crowd of constables was on the scene, speaking to the public, taking notes, and guarding the house. Hargrave, however, was nowhere to be seen. Luciana looked about in dismay, wondering what to do, when she spied Brown on the sidewalk nearby.

"Constable Brown!" she called.

He looked up, startled, and gazed at her uncomprehendingly for a moment. Then recognition lit his eyes and he approached. "Good afternoon, Miss," he said, doffing his cap. "Something I can help you with?"

"I must find Inspector Hargrave," she said quietly, aware of the cabby's presence. "Is he here?"

"I'm afraid not, Miss," he said. "He was here this morning, but he can barely stand up; he hasn't been sleeping much with these goings-on. He's gone home to have a bit of a rest and

~ Undercurrents ~

something to eat, but he'll be back. Can't think of much else while all this is on his mind. Anything I can tell him for you?"

"No, I must speak to him personally," said Luciana, feeling strangely reluctant to give up her original plan. "Can you direct me to his lodgings?"

Brown looked a little shocked, and glanced at Alice; Luciana was painfully aware that Alice was not really chaperone enough for calling on a single man. Still, Brown recovered quickly and gave the cabby the address, and tipped his hat again as they left. By the time they reached the tidy brick house where Hargrave had his flat, her cheeks had nearly stopped burning.

Luciana stepped down from the carriage and approached the door while Alice paid the cabby. She gripped the cool brass knocker, and suddenly wondered wildly who would answer the door and what she would say to them. A servant, who would ask no questions? A landlady, immediately suspicious of young women who called on bachelors? Or—had she been wrong all along? What if Hargrave was married, and his wife answered the door? *That doesn't matter,* she thought firmly. *This is a business call only.* She knocked.

A moment later, the door opened to reveal Hargrave himself. He looked wearier than she remembered, but his face softened into a puzzled smile. "Miss Morgan?"

"Inspector," she said, nodding. "I must speak with you."

"Of course," he said. "Please, come in." He led them into a hallway and began to ascend a narrow staircase.

"Alice, please wait here," Luciana said softly, gesturing to a chair that stood in the hall.

"Miss?" Alice said uncertainly. "I should stay with you."

"Alice, please," she said. "There are things you wouldn't want to hear."

Alice hesitated, then sat, looking troubled.

"I won't be long," Luciana promised, following Hargrave up the stairs.

"Miss Morgan," he said quietly, "I appreciate your discretion, but I shouldn't like...that is, I would rather have your servant hear our discussion than have your character compromised." He opened the door into a small sitting room. There was no hint of a woman's influence, although two comfortable chairs stood before a clean hearth, and fresh white curtains hung in the window. A low table near the window held a vase of fresh flowers.

"She mustn't hear; it would only upset her," Luciana said. She was distracted by the flowers. Alongside the ruffled blossoms of thornless roses, graceful heads of red and yellow tulips thrust up out of clusters of golden daffodils, and frothy sprays of white pear blossoms wreathed the whole. It seemed decidedly out of place in a police inspector's sitting room.

Hargrave shut the door. "I assume you've heard the latest. I'm sorry; it must have frightened you."

The terrible weariness washed over his face again, and Luciana had to struggle not to take his hand. "I'm afraid there is more to it than you know," she said, taking out his notebook and the letter. She explained to him her realization about the sewer line.

At once the animation of work returned to him. "Then you were right!" he exclaimed. "Miss Morgan, I apologize; please forgive me for doubting you."

"Please, Inspector, think no more of it," she said. "I'm afraid I have more to tell you." His expression turned grim as she told him of her sense of the killer's presence in her house, and handed him the letter.

He read silently, fury clouding his face, and then strode stiffly from the room. "A moment, please," he called in a choked voice.

Luciana was somewhat astonished by his reaction. It was shocking, surely, but it seemed unlike Hargrave to be so overcome. She felt awkward, standing alone in his sitting room. Her eyes fell again on the flowers, and this time she found herself reading the meaning of the blooms.

The tulips and daffodils spoke of a hopeless, one-sided love— love at first sight, in fact, considering the roses—while the pear blossoms promised enduring friendship. It was a sad and sweet arrangement, and having read its message she was no closer to understanding why it was in Hargrave's flat. She took an unconscious step towards the flowers, puzzled, and noticed a small folded card tucked in amongst the foliage. Unable to resist, she began to reach towards the card when she heard Hargrave returning. Immediately she stepped back, folding her hands.

Hargrave's gaze fell on the flowers as he entered the room, and he appeared confused for a moment; she was surprised to see him blush, and realized with a guilty start that she was being nosy. He composed himself quickly, however, smoothing out the letter—which he had apparently crumpled when out of the room —and folding it neatly. "May I keep this, Miss Morgan?"

"Of course," she said with a shudder. "I surely don't want it back."

"I'm sorry that wretch insulted you so," he said softly, gazing at her again in that earnest way that made her stomach flutter.

"It's certainly no fault of yours, Inspector," she said.

"But it is. This letter and your story have made me most keenly aware of how wrong I was to involve you in this matter. If I had been more patient, continued to follow the proper channels —"

"The man in the shack would have died," she said firmly. She laid a hand on his arm. "You must believe me; if my involvement will help you catch this man, then I do not wish myself out of the situation."

He nodded slowly. "It is not easy, though, to think of this man in your house—to read his personal threats to you." His hand closed over hers gently. "I would never wish for you to be in danger."

Luciana was suddenly far too aware of his kind grey eyes, his hand on hers, the beating of her own heart. The sense of his physical nearness, combined with his true and open presence, was overwhelmingly delightful. She found herself beginning to lean into him, reveling in the sense of being enveloped by blue sky and fresh wind.

Abruptly he drew away, striding over to take his coat from the rack. "If we can believe that madman's note, someone nearby is likely in danger of becoming his next victim. We'd best be on the lookout."

"Of course," she said. *What has come over me?* she thought. *Scarcely two days with this man and I'm...* Her thoughts trailed off. There were more important things at hand, and she could puzzle out her odd reactions later. Or not, as it mattered little; she would likely never see Hargrave again once this case was concluded. That thought gave her a pang, but she brushed it off. Hargrave was waiting expectantly by the door. "Perhaps if we go into the street I can get a sense of where he's been," she said.

They descended the stairs, and Alice followed them outside. While Hargrave sent a boy to fetch some constables, Luciana considered Alice. The maid looked exhausted, and had obviously been weeping while she waited in Hargrave's hall. Luciana took her hand. "Perhaps you should go to your mother's for a few hours, Alice. I can call for you before I go home; no one will be the wiser."

Alice's face twisted in indecision. "I shouldn't leave you, Miss. Mrs. Morgan's likely to turn me out as it is, for having gone along with this plan."

"She'll do nothing of the sort," Luciana said fiercely. "When this is all over, I'll explain everything to Mama; I'll catch it, but I promise nothing will happen to you." She squeezed Alice's arm. "Today has been hard enough for you; there may be some danger, and I don't want you getting hurt."

Alice reluctantly allowed herself to be tucked into a cab, and only after receiving promises that Luciana would be careful and would call for her directly when things were resolved did she allow the cabby to drive away. Luciana again found herself alone with Hargrave, and set her mind to business in an attempt to forestall the quickening of her heart and the not-unpleasant swooning sensation in her stomach.

"The note suggests he plans to strike near you, next; perhaps we should begin by checking the area around your home?"

Hargrave nodded. "Yes, that makes sense. We can work our way outward." He looked up and down the street, hesitating.

"Should we not begin?" she asked.

He grimaced. "I was hoping the constables would arrive. It seems I have again put you in a rather compromising situation; your maid is gone, and we have no other company."

"I appreciate your concern, Inspector, but I'm afraid society's codes do not encompass a situation such as this one. And since the Academy became coeducational, people have had to relax their ideas a little about men and women who are working together." *With the exception of my mother,* she thought acidly.

"If you're certain, then. I wouldn't want to...hurt your chances," he said delicately.

"There's no need to worry, Inspector. We are on a public street, after all, and at any rate my fortune ensures me more leeway than those less fortunate." Her tone was wry, but his reply was surprisingly sombre.

"Yes, I'm certain there is no doubt of you marrying well. Let

~ Undercurrents ~

us go, then," he said, setting out.

They began by circling the house itself, and then the block it occupied. They passed a sewer grate on the way to the next block, and Luciana found herself doubled over, trying not to retch. Hargrave was at her side in an instant, supporting her. He helped her to the other side of the street. She pressed her forehead gratefully against the cool brick of a wall, taking deep breaths to quell the heaving in her stomach.

"I take it he has been here," Hargrave said.

She nodded, still gulping air.

"It seems worse," he continued, a worried crease forming between his brows as he examined her.

He was right. It was worse even than when she had felt the killer's presence the night before. "Perhaps the murders... perhaps each one taints him more," she murmured, thinking hard.

"It can change?" Hargrave was puzzled. "I was under the impression that these presences you feel were constant—like someone's face, you said."

"They are, for the most part. But I have noticed that certain powerful things can alter them; marriage, for example, tends to mingle two presences a little."

"Ah. So a marriage or a murder might affect your sense of someone, but you wouldn't be able to tell if someone simply conceived a great hate for someone else. Or fell in love."

She nodded. She was about to make further reply when a constable rounded the corner.

"There you are, Inspector. Miss," the constable said, tipping his hat. "I'll have the lads come down this way, then?" At Hargrave's nod, he ducked back around the corner, returning a few moments later with a group of men, some of whom Luciana recognized from her first outing with Hargrave.

By this time she had composed herself enough to continue, and she was able to slowly explore the area. Hargrave stood nearby, his face showing both concern for her and excitement at the fresh development in the case. It did not take long for Luciana to realize that the murderer had left traces of himself around one house in particular.

"This must be where he plans to strike," she said. "He's been all over the yard and the surrounding streets."

"We'll be ready for him, then," said Hargrave. "I'll speak to the residents, arrange to station some men inside. I'll send one of the men to fetch an Enforcer or two from the Academy, now that we've gotten close to him. He seems to have more tricks up his sleeve than we can handle on our own."

As it happened, there was no one at home. Hargrave had to content himself with ranging constables around the house and the adjoining street.

"I should have someone see you home, Miss Morgan," he said. "We may be here a while, and I do not know what may happen if he actually makes his appearance."

Luciana was reluctant to leave, although she had no desire to encounter the man they had been pursuing. She could think of no good reason to stay, however, and was about to consent to go home when a constable directed a messenger to Hargrave. The boy handed over a letter, bobbed in thanks for the coin Hargrave gave him in return, and raced off.

Luciana recognized the indigo wax seal on the letter at once. "Why, that's from the Academy!" she exclaimed.

With a thoughtful frown, Hargrave broke the seal and began to read. "You are correct. And it seems I may not have you taken home just yet. It's from one of the archivists; he's been following the case, he says, and thinks he has come across something that may help us. He's even gotten word that you were assisting me. We're to visit him at one of the storehouses as soon as may be; evidently the information was in a text that was being kept in storage."

Luciana could not keep a smile of delight from her face. "This is happy news," she said. Her heart thrilled at the thought of visiting one of the Academy archives, even briefly, and she was very satisfied by her continued involvement in the investigation. Her happiness even overcame the attendant awkwardness of being once again alone in a cab with Hargrave; or perhaps, she reflected, it was simply that they had spent more time together now. At any rate, she was perfectly composed as she settled into the seat across from him—at least until he spoke to her.

"It is most reassuring to see you looking well again. You frightened me a little," he said, his lips curving in a gentle smile.

"I-I am quite well, Inspector, thank you." Casting about for something to say, she noticed that once again they had entered an unfamiliar part of London. "I don't think I've ever been here before."

"I daresay you haven't. These warehouse districts are certainly no place for a young lady such as yourself. Unless, of course, she has the protection of a Scotland Yard inspector." This time, when she looked at him, his eyes were positively twinkling, and she could not help smiling in response. "Ah, here's the place," he said, as the cab drew to a halt. He helped Luciana down onto the broken curb of a very quiet street.

"Shall I wait, Sir?" the cabby asked.

Hargrave shook his head. "We may be some time."

With a nod, the cabby drove off, leaving them on the deserted street. They were outside a low gate, behind which Luciana could see a warehouse at the end of a long walk. Hargrave held the gate for Luciana, careful to keep it clear of her skirts.

"I'm afraid I'm not really dressed for this outing," she said. She felt a sudden urge to explain to Hargrave why she had turned up in such a sumptuous outfit. "I must confess, my mother thinks I am attending a concert."

"I'm not sure what is the proper attire for visiting a magician-archivist; perhaps I'm quite underdressed," he said kindly. "However, it seems there is no one about to witness our shame." He smiled at her again in that unaccountably pleasing way as he accompanied her up the walk.

They reached the warehouse and knocked, but when no response came, Hargrave tried the door. It swung open easily, and they entered to find themselves in a large open space whose walls were heavily laden with shelves of books and scrolls in various states of repair. It was dim, but shafts of sunlight slanted in through high windows, their soft golden rays sparkling with dust motes.

"Hallo?" Hargrave called. "Master Arcturus?" Only the faint reply of Hargrave's own voice echoed softly from the high ceiling. He pointed towards the back of the room, where a door opened onto another large chamber, one which seemed to be full of library stacks as loaded as the shelves in the present room. "I expect he's just back there. We'll wait a moment."

The moments stretched on, and Luciana began to feel concerned. She knew scholars could be somewhat eccentric, but it seemed odd that the archivist would send for Hargrave to come immediately if he was not nearby. "You're sure this was the address?"

Hargrave double-checked the note. "Yes, this is the place. It certainly looks like an archive." He paused, turning the note over in his hands. "Forgive me if this is impertinent, Miss Morgan, but I've been thinking about what you said—about your mother thinking you are at a concert. It's a shame you couldn't convince her of something similar so that you could attend the Academy; perhaps you have some cousins in the country whom you could be supposed to be visiting? You seem to be happy when you can use your talents."

It *was* an impertinent thing to say, given their brief acquaintance, but his tone was very kind. "I'm afraid not, Inspector. My mother requires very particular accounts of things; I shall be hard-pressed to come up with a suitable description of this afternoon's music to content her."

She smiled at him, but something about his comments troubled her. Their acquaintance had been brief and...they had discussed little but the investigation at hand. "Forgive me for asking, Inspector, but how did you discover that my mother forbid my attendance at the Academy?"

He looked a trifle guilty. "I apologize, Miss Morgan; I should not have commented on the matter, since you did not explain it to me yourself. The archivist mentioned it in his note." He unfolded the paper again and read aloud: " 'I'm certain the young Miss Morgan will be delighted to accompany you, since it is her mother's will and not her own that prevents her from pursuing knowledge of the arcane arts.' "

He frowned. "It was improper of him, really, to suggest taking you along when he knows it is counter to your mother's wishes, but scholars sometimes have odd ideas about society's rules. I cannot excuse myself the same way, though; I knew it was wrong, even though you seem very capable of making your own decisions. I really should see you home; I'll see if the cab—" He stopped in surprise as her hand closed convulsively on his wrist.

"Inspector," she said in a low, distinct voice. "I never told the Academy why I wasn't attending. There is no way the archivist could know that."

He drew back in surprise, but quickly shook his head. "He's an information gatherer; he even knew you were assisting me.

~ Undercurrents ~

Surely he just found out the reason somewhere, and forgot that it had not come through official channels."

"No—no one knew why. It was not discussed. My mother and I argued about it, but not when other people were near." She gasped. "That night—the night the murderer was in my house— we argued about it again. He might have heard the whole thing."

Hargrave's grey eyes grew steely, and he looked about the room sharply. "Miss Morgan, we'd best leave at once."

The door, however, refused to open.

"There must be another way out," he said, taking her by the arm. He picked up a loose board that lay against one of the walls; holding it like a club, he began to lead her out into the room.

When they reached the centre of the room, everything changed utterly.

The shelves of books disappeared, as did the neatly-swept floorboards. They stood instead in a barren room with a cracked concrete floor, which had several rough depressions around its perimeter. Into each of these depressions was set a sewer grate.

"This is no archive," Luciana whispered, tightening her grip on Hargrave's arm.

"No. It's a slaughterhouse," Hargrave said unsteadily. His face twisted in anguish. "I should have sent you home." He hefted the board and began to advance again, then paused. "What's that noise?"

A soft, scraping sound filled the room, seeming to come up from the floor. It grew louder, fracturing into many smaller sounds—the sounds of hundreds of tiny feet. Rats erupted from the grates in a dark wave, streaming towards Hargrave and Luciana in a seething, squeaking mass, their black eyes glittering evilly in the dim light.

Luciana sank to her knees amongst them, overcome as the essence of evil clogged her nose, her lungs, her very being.

"Miss Morgan! Luciana!" Hargrave cried, swiping furiously with the board in an effort to keep the rats away from her.

"He's here!" she shrieked. "He's one of them!" Vainly she searched for some distinguishing feature in the grey bodies as tears blurred her vision.

Hargrave whirled around wildly, kicking at the rodents now trying to swarm up his legs. "How can we know which one?"

Luciana, to her horror, saw one of the animals unfold with

sickening swiftness behind him, straightening into the form of a tall, disheveled man. The man's fist rose and fell as Luciana choked out a belated scream of warning. Hargrave slumped to the floor.

At once, the rats went silent, and retreated to crouch near the walls.

"Miss Morgan, I cannot tell you what a pleasure it is to finally meet you."

The man's courteous speech and air of shabby gentility did nothing to make his presence less revolting to Luciana. She felt as though she were breathing thick black muck. It was all she could do to cling to consciousness as he went on.

"Did you like my little trick?" he asked, gesturing to the walls. "I had an acquaintance set it up for me, so as not to ruin the surprise for you." He seemed to wait for her to respond, but as she was silent, he continued, pacing slowly.

"It has been such fun, this little game we've been playing. It's a shame it has to end. But your Inspector, you see, he's rather clever; he was getting a bit closer than I liked. Still not clever enough, of course, or he wouldn't have come here—especially not with you." He leaned forward as though to pat her on the cheek, and Luciana flung herself away, retching.

"I'm a bit much for your talent, eh, Miss Morgan? I suppose those dandies who dance attendance on you haven't much on their souls—not much to toughen you up. It's a good thing you can't sce their thoughts. I'm sure even the good Inspector Hargrave would have given you a turn if you could have read his mind when you turned up in that lovely gown you're wearing." He leered at her.

Luciana struggled to drag herself back to her knees, scrubbing at her mouth.

"Perhaps if you'd witnessed more ugliness in your life, you'd be able to stand up to it better. Not that it matters now. I can't let you live, of course, as you're the only one in all of London who can track me down. After you've watched me finish off this chap, you might have the strength to stand on your feet and face me. You deserve that much dignity at the end, I suppose." He turned to Hargrave's prone form, frowning in concentration.

Luciana was suddenly aware of a dull throbbing in the air. The sound slowly grew louder, and her stomach dropped

~ Undercurrents ~

sickeningly as she realized it was Hargrave's heart.

This is how we die, she thought dully. *And no one will know where to find us.*

The throbbing quickened. "It won't be long now," the murderer said.

Hargrave trembled, and his head tipped to one side. His face was turned towards Luciana, his eyes closed as if in sleep. She thought of how he had looked at her earlier in the cab, and how horrified he was when he realized what a trap he had brought her into. She thought of how he had said her name.

Heat blossomed in her stomach as she realized the significance of all she had felt since meeting Hargrave. But instead of simply bringing another flush to her cheeks, this heat spread through her entire body, enervating her weakened muscles and flaring along the length of her limbs.

"No," she growled.

The throbbing subsided a little as the killer glanced at her, distracted. "Did you say something, my dear? Going to beg for his life?"

"No," she said more strongly, and she heaved herself to her feet. The heat prickled over her skin now, almost painfully.

"Oh, trying some heroics perhaps? That would be entertaining. Are you going to slap me?" He chuckled.

The sickening blackness of his presence lay on Luciana's mind like a slick of oil. Remembering how she had fought it once before, she reached out for Hargrave's presence, but she could find mere wisps of it. Her body flared again, but she felt the blue sky slipping away, the blackness threatening to obliterate it.

"NO!" she cried, frightened and enraged. Sheets of flame roared from her hands, leaping towards the murderer, devouring him as greedily as they would kerosene.

He screamed, his entire body suddenly alight, and fell to the floor, writhing. The rats cowered away from the flames.

Sobbing, Luciana grabbed Hargrave's arm, struggling to drag him out of the way. He stirred at her touch and quickly managed to stagger to his feet. They stumbled to the wall, Hargrave clutching his chest, and he turned to look at the agonized killer in astonishment. The flailing man's shrieks were becoming more horrible, and Hargrave swiftly tucked Luciana's head to his shoulder, murmuring softly for her not to look.

~ Undercurrents ~

The screams died away abruptly, and there was only the crackling of the flames. Still Luciana and Hargrave clung to each other. It was several long moments before her sobs and the shuddering aftershocks of the murderer's spell subsided enough for them to speak. Finally Hargrave tipped her head back gently, his thumb smoothing the tears from her cheeks.

"It's over now," he said soothingly. "But, Luciana—Miss Morgan—whatever happened? Did you do that?" He cast his gaze over her shoulder meaningfully, but prevented her from turning to look.

She nodded, and looked at her palms in wonder as she clearly recalled what had happened. The smooth skin was unblemished, only perhaps a little warmer than usual.

"But how? I don't understand. If you could do that, they never would have let you avoid the Academy."

"I couldn't do that. Never before. Until...until I thought you would die." She ducked her head as her cheeks flamed—a perfectly ordinary heat now—trying to ignore the sweet pressure of his arm around her waist.

His fingers under her chin tilted her face up again and he studied her carefully, something new and unfathomably cautious darkening his eyes. Her eyes met his, and he must have read them correctly, for he tenderly lowered his mouth to hers.

Luciana's heart pounded, every shred of the killer's presence blasted from her awareness as she soared on warm winds through a sun-lit blue sky. Though she had tried to ignore it, she had been yearning for this since, descending the stairs, she first sensed Hargrave's presence.

Reluctantly, slowly, she drew away, recalling that his affections lay elsewhere. Hargrave immediately attempted to release her and began to apologize.

She clung to his arm. "It's not that," she said. "It's just...don't you care for someone else? I thought—the flowers..."

To her surprise, he laughed, a delicious unrestrained sound that made her feel as though she had never truly heard anyone laugh before. "Luciana—dearest—they were for you. I bought them the day after I met you, and then I cursed myself for a fool. Of course I could never send them to you. Then I feared you'd sense it anyway, and pity me." A worried crease appeared in his brow, and she reached up to smooth it away.

~ Undercurrents ~

"You may send me as many flowers as you like, although I'd prefer it if you brought them yourself," she said, smiling up at him.

He smiled, his eyes crinkling in a way she was coming to enjoy very much, and kissed her again. "But—what about your mother? Surely she won't like it if a police inspector comes courting. And she's right—you deserve better, truly."

"My mother will have to accept some changes. She does want me to be happy, really; she just thinks she knows how best to achieve that end." She lowered her head and looked up at him shyly through her lashes. "I simply can't imagine anyone better than you. Besides, I think a police inspector may safely call at the Academy; they don't have much regard for society's ranks there ."

His eyes widened. "That's right—she'll have to let you go now, won't she?" He hugged her tightly, lifting her and twirling her around. "How wonderful!"

"Yes," she said, giggling as he set her on the ground again. "But I may not even tell her about..." She spread her hands, looking at her palms again. "She only needs to know that it is my decision; I never should have let her make it for me in the first place. And...Papa made sure some other decisions were left to me." She gave him a shy smile, and then smoothed her ruined skirts ruefully. "It's a shame I'm such a mess; Mama is always easier to deal with when one is well dressed."

"I shall keep that in mind, although you, my dear, would look lovely in a burlap sack."

She giggled and took his hand. "I suppose we'd best go; the sooner I speak to Mama, the better. But...just one more thing before we go?"

"Anything."

"Could you say my name again? Not Miss Morgan, but—"

"Luciana," he breathed, pulling her into his arms again. The murmured sentiments that followed rather delayed their departure, but when they did step hand-in-hand back into the fresh air and sun, Luciana felt that the skies had never been more cloudlessly blue.

⁂

~ *Undercurrents* ~

Krista C. Miller was born in Sydney Mines, Nova Scotia. Early in life, she developed a tendency to become anxious when not surrounded by large piles of books, and has carried this trait into her adult life. As a result, it was imperative that she study English at university, a path that conveniently crossed that of the incomparable Bruce Miller, a man whose passion for postmodern literature and awareness of hours and minutes provided a fitting contrast to Krista's love of Victorian fiction and more abstract concept of time. Krista is now a high school teacher, and lives in rural Cape Breton with her wonderful husband, Bruce; many books, plants, and half-completed art projects; and a field that is sorely in need of a horse.

www.ingramcontent.com/pod-product-compliance
Lightning Source LLC
Chambersburg PA
CBHW071834020726
47502CB00004B/1356